Fire:
The Elementals Book Three

First Printing, 2021
ISBN:
Imprint: Imagine Nation
Imagine Nation
Chenoa, IL 61726
AuthorJenniferLush@gmail.com

Chapter One
The Son of Lars

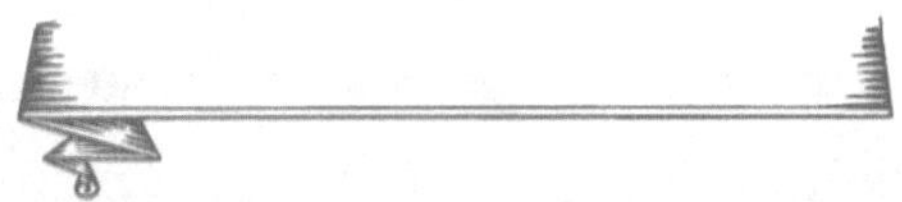

Fire looked around the cobblestone alley, hearing the people gasping over his appearance even before he could see them. Townsfolk were already passing on the nearby street of the village the moment he emerged from the rock in the location the Divine Spirit chose for him. He had only been in this plane for mere seconds before he had been noticed. *'This was intentional,'* he declared internally, feeling the anger rapidly swell within him.

"Whoa. Where did that come from?" he muttered, eyeing the alley for any other possible exit routes as opposed to the obvious one.

It had been less than one minute since he arrived on this plane, and he was already making false accusations against the Divine Spirit such as these wayward souls had been doing since the beginning of their existence. Fire had chosen to stay on the rock until all of the other Elements had gone on ahead. Regrets had begun to settle into his mind as soon as he materialized in human form in the place between the veil and the material world. He couldn't explain it, but he immediately filled with trepidation that he may never return to his rightful place behind the veil. As hard as he tried, he could not pinpoint the reason why. He hadn't cared one way or the other about experiencing life as a human himself from the time Water first approached him, to the moment all four Elements stood before the Divine Spirit as a united front supporting Water's request. As soon as his essence was trapped inside this shell of flesh, he began to dread his decision to not decline Water outright. Air had also been unsure of the idea and would have never swayed his mind if Fire had said no as well.

He stayed on the rock, considering the notion of never leaving it during the entire year his companions spent in the human realm. The slow passage of time humans experience would soon become agonizing when all he had to entertain his mind was the view of a small meadow at the edge of a forest. Until now, boredom was as foreign to him as the pains growing in his abdomen that he would learn shortly was caused by hunger. Because of this, he was the only one present during Water's request. It seemed trivial to him now, but it would be the key to unlocking more than one mystery in the millennium ahead. If only he had stayed a short while longer, he would have had the knowledge to unravel the biggest mystery and threat that he and the other Elements would ever face.

Blaming the Divine Spirit for his current predicament was both unexpected and not based in truth. On the other side of the veil, he would have never dared to displace the fault of his current situation. Human thought process and emotions had begun to take hold far faster than he had believed they would. The only one to blame for his current predicament was himself for not leaving with the others as had been expected of him. Judging by the early light filtering through the buildings, he could assume it would have been the middle of the night when he stepped out into the alley if he hadn't hung back for so long.

As it stood now, there was nothing he could do to avoid violating the rules laid out for the Elements. He had already been seen. It was too late to prevent that. The pains he felt grew aggressively once he left the rock and was fully encompassed by the mortal side of the veil. His midsection screamed at him for food. None would be found in this alley. It wouldn't be possible for him to hide here for a full day until the cover of nightfall allowed him a chance to explore the area undetected. With his growing hunger, he wouldn't be able to last that long.

While he tried to decide what he should do, a voice called out to him. Fire faced the man at the entrance of the alley. The language was familiar and guttural. *'Europe,'* Fire told himself. *'Possibly Germania.'*

The decision had been made for him. Without an alternate exit, the only option for him was to deal with this gentleman and leave. Fire walked toward him, and the man began frantically calling out while looking around him for a means to escape, or possibly for someone to aid in his defense against this stranger.

It was the robes he was wearing. Fire was well aware of the cause of the man's apprehension. The clothing didn't match the customs or style of the area. All of the Elements were sent as equals. They were given no supplies to bring with them except for the identical robes that adorned their bodies. While at one time they may have blended nicely with some civilizations, this was not true of the region where he found himself or the times.

The bystander was yelling at him to stop. Fire paid him relatively no attention. The man was far too afraid of the menacing figure approaching him wearing unusual attire. He would surely have run if Fire stopped and looked him in the eye. Instead, he continued on past as though the panic stricken gentleman wasn't even there. In the street, he quickly walked with his head down checking every road he crossed for the safest location to hide out until darkness fell.

The stare of every passerby could be felt boring into his skin. It was still early, allowing him a short window to escape the onslaught that would await him once the entire village had awakened and become aware of his presence. A foreigner such as the looks of him would not fare well in these parts. Nearing the edge of the village, he veered off toward the tree line hoping to take refuge in the woods until he could devise a plan.

Food and clothing were his top priority, but he had no means to acquire either of them. He hoped he might happen upon something edible growing wild as he made his way through the forest outside of the village because it was the only viable option at present. As he walked, he scoured the ground all around him searching for anything he could make into a meal. If not for the smoke that billowed from the fire in the near distance, he would've walked straight into the camp ahead.

His feet screamed at him with every step, seeming to find every lump of hard dirt or sharp twig on the forest floor. Almost every time his feet touched the ground, a stab of pain shot through them. It amused him the first few times having a new sensation to experience. He hadn't made it far into the tree covering before he started to hesitate and felt apprehensive about continuing his chosen path. The only upside was he no longer paid attention to the growls coming from his abdomen demanding to be fed.

Fire could smell the smoke before he saw it. Curious, he slowly approached the area to investigate. A group of travelers had set up a site for the night, possibly longer. The fire was smoldering and almost out. It had last been tended quite some time earlier. There were no movements in the area, and only one soul could be seen. A man dozed awkwardly on the ground not far from the fire. He appeared to have fallen asleep while on watch. This told Fire no one else was up for surely the man would've been scolded awake for failing to keep his post. Any others accompanying the man must still be asleep under the roughly thrown together shelters strung between the trees. He would need to move carefully to avoid waking anyone.

He hung back in the undergrowth to not risk being seen in case he was wrong or if someone woke and left their tent before he could take cover. As he surveyed the layout of their campsite, he noticed clothing hanging on the lower branches of a few trees about twenty yards from him. They had been placed there to dry, and the temptation to help himself to what he needed struck hard.

Intuitively, he could see while looking at the garments that this group had recently pillaged many of the belongings from a man who had passed away during his travels. On the other side of the veil, all was known to him, but here it was muffled. It was more like bits of memories he couldn't quite piece together coherently. What he could see told him that while this group didn't take the man's life, they did help themselves to his possessions. They barely noticed the body except to flip it over to avoid having to look in his eyes.

'It would hurt none to take a closer look,' he told himself, encouraging the decision to check it out. There appeared to be a surplus of clothing for the number of makeshift tents. They might not even miss a couple of pieces. *'Besides, humans lie, cheat, and steal every day. How is one to study the human experience without partaking in these actions for oneself?'* he thought. These travelers were all the same. Chances were that the whole lot of the items on these trees were obtained from ill-gotten ways.

Not to mention, these people were opportunists. They happened upon a poor soul who had stumbled in his walk, hitting his head hard enough to bring about his demise. Since he had no more use of his belongings, they claimed them for their own. *'Am I not an opportunist myself in this moment? I discovered this poorly guarded camp which bears the items I am now in need of most.'* Fire finally made a convincing enough argument to allow himself to take from the items left unguarded.

A voice spoke inside his head, uttering a single word. It was a name. Fire couldn't be certain if the Divine Spirit was merely giving him an identity or trying to reprimand him out of what he was about to do. If the latter were the case, it had ill effect to serve its purpose.

"What is that?" Fire whispered, pulling a pair of britches off a branch. He pulled them on his legs and fastened them. The fit was off, but they were a far sight better than how he had been dressed. Grabbing a shirt, he quickly tore off the robes, and slid it down his arms waiting to do up the buttons on it until he was a safe distance away. "Was that a name? My name?" he asked softly, aware the Divine Spirit was listening even without an answer returned.

A pair of boots laid nearby, and he picked them up, noticing he could see the ground through the opening for the feet. Fire turned them over and saw the soles were worn through with holes. They were still better than no foot coverings at all. He tossed the boots into his robes to carry. The urge to sit down and pull them on now was overwhelming, but he didn't want to press his luck by waiting any longer to leave the camp. Next to the boots was a bag with a long loaf of bread sticking out of the top. He grabbed it too then hurried off through the trees until he felt he was far enough away to safely stop for a spell.

Fire bit into the end of the loaf not caring to waste precious moments breaking it apart. The pains being howled from his mid-section were almost louder than his thoughts. "That name will not do," he said, between large bites of bread. "I shall have to find one that fits."

Finishing his meal, thirst replaced his hunger. Fire listened to all the sounds of the forest until he heard what he was looking for at last. Areas like this, while becoming modernized, were still centered near a water source from the early days of their settlement. He slipped the boots on and tied them before fastening the buttons of his shirt. All that was left were the robes which he wasn't sure if he needed, but he felt an odd urge to hang on to them all the same. He tossed them on his shoulder and headed in the direction of the stream he had heard where he would at long last be able to drench the dryness that was scratching his throat.

Sitting along the banks, he studied the landscape trying to determine his precise location. It would not have been his first choice to spend his days under the rule of the boy king who became emperor. There would be wars trying to regain the lands to the south that had been lost as he aimed to unite the western and eastern parts of the empire once again. Amongst the many battles littering the countryside, there would be far fewer places to remain hidden with armies marching through the land. He began walking east trying to decide if he wanted to stay in Europe or cut back north and stow away on a ship somewhere else altogether.

Before long, he found another road cutting through the woods. If he went one direction, it would lead him back to the village. He decided it would be best to avoid that area for a few days until talk of the peculiar visitor from the morning had died down. While walking farther away from the village, he began thinking about what to do for the next year. It was off to a dreadful start. He'd been spotted by many individuals, stolen, and showed a disrespectful attitude to the Divine Spirit. For that last part, he was most remorseful.

The Elements had spent an eternity watching people turn away from and spite their Gods one moment then claiming to honor and worship them in their next breath. It was something he had looked down on this species for doing almost since their beginnings. He had been human for less than a day and was already acting in that manner. It filled him with anguish and regret.

He couldn't waste spending precious time having internal conflicts with himself. He needed weapons to hunt and a place to make his own camp. There had to be a remote area where he wouldn't be discovered for who he really was and could hunt to provide for himself. Perhaps he could trade meat and furs for more clothes. Since he'd already been seen, the effort put into avoiding people would be a waste of time. The orders weren't that crystal clear after all, so it may even be something that was allowed.

Fire walked on trying to remember exactly what the Divine Spirit had told them. Leave together; complete the Return together. That was easy. None among them would have any cause to want to stay in this troublesome form in this wretched place for longer than necessary. They were to observe and not interfere. Their presence should not be felt, and their absence undetected when they left. It might not be verbatim, but it was close to the precise words spoken when the rules were laid forth.

After rolling the words around in his head for a stretch, he came to the conclusion that it didn't necessarily mean they couldn't interact with the people of the land. They merely couldn't have a lasting effect on any society they encountered. It made more sense why he was delivered to the heart of a village instead of the outskirts. While he left the other side believing he couldn't be detected at all, he managed to convince himself he just had to stay in the background as much as possible and not make waves when he was in the mix.

As he proceeded on foot down the road, the scenery changed around him. Where once stood giant trees, guardians of nature, there were now open meadows. Some of the land appeared to be cultivated. There would be a home nearby. These land ownings could stretch for miles, but he was closer than he was when he started. Perhaps there would be a chance ahead for him to find more suitable attire, and more food, preferably a full meal.

Quickening his pace, he wanted to find the main entrance to the property. It was broad daylight, and it wouldn't be wise to attempt to sneak onto the grounds until nightfall. He could scope the place to see if it would be worth hanging around somewhere close by until the time was right.

Walking nearer, the out buildings started to appear. Near the barn, Fire could see workers bustling about. He could be spied by them, albeit from a distance. That was no matter. He would continue on his trek making mental notes as he went.

Soon, a man on a horse rode his way. He felt a surge within his chest and abdomen, and he smiled coyly at the sensation. Although he had never experienced it, he could recognize it. The fear of not knowing what was coming or how he would be affected by it, and the demand for a decision about his next move was causing him to panic.

Taking a deep breath, he walked to the stone wall at the front of the property along the road and waited by the end of the path that would lead to the main house. It was set far back behind a fence of trees and couldn't be seen from where he stood. Physical sight wasn't necessary to know it was there.

The man on horseback approached him and called out, but Fire remained quiet. Coming within several feet of him, the rider brought the horse to a stop, and asked, "Are you Ulric?"

Fire hesitated to answer, unsure of what to do.

"You there, boy!" the man called out. "Are you deaf as well as stupid?"

The urge to leap at the horse, pulling its rider off in retaliation swept over him, and Fire took a deep breath to control his temper.

"Are you Ulric, son of Lars?" the man asked again, his tone sharper than before.

In his mind, the image of the body the travelers flipped as they ransacked his bags flashed, and Fire knew there would be no worry of the person who authentically bears the name ever arriving. "Yes, sir. That I am."

The horse circled around behind him, and the rider struck the back of Ulric's knees, buckling him to the ground. Fire was burning with rage, but he heard a familiar voice telling him, *'Stay calm.'* It was his own conscious trying to keep him settled.

"You were expected days ago. Word has been sent to your father inquiring why he did not uphold his end of the bargain."

'Great. I've been traded for labor such as a fate a mule would receive.' He kept the pretense, but Fire knew he would not stay long.

"My apologies, sir," Fire said, hoisting himself to his feet. "I encountered a group of travelers who robbed me. My journey was delayed," he told him, giving a slight bow of the head. It was hard to stifle the smile from knowing he had told his first lie, or from the thoughts of what he planned to do to this rider to thank him for the warm welcome he was receiving. Being human was starting to feel pleasurable to him.

The man on the horse looked him over and frowned. "Come. There is much work," he barked, guiding the horse around to ride off.

'Ulric Larsen,' Fire thought. *'It's still horrendous, but a vast improvement from the name I was previously given.'*

He followed the man on horseback and walked toward the main house, thinking he would be given instruction of some form, or a tour of the grounds. It would be the last time he would assume the best from anyone.

The house loomed into view before him as soon as he cleared the tree line. It was humbler than expected given the size of the estate. Ulric stopped for a moment assessing his current situation. A few days should be more than enough time to survey the operations of the grounds, and he could see what he could manage to lift before leaving that would help him survive until he found a more permanent plan. With any luck, this would turn out favorably, and he'd stay longer considering the winter that would be fast approaching.

Too busy contemplating his options, he paid no attention to the man who oversaw the grounds for his new master. Ulric didn't notice how he turned back around on the horse to circle him until he felt the sharp edge of the whip cut into his back. He was knocked off his feet and landed face first in the ground swallowing a mouthful of dirt, and the horse's hooves barely missed his head as it trotted past him.

The pain was intense, and he didn't quite understand what had happened or why. Ulric saw the man's feet hit the ground as he climbed off the horse and approached him. Thinking the man had come to assist him, he raised onto all fours and reached out an arm for help righting himself. Instead, he was knocked onto his back when the man's foot smashed into his side, hitting his head hard on the dry ground when he fell. His ears were ringing and his vision blurred. Every image in his sight doubled, then tripled. The man's voice echoed around him as though a crowd were speaking in unison.

He was being yelled at and ordered to get to work. Anything would be better than dealing with the rider another moment only he wasn't sure where he was supposed to go, or what he was expected to be doing. It was obvious these questions would not be received well. Under threat of more pain, he scrambled to stand upright as quickly as possible which was almost unachievable as the ground around him was spinning fast.

The anger inside of him burned so hot he felt certain his flesh had boiled red along with it. If he wasn't so unsteady, he would have lunged at the man in front of him who hit the ground with the whip, illustrating his displeasure with Fire's slow pace.

An old man dressed in rags appeared from nowhere and put his arm around Ulric, leading him off. "Keep your head down," he muttered nervously. The old man then asked him what he thought he was doing.

"I don't know."

The old man repeated the question, yelling this time, "What do you think you are doing?"

His voice was filled with disgust, but Ulric could sense it was for the benefit of those who had their eyes on them, looking for any reason to intervene.

Ulric whispered, "I don't know what I'm supposed to do."

After they stumbled a ways off and were out of ear shot from the man on the horse, the old man's tone grew softer. "You are the servant we've been expecting, aye? Two years of service to repay your father's debt."

Ulric responded, "Yes."

"Follow me. Do as I do, and pray you're a fast learner."

He spent the day in the fields working the remains of the harvest, trying to learn as much as he could about those around him as well as the man they served. It was difficult to understand why they did not revolt and gain their freedom. They had the numbers to overtake the house. It was terror that kept them in their place. For most, their freedom would be short lived. They would be hunted down and discovered. Their fate would be death, if not worse, for their treachery.

By day's end, he was certain of three things. He would leave that night. There was plenty of bounty from the field's harvest that had been collected since before he arrived to take with him. Clothing and blankets suitable to survive the winter should he have to survive on his own in the back country would also be secured.

Secondly, it was definite there would be no threat of capture and punishment. While the estate would put out word of his disappearance once his absence was discovered in the morning, the search would be short lived. The body of the true Ulric Larsen would be discovered. Since no one of stature gives a peasant so much as a passing glance, they would be hard pressed to notice the glaring differences in their appearance. Even if they could, the letter found in what remained of the deceased man's possessions spelling out the details between his father and the estate owner would be proof enough to identify the body.

And lastly, he would have his revenge on the rider and the estate owner before his year was over.

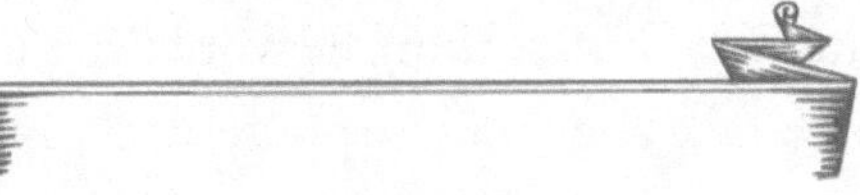

Chapter Two
The Proposal

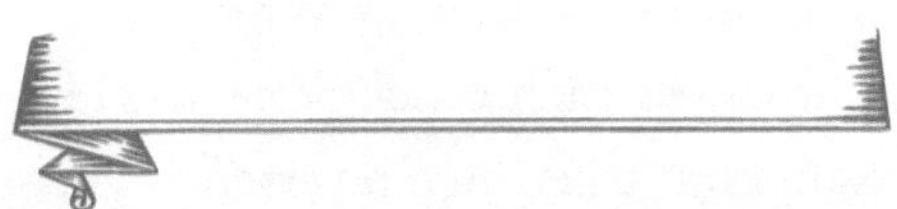

Ulric knew what the answer would be by the look on her face. She was anything but conventional. As long as he had known her, she lived her life according to her own terms. It was what attracted him to her in the first place.

"Married?" Camilla scoffed. "You actually want to get married?"

"Don't you think it's the right thing to do? We're going to have a baby."

Camilla rolled her eyes and shook her head. "So, you want to marry me because I'm pregnant?"

He burst into sudden, loud laughter, but cut it short when he saw her face. "No," he said, cupping her chin in his hand. "I want to marry you because I love you. Same as the three other times I have asked you. I'm hoping now this baby will be enough to convince you to say yes."

She raised her head and gave him a quick peck on the lips before sitting upright. "Why do we even need it? It's merely a piece of paper. It's not important."

"It's important to others. Think of our child who would be growing up with parents who are living in sin."

"You're showing your age. The world has changed a lot since you arrived," Camilla said, lifting the blankets and tossing them aside to get out of bed.

"Where are you going?" he asked.

"Work. It's called a job. I have one, remember?"

He sighed and laid back on his pillow as she walked down the hall to the bathroom. None of this had been expected since the moment they met, except possibly for her reaction to the proposal. All of his proposals for that matter met the same resistance. Their romance hadn't been planned and falling in love with her was the last thing he would've thought possible.

Sometimes people talk about their spouse declaring it was love at first sight. They would say the moment I laid eyes on her I knew she was the one. That was hardly the case for him and Camilla. The saying opposites attract might more aptly apply. They couldn't be more different. Most would assume, as he once did, that they would only serve to stifle one another, not provide any form of support. They were more like yin and yang. What set them apart complimented each other perfectly. His strengths were her weaknesses, and the same was true when reversed.

When they first met, it was an uncomfortable scene. One he didn't much think about afterward. As time wore on, they bumped into each other more and more. They settled into an awkward friendship. That alone was enough to surprise the man who had thought he'd seen it all before dozens of times over. Then one night, romance was in the air as they say. The moon and the stars were perfectly aligned for new lovers.

What they had together was electric. From their first touch, he knew their affair couldn't hold a candle to any woman he'd ever known. Ulric was only caught off guard when he found himself so hopelessly in love. There had been no one since that tragic day lifetimes ago, and he made every attempt to keep those memories buried deep.

No woman had captured his affection for a very long time. That was what he wanted. He derived pleasure from having the heart of stone that no one could pierce. Camilla managed to find her way through the centuries of walls he had built, and he was certain she accomplished the feat without even trying.

He had long known her past. It didn't matter to him because he honestly believed she loved him in return. Whatever paths she had taken, whatever choices she had made weren't important. It all led her right to him, just as he thought she forgave his past wrongs out of love for him as well. The only thing that mattered was feeling her close in his arms. He didn't yet know that he was merely a detour on the road she was traveling, and he wouldn't be able to hold her for long.

The pregnancy had been the biggest twist of all. It even surpassed the miracle odds of their romance. Ulric was aware he could produce children, but hadn't tried for centuries. Camilla had always been certain she was incapable since after her first pregnancy. The term barren had been used by more than one doctor throughout her life even though none of them had ever found a medical reason why she was unable to reproduce.

Camilla had been seriously ill for weeks. She made several visits to the doctor with no solid results. Whatever the ailment was she suffered from only seemed to worsen despite how much rest she had or how many different medications she was prescribed. He had offered to attempt to heal her on multiple occasions and practically begged endlessly as her condition worsened even though they both knew his blood probably wouldn't have the desired effect on her. Camilla always refused. It didn't matter how long he had been in the flesh. She would tease him that he didn't know squat about living. "Being a vampire," she told him, "meant he missed out on this part of the human experience."

She was certain it was merely a bug, and it would eventually go away. He couldn't help but worry and finally convinced her to go to the hospital. It had been relatively quiet in the emergency department that day. Ulric shared the waiting room with two others: a freckled faced boy missing his two front teeth and the boy's mother.

The boy smelled rancid as though he had managed to get away with skipping his bath for a month. Ulric pictured him splashing the bath water with his hands for several minutes before dressing for bed, tricking his mother into thinking he had in fact bathed. It was impossible to understand how she could be blind to his smell. Even now, Ulric's face still scrunched up at the recollection of the stench. The visions of the boy picking his nose and wiping his fingers under the seat of his chair haunted Ulric as well.

Today's era lacked a certain sophistication that he yearned to experience again. The days of long ago were filled with more raucous debauchery than anyone in the present time could imagine, but propriety held a certain place and was respected when it counted.

The boy had a yo-yo that he kept extending to hit Ulric's newspaper as he was skimming, trying to unsuccessfully pass the time. His mother was oblivious to not only the stench, but also to the ornery faces the boy would throw to Ulric after every disruption. Everything about the child grated his nerves from the dirt lined fingernails to his croaky voice when he spoke. For the first time since the rules of the Fire Elementals were laid out, rules Ulric helped to devise himself, he thought about breaking them.

The stress of the morning was getting to him, so he walked down the hall to get away from the brat. That was when he heard Camilla screaming at the doctors to run the tests again because there had to be a mistake. Running toward the sound of her voice, he made his way to her side fearing the worst. It had to be a terminal illness. Unbeknownst to the doctors, his love wasn't at risk of dying, but they'd be forced to move from their home, community, and friends they'd made to avoid the scrutiny of a miraculous recovery. Camilla could get ill and think she could taunt him about not being able to have the full human experience, but she wasn't going to die. He was certain of that.

He sat frozen and numb after hearing the word pregnant. Voices swirled around his head, and he felt close to passing out. Camilla insisted there was some mistake. She repeatedly told the doctor she wasn't able to have children. The doctor delivering the news assured her the only mistake was made by whoever told her she was infertile.

Leaving the hospital with her, he walked by the boy and his mother who were still seated in the waiting room. Nightmarish visions floated through his head of what could be in his future, but he resolved then that any child of his would not be raised to act in that manner.

That was two weeks ago, and Camilla was already almost three months along when they found out. Her attitude toward the pregnancy had been indifferent at best. The night of the emergency room visit she appeared hesitant but optimistic. Her mood had gradually gone downhill ever since. He tried to be patient with her and understanding of how hard the shock must have hit.

Once the spray of the shower could be heard down the hall, he got out of bed and went to talk to her while she couldn't easily walk away and avoid the topic. He gave the door a quick knock before opening it so as not to scare her. She could call him old fashioned all she wanted. He'd been called far worse.

"Listen. I know it's a different world now, but people are still looked down on for less," he said, leaning against the sink.

"What name?" she yelled from behind the curtain.

He misunderstood what she was asking. "Baby names? For our child?"

She peeked her face out from one side of the shower curtain, and answered, "No. What name would you use if we got married?"

"Ulric Larsen, of course."

"Ugh," she groaned, snapping the curtain back. "I hate that name."

He crossed his arms and laughed. "I don't know how you would possibly like the other one if you ever found it out. Besides, it doesn't have a surname anyway."

The water stopped, and she groped her hand along the wall for the towel.

He reached for it and handed it to her.

A couple minutes later, she pulled the curtain wide open and stood before him with the towel wrapped around her body. "It's last name. No one says surname anymore, Gramps. Make one up."

Ulric pulled the corner of his mouth back thinking about a bygone era. A surname had been devised for it long ago at a time when he thought he would have use for it. "If I use my real name, you'll marry me?"

Camilla stepped out of the shower and grabbed a second towel to wrap around her hair. "Do we have to go through the horse and pony show? Can't you have one of your contacts draw up some papers that will say we're married without suffering the whole production of it? You know that kind of attention is not for me."

He tilted his head to the side while he considered it. This wasn't what he had in mind, but they'd still be legally wed as far as anyone was concerned. Camilla would be his wife which is all he longed for in the world. Following her back to the bedroom, he agreed. "I'll get the documents and use my real name, but," he bargained, "you stop working."

Immediately, she glared at him. "Fine," she forced the fakest smile. "Call me Mrs. Larsen then because I'm running late for work."

Ulric laughed at her. He had hoped for something a little more romantic when he built the courage to propose.

Again.

For the fourth time.

It worked out well in the end. The last thing he ever wanted to do was use his given name. The name was utterly outrageous, barely worthy of a soap opera character. It would not do for a presence like Fire.

AIDEN WAS PERFECT FROM the curly tufts of hair on the top of his head to the tiny nails on his toes. Ulric couldn't get enough of his son. Not having a job to trudge off to every day allowed him to spend every moment he could with his boy.

If only Camilla looked at their son in the same way, life would have been perfect. The baby blues hit her hard after he was born, but they didn't seem to be letting up. Someday, he would be honest with himself and admit her coldness toward their baby began long before the night she went into labor. Every book he read and every doctor he asked said her behavior was normal, and it would ease. Nothing was getting better. Instead, it only continued to get worse.

The first few days after she had him, he didn't think much about it. Camilla was exhausted and needed to recover from bringing a life into the world. He didn't mind stepping up and taking care of things, but he had wished she would have at least given nursing a try. There was no convincing her. Even that worked out in his favor because it was more time for him to bond with his son while he fed him.

As soon as her body would allow, she wanted to go back to work. That's when the fighting began. If she wouldn't give up the job altogether like he had wanted her to from the beginning, she could at least take the leave of absence offered to her. Camilla refused. "That isn't who I am," she repeated time and again.

He had always known she wasn't one for a classic family life, but his love for her blinded him to so much that should have been obvious to see. Somehow, he thought that not folding to traditional roles or caring about marriage wouldn't cross over to motherhood. It's supposed to be instinctual after all.

Days turned into weeks which turned into months. He tried everything he could think of to do to win her back. They had been in love for a long time before Camilla found out she was pregnant. It had been quite the shock for both of them, and he wasn't sure how he felt about it at first. Having more children wasn't something he had planned. As the idea of being a father again took root, he became overjoyed that they were having a baby.

The same couldn't be said for her. From the moment she found out, she started to draw away. It was so slight at first that he didn't notice it until after Aiden arrived. Thinking back, he saw all the signs he had missed. No, they weren't really overlooked at all. He had done as he always had and made excuses for her.

"It was quite a shock."

"She's overwhelmed."

"She's in denial. It takes some getting used to when you never thought it was possible."

The glaring truth was she never wanted to be a mother. If she had been truly honest with herself about the choices she had made long ago, it wouldn't have been a secret why being a mother was something she couldn't face. Once their son was born, Camilla really changed. She was always working long hours or just too exhausted to do anything except sleep.

Before long, Aiden's first birthday was fast approaching. Ulric had spent weeks planning a party and invited all their friends and everyone he knew who had a child. The morning of the party, Camilla got up and got ready. It appeared like maybe she was going to enjoy the day with them as a family for a change. Once she was dressed, she dropped the news that she had agreed to come into the office on her day off because the staff had fallen so far behind.

Ulric let her go. He knew it was a lie, but he didn't try to confront her. Later, he wondered where she had really gone and how she spent her time while she claimed she was working the extra shift, but thoughts like those would only lead him down paths that are better off not traveled. Aiden's party was the first time he let himself accept the idea they wouldn't be a family for much longer.

After that, Camilla started traveling for work. Another lie. It wasn't part of her job. He stopped by the office with Aiden one afternoon to surprise her only to learn she didn't work there. No one by the name of Camilla Sabry or Camilla Larsen had ever worked for the company.

He went home hell bent on confronting her when she finally walked through the door. The hours ticked slowly by. Aiden played and laughed, and pulled him out of his anger. By the time Camilla arrived, he didn't care anymore. Their relationship ended when the pregnancy started. It just took him far too long to realize it.

The tricky part would be ending it. While she wanted nothing to do with their son now, that didn't mean she wouldn't try to take him with her when they went their separate ways. Having an heir was far more important to her than it could ever be to him. She may not have any interest in his raising, but Aiden would be especially vital to her when he was older. It was a fear that settled in his core and affected every decision he made from that point forward. The dread still controlled him even after Camilla made things easy by walking out on him.

After returning from the first of what would become an annual camping trip, he found his son asleep in his bed, but the woman who was his wife only by forged documents was nowhere to be found. Of all the Return attempts he had succeeded in making an appearance, this one seemed both the most trifling and of the greatest consequence. The world had long been in peril from the elements that raged war against it. There was no rhyme or reason to the natural disasters that plagued the planet anymore. Balance was lost.

Aiden had opened his eyes to the reality that they needed to go back. The Elements needed to take up their post and correct this collision course. The family he had previously did make him think of their future, with and without him, if he crossed the veil. This was different. It was crystal clear to him that if the Elements didn't manage to pull it off soon, there wouldn't be a world for them to watch over anymore.

It was his want of a long life for his son that forced his hand that year. Unfortunately, Camilla stayed at home with their boy. They had originally planned a getaway together to a picturesque cabin in the middle of the mountains. It was miles from the nearest neighbor. This was supposed to be a romantic getaway for the two of them, a chance to reconnect. It was a last ditch effort to save their relationship and make things right. Friends were going to keep an eye on Aiden, and all the documents had been drawn up for his future if the Return did occur.

At the last minute, Camilla backed out, claiming she had a stomach bug. It didn't fool Ulric. He knew the last place she would want to be that weekend was at a remote cabin with him. Funny, though, he never worried that she'd leave him and Aiden behind. Ulric feared she'd take his son away from him more than anything. Even though Camilla couldn't feign interest in their son, he knew her family would never let her walk away from the boy once they learned of his existence.

The previous year he had skipped the Return to be with his new family. He made an inner pact that night not to miss another one until they reached a millennium in this realm. With Camilla's refusal to come along and his sense of foreboding, he almost broke the covenant he made with himself. In the end, he went if for no other reason than he didn't want her to have an inkling he no longer trusted her. He departed for the Return, but not before having an old confidant keep tabs on her while he was gone. If she did flee with Aiden, he wanted a trail to follow.

Most of his distress proved to be false. Camilla had no designs for taking their son away. The glass of wine she had poured was on the counter only half drank when he walked in the front door of the house, and the bath water was still running upstairs. He assumed she fled the house as soon as he pulled in the driveway. He had left the cabin earlier than he had planned coming home the night before he said he'd be back, so Camilla wouldn't have expected him until the next afternoon. Perhaps that was why she never left a note. Briefly, he considered the possibility something had happened to her, but even if it had, she was more than capable of defending herself against any adversary.

The friend he asked to keep an eye on her didn't see anything strange. He never saw Camilla leave the house. It was possible she realized she had a tail, or acted out of caution in case there was one. Near as he could tell, she walked out of the back door and vanished.

There was never any relief from having her voluntarily leave the picture. He never felt safe with the constant torment that she may one day come back for their son. A life of checking locks and always looking over his shoulder was not one that he was accustomed to, nor was it one he would tolerate long. The only answer was to move and try to hide where they would never be found. The burning question was where they would go.

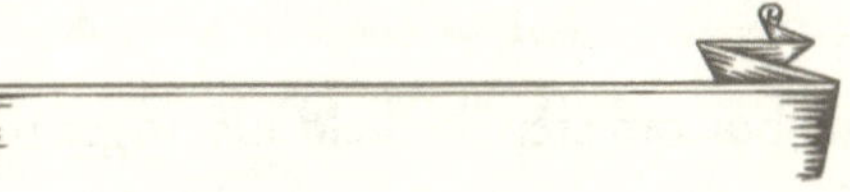

Chapter Three
The Babysitter

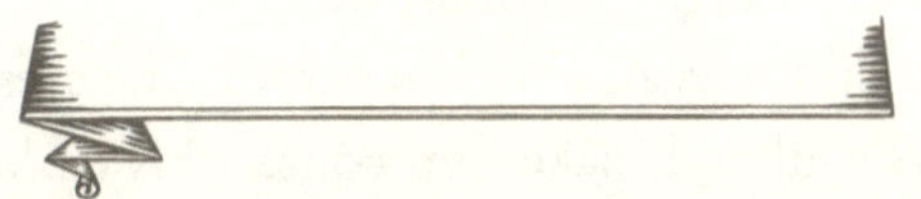

It didn't take long to find her. With all of his contacts working on it, he hadn't expected it too. One proved more valuable than the rest and was rapidly becoming a dynamic ally. After one trip to verify it was her, he put his house out east on the market and began the process of moving over six hundred miles away.

The new house was purchased without ever having viewed it in person and very few items were brought with them to their new home. New identities were created for him and his son. It was a matter of days before they were on the road to start over in a small town that wasn't far enough away from Camilla's roots as he would like. Even so, it was the safest neighborhood he could imagine for them.

He drove around the block several times before gathering the nerve to park out front. Their history would mean nothing to her the moment she laid eyes upon him for having the audacity to put her at risk. For the sake of not causing a scene where she lived if for no other reason, he hoped she would hear him out before resorting to drastic measures to force him to leave. Their arrival would not go undetected, or at least his son's presence would not be unnoticed. It was no surprise to see her waiting on the porch after collecting his son from the backseat of the car.

She braved a wide stance trying to appear larger than she actually stood which amused him. Her arms were crossed, and her mouth was drawn into a thin line. Once she recognized him, her eyes softened, but the rest of her demeanor held firm. It wouldn't take much for her to turn him away. Quite the opposite as he considered it. Receiving a cold shoulder was an almost certainty. The only hope of receiving any hospitality rested solely on her love for family and children.

Approaching the bottom step, he held his finger to his mouth, warning her to stay quiet. He couldn't risk the wrong thing being said. Not now. Not when they were so close to safety. Shifting his weight, he moved his sleeping son to a more comfortable position in his arms.

"Hello, ma'am," he said cheerfully. "We're new in town, and I'm in need of a babysitter. You came highly recommended."

Her arms fell to her side, and her lips parted. The eyes which could bore into a grown man's soul and make him confess his darkest sins grew wide until they consumed the rest of her features. "This is your son?" she asked in disbelief.

"Yes, ma'am," he smiled, relishing her surprised reaction.

"You have a son?" she asked again.

He narrowed his eyes and put his finger to his lips a second time. Looking side to side, he scanned the street in both directions to see if anyone was around.

The worried way he demanded secrecy didn't go ignored. "Come inside," she offered, sounding as though she was aware of the mistake she was making as she extended the invitation. "We can discuss things over a glass of iced tea."

He walked up the steps with his son in his arms, and she held the screen door open for him. Giving the neighborhood one last once over, she followed him inside.

In the living room, he felt his nervousness melt away. There was still a great deal of unease caused by the woman standing behind him, but he knew her well enough. This home would be spelled. No one would gather any information on what occurred inside these walls if anyone were to try. He laid his son on the couch. When he turned around, she was spitting daggers at him with her eyes. "I know," he said, holding up both hands. "I'm sorry. We need help."

"More like you will need help when I'm through with you. Showing up here unannounced like this! How did you find me?"

Looking at her coyly, he answered, "I have my ways."

She sighed heavily. "What do you want, Ulr-,"

"No," he said hastily, motioning for her to stop speaking. How quickly he forgot this home was a safe zone. Old habits die hard. Realizing his tone was a little too sharp, he took a deep breath. If she even suspected there was more to the truth than he was willing to let on or that he was about to lie to her face, he'd be on his own without her ever giving it a second thought. "Don't. That's not my name. It never was," he said, looking out the front window nervously.

She looked down at the boy sleeping peacefully on the couch, and he could see the wheels turning in her mind. The weight of the situation, while still unknown to her, was starting to settle. The rest of the visit needed to unfold the way he had prepped himself to handle it. There needed to be just enough information for her to understand his trepidation without revealing the big picture, and how deeply it terrified him.

"Who is this little guy?" she asked, not taking her eyes off the child.

"This is my son, Jackson Montgomery," he told her, holding out his hand. "I'm Judd. Pleased to meet you."

She looked at his extended hand and scoffed. "Judd Montgomery," she huffed with another icy glare, refusing to shake his hand. "How can I help you?"

"I really am in need of babysitting services."

Straightening up, she balled her hands into fists. "You're kidding," she growled.

"No, ma'am," he grinned devilishly. "I was told that you're the best."

She closed her eyes and took a deep breath, and he knew she was summoning the strength to resist knocking him to the floor. "Come on," she bade him, walking into the next room. "Let's discuss details then. Your unexpected arrival intrigues me just enough to humor you, so watch it," she warned.

Judd sat at the table and waited while she got two glasses from the cabinet. He looked around the kitchen. It was bright and airy. "Beautiful home you have," he complimented.

"Humph," she snorted, pouring tea into the glasses. Bringing the drinks to the table, she eyed him carefully before sitting down. "It is rather lovely," she agreed then added, "and I used to think it quite safe too."

This reaction to seeing him was expected, but he quickly steered the conversation away from her misgivings about him. They started talking about the neighborhood and the quiet community she lived in, but it was

Eloise's eyes widened, and she opened and closed her mouth several times. Words didn't often fail her.

"In the bathtub," he looked down at the table, trying not to smile. He knew how ridiculous it sounded. If Eloise would buy it, then anyone would. Time to tell the tale he concocted on the drive.

"She, uh... She had a hard time after Jackson was born. You know," he stumbled around his words, pretending it was hard to discuss. He rubbed his hands together and rested his elbows on the table. "The doctor said it was normal. Nothing to worry about."

"Ah," Eloise nodded. "Yes, quite common."

He stretched his neck from side to side. "They put her on some pill. Said it would help her sleep," he looked back at Eloise. "Something about better sleep would help her mood during the day," he said, cutting his eyes to the side.

"Did it help?"

Judd shrugged. "I don't know. I don't think so, but maybe it did. Maybe she'd have been worse without it."

So far, every word of his story was the truth. Camilla had been prescribed sleeping pills to help with her baby blues as they called it back then. They didn't seem to help her mood in the least, and Judd had never been certain she was taking them. If she was, it wouldn't have been pretty to see how much worse she was without them.

The sound of running feet caught his attention, and he turned toward the hall. The children never appeared in the doorway. They got close then ran back the other direction again. It reinforced the idea he had made the right choice in coming here knowing Jackson had a friend to play with who would someday understand his origins.

"The medicine knocked her out soon after taking it," he began again, looking back at the table. "One day...for whatever reason...she took a late night bath, and...," he paused, performing his best to appear as though it was a hard subject to discuss. "By the time I found her, nothing could be done."

He let his story hang in the air for a moment and took a long drink from his glass. "There are those who aren't convinced it wasn't intentional," he managed to force his voice to crack.

Eloise sucked in her breath, "Oh, my." She reached over and patted his hand.

Judd couldn't look directly at her. If he did, he'd smile and blow the whole cover he just sold her. Instead, he wiped at the corner of one eye for added effect.

Neither of them said another word for several minutes. They sipped their tea and fidgeted around in their chairs as the silence grew uncomfortable.

"What was her name?"

He put his finger to his lips then pointed to his ear. "You and I are both aware there are people proficient at honing in on conversations if they choose."

"Judd Montgomery, are you implying you think I'm incapable of keeping my home protected?" she asked indignantly.

"Not at all," he shook his head. "It's simply something I need to make the norm. I need to get into the habit of not discussing her." When in reality, if Eloise learned her name, she may be able to learn the truth.

Eloise nodded and leaned toward him. "Are you in trouble? What exactly is it that has you so concerned?" she asked quietly.

"Her family." He was broadening his lie, but it was based in fact.

"They're after you?" her eyes widened.

He drummed his fingers on the table. "They don't even know me. We've never met. I'm just worried they may find out about my boy and try to take him."

Judd stretched back and clasped his hands together on the top of his head, staring out the small kitchen window. "I can't go through it again, Eloise. You remember what happened. If I hadn't run into Thomas... If I hadn't directed my anger to saving our kind rather than killing them, I don't know when I would've stopped. I can't go through it again," he said, bringing his arms down and resting them on the table. "I can't lose my son."

That softened her features, and she nodded. Family had always been the focus of her world. Eloise treated all children as her own. She would move heaven and earth to protect an innocent babe. That is why he came here. There was nowhere more free from harm for Jackson than in the care of this woman. He knew she was thinking he might be a little too overprotective. That was fine by him because what she didn't know could hurt her, but it could also protect her. Time would tell which was which. He hoped what he had told her was enough for her to would accommodate him.

The children's laughter drifted down the hallway. "That explains why they hit it off so quickly," Eloise thought aloud.

Judd narrowed his eyes and waited for her to explain.

"Everleigh lost her mama too. Remember?" she sighed. "In childbirth."

"I'm sorry, Eloise. I didn't realize this little girl was her child."

Eloise slowly nodded. "It was hard, but I suppose I'm used to loss by now," she said, looking off toward the sound of the laughter drifting down to the doorway. "Children sense these things, you know. Those two won't be able to put it into words, but they can feel the connection bringing them together. They both know life without their mama."

"Yes," Judd agreed, seizing the opening, "and it's not their only connection either. That makes our job even more difficult, doesn't it?"

It was her turn to not understand. "What job?" she asked, ignoring his reference to their shared connections.

"Raising them. You know all too well, Eloise, our children need to have a careful upbringing. He wouldn't be safe with someone who didn't fully understand our way of life." Judd made one last appeal to drive home his undertaking.

Eloise sighed, "How long do you need me to watch him? Do you need to be out of town for a few days to make the arrangements?"

Judd pitched his head to the side, and said with a glint in his eyes, "Actually, I was hoping it might be a reoccurring, as needed thing."

She raised an eyebrow. "Reoccurring?"

"Well, yeah, a single father might find himself in need of a babysitter from time to time. Even one who doesn't have to work for a living like me," he said, taking another swig from his glass.

The gears were grinding away in her head again, and he could tell she was pondering the questions she wasn't sure she wanted answered.

"Right now, I could use someone to keep an eye on him while I do some shopping. We need furniture."

"Furniture," she repeated, sounding unsure.

"Our house is pretty much empty."

"Ulr-," she caught herself. "Judd Montgomery, where exactly is this house of yours?"

He smiled mischievously at her. "From here..." he looked out of the corner of his eye as he counted. "I'd say it's about seven, maybe eight blocks."

Eloise's eyes rolled back. "Fairview has gone to hell in a handbasket if they'll let a vampire move to town." She pointed toward the hallway where the kids were playing and added, "And soon there's going to be two of you."

"Now, wait just a minute, Eloise," Judd spat at her with a knowing grin. "You don't know that for sure." He picked up his glass and held it near his lips. "He might take after his mom."

She narrowed her eyes and scowled at him.

"Jackson may turn into a wolf," he concluded, taking a drink.

Her eyes burst wide, and her mouth fell open. He expected her to be shocked, but the expression on her face caught him so off guard he choked on the tea. It sprayed from his nose and mouth across the table. He coughed several times, gasping for air before regaining his composure.

Eloise stared menacingly at him as she lifted a napkin to her cheek to wipe off the tea that had shot from his mouth far enough to reach her face.

Judd lost it as he watched her and laughed until he wheezed.

"Get out," she demanded.

He waved his hands in front of him finding it hard to speak. "I'm...so sorry. Really."

Eloise stood up and pointed toward the front door. "Now! Maybe by the time you're through picking out your bedroom sets, I'll have calmed down enough to let you in to gather your boy."

He stood, smiling at her. It wasn't the first time he'd angered her, not by a long shot. It most likely wouldn't be the last time either. "Yes, ma'am," he told her, still laughing.

"Out!" she screamed.

"I'm going. I'm going," he said, picking up the pace as he walked through the living room.

Judd opened the front door and stepped onto the porch. Before closing it behind him, he peeked his head back inside, "Can I get you anything while I'm gone?"

Eloise growled, and he jumped back, shutting the door just as the vase she threw hit the other side and shattered. He blinked at the door a few times and shrugged. "Guess not," he mumbled out loud before exploding in another fit of laughter.

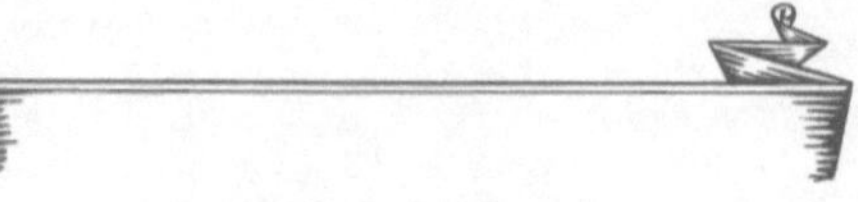

Chapter Four
Revenge

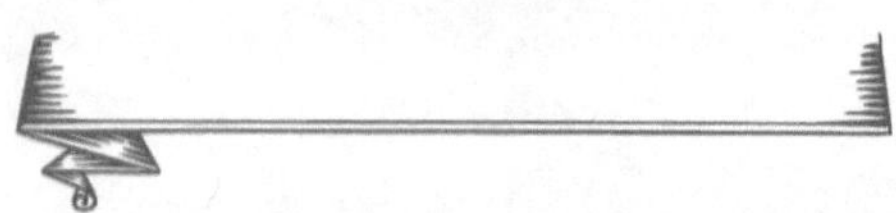

These people were crazy. It was beyond his comprehension why Water ever wanted to go on this quest of exploring earth in the flesh. There was no reason or logic to the maddening way they constructed their society. Across the water, starving people were killed for hunting in the king's forest. If you could not afford to pay and were caught, the punishment was public mutilation and death. And for what? A wild hare? Meanwhile the people of privilege had more than they could consume, letting most go to waste without nary an afterthought.

The most preposterous act of all was to erect a gallows in the front of a church. As if their God, or any God, desired to be associated with public executions. It was blasphemous.

The vicious acts were well known before any of them came to this land. Whether or not any of them agreed with what was happening wasn't their place to say. Still, his knowing how these miserable creatures went about their lives couldn't prepare him for being there to see it in the flesh. It's not the same when you are watching from worlds away. Only the grand scheme can be seen from beyond the veil, not the details. The small bits are what make the acts so vile.

Public executions are not for the purposes of punishment at all. That's only a guise to make right their morbid actions of the macabre. It's for sport. These heathens gather and cheer on the executioners. No manner of crime ever received a proper sentence. Stealing a loaf of bread to feed your family could land you with your entrails wrapped around your neck while your fellow countrymen shout obscenities and throw rotten food your way. The very people who were your friends and neighbors yesterday would be there in the crowds today, hollering in delight as the sword cuts through your flesh.

The crime and punishment he bore witness to his first summer alive cut the deepest. He did not witness the crime as much as heard it, but by the time he found the poor young girl he was too late. For almost an hour, he searched through the woods trying to follow the sound of her cries. The echoing from the rock walls of the caves bouncing off the trees made it hard for him to pinpoint her location. If only he had the heightened sense capabilities as he had in spirit form, he could have discovered her in time, preventing her from suffering all the horrors she had been subjected to endure.

When he found her, she lay dirty and bloody in a heap on the ground. Minutes sluggishly ticked by before he could be certain she had lived through her horrible attack. The soldiers laughed and told stories near the fire with their drink as though nothing out of sorts had been carried on by one of them that night, much less by all of them in turn.

Fire waited and pondered how to make a move. Anger was the prevalent emotion fueling him since arriving, and it burned to new heights throughout his body watching the men in their revelry. It didn't take long for one man to step just inside the tree line to relieve himself. This was his chance. Fire jumped from where he'd been crouching in the shadows and took the dagger from the soldier's side, stabbing him through the neck.

The soldier fell to his knees, urinating on himself in the process. Both hands clawed at his neck trying in vain to remove whatever force yet unseen by his eyes that was choking him. The dagger dripped with blood, and Fire stared at it mesmerized by the dark, sweet smelling liquid that covered the blade. Lifting it slowly to his mouth, he licked the side of the dagger savoring the metallic flavor unable to tell if it was the steel of the weapon or the iron in the blood that overwhelmed his taste buds.

The soldier's eyes filled with terror watching his murderer relish in the added torment of enjoying his blood as the life drained out of his body. The last thing the soldier saw before his death was the homicidal man in the woods smile in delight, watching the spark of life leave his eyes while his own blood dripped from the corner of the stranger's mouth.

Fire's thoughts soon turned to the remaining soldiers nearby. From the shadows of the trees, he watched them for several minutes. How blissfully unaware they were that anything had happened to their comrade mere feet from where they laughed heartily, imbibing their spirits. Circling around to the north, sticking to the darkness, he waited for his moment to attack.

Two of the soldiers fell to the blade he still carried before the third one managed to stumble to his feet. Ulric knew he could take him out swiftly, but he welcomed the novelty of a fight. Even as this ghastly man's condition rendered his odds of triumph to the bare minimum, the soldier made one lunging move toward Ulric and tripped into the fire. He rolled and moaned on the ground. His skin blistering under red embers that clung to him, burning into his flesh. Ulric enjoyed watching the man's misery, appreciating how he deserved a far worse death for his crimes.

A noise caught his attention, and he turned to see a horrified look from the young woman. Not wanting her to endure more than what she had already been put through, he slit the suffering soldier's throat before rushing to her side. Blood bubbled at the corner of her mouth, and one eye was nearly swollen shut. She whimpered, trying in vain to scoot backward and away from him, filled with fear. His heart broke over her reaction. There was no way he could ever harm her, not his beloved Sophie.

He had been spying her for months ever since spring broke and gave way to summer. The village came to life again, and he immersed himself in the bustling day to day lives of the townsfolk while maintaining a low profile. He only caught glimpses of her at first and accidentally stumbled upon learning her name. He had long been aware of who she was and unfortunately, her family. Regrettably, the original plan for revenge he vowed on his first day here would've included her as well, even if he hadn't planned the exact manner in which he would carry it out. It would not have been near as disgusting as the torture these animals put her through.

Ulric had long allowed his lust for her to rage unchecked. At night, he would close his eyes and see images of her behind his eyelids. His thoughts hadn't been much better than the actions of the soldiers tonight. Only his thoughts would've remained simply that - thoughts. Never acted upon. Physical passion had been the only thing he was aware he ever felt for her until now.

Sophie lay trembling from the terrors she had endured, and she was pierced with fear over what this murderous man who appeared from nowhere might have in store for her. As he gazed upon her, lust was the farthest thought from his mind. Replacing it was a feeling he didn't recognize. It was soft, careful, and gentle. It was everything he was not.

Scanning the camp, he found water the soldiers had collected. He used it to clean her wounds as best he could. Gently, he lifted her even as she tried to protest and began the walk through the forest back to her father's estate. It was several miles away. There was no need for her to give him any information or direction. Ulric was already acquainted with the miserable property she called home.

She passed out in his arms, and he stopped several times on the trek to check on her and allow her to rest. The sun was beginning to rise by the time he arrived. He was confident the servants would already be awake, and he would have to make a hurried getaway to avoid being seen. At the doorstep of her home, he laid her down carefully, but she awoke. She looked around to see where he had brought her, and she became terrified again, trying to tell him no once she recognized her surroundings.

Ulric couldn't understand why she wouldn't want to be there. Her home should make her feel safe. The security of her family is what she needed most in her recovery. He fought the urge to keep her by his side. The desire to nurse her wounds and heal her heart was overwhelming. He suspected it must be the nightmarish ordeal she went through that was causing her to act irrationally. Even as she objected, he left her and disappeared back into the forest.

Days later, word spread through the village when the bodies of the commander's hunting party had been found brutally murdered. It didn't go unnoticed by anyone that the bodies were discovered just days after shame was brought upon the Addler estate by his eldest daughter Sophie. The girl's father turned her in for murdering the soldiers. It was absurd that anyone could think she was capable of such an attack, or had even the strength to lift a dagger after being raped and beaten so severely. Her father was happy to be rid of her and her disgrace all the same.

As retribution for the soldiers' crimes, the army quietly paid Sophie's father a hefty stipend. The payment would never reach her which inflamed Ulric. The idea that a father would profit off his own daughter's violation filled him with rage.

Sophie's fate was far worse. The punishment for the murder of soldiers in the service of the emperor was death. She would be publicly hanged. Deep down, Ulric knew her father didn't believe she was guilty of the crime, and the only reason her father turned her in was to make money off his daughter's death with the collection of the reward. In his mind, her father was killing two birds with one stone since his estate was facing difficulties. He could rid himself of the shame while achieving financial security.

Ulric scanned the large crowd gathering in the village. The weight of knowing he was responsible for Sophie's fate bore upon his every thought. Leaving Sophie at the door of her father's house had been the hardest thing he'd done since arriving here last year. Not even the horrid depths he had to go to in order to survive the bitter cold of the winter could compare to walking away from her that night. Sophie's eyes had begged him not to go, or rather to take her with him. At least that's what his hopeful mind wanted to believe she was trying to tell him with her look. He had been certain he had acted in good conscience by bringing her home.

Sophie had captivated him since the moment he first laid eyes on her. For months he had watched her in secret, memorizing every inch of her, the way she laughed, the way she tilted her head when she was curious about something. If his time here wasn't finite, he'd have moved the heavens to be hers. She alone would have been enough for him to leave all thoughts of revenge on her father aside if she would have him, and if he was free to ask her. There was also the pesky matter of not interfering with the lives of those he came in contact with to consider when deciding how deep to make his acquaintances.

Still, when he found her in the forest not even a week before, he wanted to take her to his makeshift forest home. He wanted to hold her while she wept for her lost innocence and what couldn't be undone. He wanted to nurse her physical wounds, and he longed to be the guiding voice to help ease her mind and soul. If there was a way in which she could ever experience life as fully as she had before, he wanted to be the one who showed her the way back.

When word reached his ears a couple days later about the aftermath of her attack, he saw red. His anger consumed him until he could feel the fires of his rage surging through his veins. Sophie never wavered in her recount of the events that unfolded the night of her attack. Her recollection stayed strong right down to the unknown man who carried her several miles through the forest to deliver her home. Yet, her tales were discarded as insubordinate fantasy. No one took her word as more than outrageous lies in a preposterous attempt to excuse her lost virtue. She was not believed until the bodies of the hunting party had been discovered by soldiers sent to search for them.

The commander of the army did pay a visit to the estate and paid her father a handsome sum in restitution for the disgrace brought on his family's name by his men. Theodore Addler received the payment, not his daughter Sophie who was the one to actually endure such spirit shattering trauma. And worse, he kept it while throwing his own flesh and blood to the wolves. She was removed from her home by force before her injuries could fully heal for dishonoring her father's name as though she had any fault to play in what happened to her. Even if Ulric hadn't already sworn vengeance on him after his first day in this realm, that alone would have brought his wrath upon the man.

Before he could find her to rescue her from the people he thought would be best to provide her aide, the situation grew exponentially worse. His beloved was arrested for the murder of the soldiers. As if she hadn't been forced to endure enough already, she was bound and given a quick trial if one could stoop low enough to call it that. The commander met with the village's magistrate and brought his own judge to the meeting as well. It was decided that the evidence in the case was overwhelmingly strong, pointing to Sophie as the murderer. Therefore, she was declared guilty with her execution by hanging to be carried out the next day. This would allow the commander to return to his post expediently.

There is no logical way such a small woman, after having been raped in succession and beaten within minutes of death, could have the strength to overtake four soldiers on her own. Their swift determination was to bring the matter to an accelerated close for the sake of the commander's interests. Possibly it could also have been a ruse to draw out the real culprit behind the soldiers' deaths if the guilty party did in fact care enough to save her life a second time. If that was the case, their plan would work far beyond what they had hoped with detrimental results.

Sophie was walked out to the gallows to be hanged in front of a large crowd that had gathered. They cheered as she emerged, rooting for her death. Ulric stood in the crowd watching the villagers celebrate the hanging with more frenzy and cheer than one would regale at a wedding. It disgusted him, and he lost what little faith in humankind he had managed to build during the last nine months. As her sentence was read out to the crowd flaming their cheers, his anger grew red hot, and he felt it physically searing his skin.

He didn't take his eyes off her until after she looked into the crowd directly at him. It would be difficult for her to have recognized him between her swollen eyes and the way she drifted in and out of consciousness when he carried her home. Somehow when she noticed him in the maddening mob, the glint in her eye told him she remembered him. The remorse he felt forced his eyes to dart away. If he had only listened to her that night, she would be safe.

On both sides of the platform was a torch, and he focused on one in a weak effort to keep his eyes from drifting back to her. As he gazed upon it, the flame shot up, tripling in size. Ulric quickly looked to the one on the other side of the platform with the same result. He realized that even in his human form his erupting temper was giving him a greater manipulation of his Element than he had been previously aware he had.

Without a moment's pause to think his actions through, he intensified the fire from both torches until it set the gallows ablaze. Not stopping after his first trick, he continued to fan the flames into the church yard. The dry heat along with the spirits they were guzzling in their revelry caused members of the crowd to soon catch fire. In seconds, the flames had spread through the horde and to the buildings in all directions. Within minutes, the fire was spreading throughout the village without him continuing to fuel the flames.

People screamed as they attempted to run from the danger. They knocked others down and trampled them as they tried to flee to safety. Some rushed to put out the fires, or to save a loved one who was dying an agonizing death in the street. Most of them only cared to save themselves.

When he looked back to the gallows, the fires had spared her. The edges of the platform around her were in flames, and fear seared in her eyes. Somehow as he lost control of his emotions and destroyed everything in sight that he could, he managed to keep her safe. The flames danced around on either side as though invisible walls protected her.

While everyone ran the opposite direction trying to escape the church yard, he ran straight to Sophie. Using his dagger, he sliced through the rope around her neck and the rope that bound her hands behind her back. Once she was free, she looked at him with the same recognition as when she found him in the sea of faces. She lost consciousness and passed out either from the heat of the raging fires or from shock. He caught her and for the second time, carried her off through the forest.

This time he brought her to the hut he had fashioned for himself from an abandoned hunting shack he happened to stumble upon months ago. He laid her down and watched over her while she slept. Ulric vowed that for as long as he remained on this earth, he would see to it that no more harm came to her. The first order of business in protecting her would be to personally make sure her father got what he deserved.

While it will always be a dark mark on his personal history that he burned through an entire village, many of the people actually survived. However, most of the buildings did not, including the country estate of Addler.

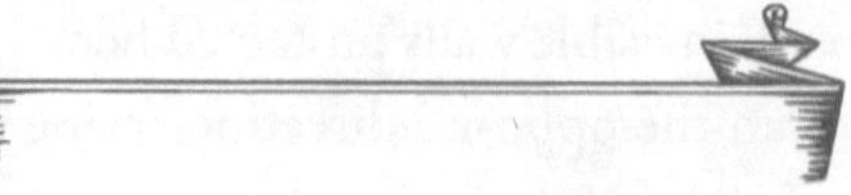

Chapter Five
Elemental Lineage

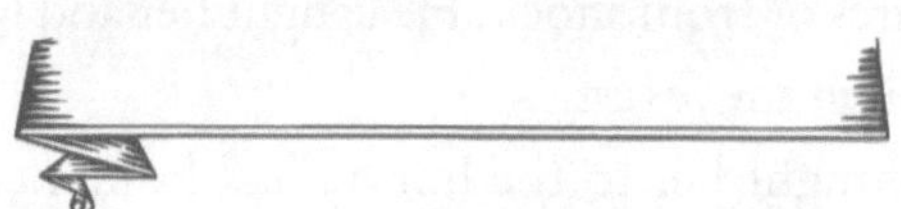

Judd waited while his son checked his phone when it chimed. He knew the text was from Everleigh before Jackson even read it. The two of them were as close as siblings and were always at each other's side. It didn't surprise him that Everleigh would want to talk to Jackson about the news right away. What surprised him was how soon she was trying to get ahold of him. He had barely had a chance to begin saying anything to his son.

Eloise had agreed it was time, and they would talk to the children tonight. He didn't expect for his old friend to be finished so soon, but it shouldn't have surprised him. Witches were an accepted part of today's world. Eloise didn't bat an eye at anyone's opinion that she might be one, not like she would have lifetimes ago. She walked a fine line, allowing people to draw their own conclusions without fully admitting anything, but around her family, she was open about being a witch. Even Everleigh had been raised with the knowledge about her family's magical history, but until tonight, Judd wasn't sure how much Everleigh had been told about Jackson.

He waited until Jackson sent a reply and set the phone back down. "Everleigh?" Judd asked.

"Yeah. How did you know?"

Judd rapped his fingers on the table, and asked, "When is it not Everleigh?"

"Hey, I have other friends too," Jackson laughed.

"So, what did she want?"

"She just asked if I was busy because she wants to talk to me," he said with a mouth full of the sandwich he was eating.

Judd nodded, "And what did you tell her?"

Jackson shrugged. "That you needed me and to give me a bit."

Straightening back up to the table, Judd asked, "Where was I?"

He watched as his son raised his eyebrows in a cartoonish pose. "You were telling me that supernatural beings actually exist." Jackson wrapped both hands around his glass and tilted it, staring inside.

Judd knew his son wasn't a believer, and the thought almost made him laugh. That would soon change. His son would be forced to believe in it once he lived through it. "They do."

"Uh-huh," Jackson mumbled.

Taking a deep breath, Judd leaned forward, and said, "Jackson."

"Yes," he said, continuing to concentrate on his glass.

"Look at me," Judd ordered.

Jackson turned his head toward his dad, and the distorted features of his dad's face filled him with fear. In trying to jump up to flee, he knocked over his glass and sent his chair toppling down behind him. Jackson stumbled backward, barely maneuvering around the chair legs, before landing on the kitchen floor hard.

Judd stood up and offered his son a hand to help, but Jackson only tried to scramble away from him. "It's okay, son," Judd told him gently.

Hesitating, he glanced quickly at his dad and saw his face had returned to normal. Gasping for air, Jackson asked, "What? What was that?" He moved inches further away until his back hit the wall. "How did you do that?"

Reaching down, Judd grabbed his son and pulled him off the floor. He picked up the chair and righted it next to him before sitting back down. "As I was saying, supernatural beings really do exist."

Jackson was shaking from head to toe when he finally sat down, sliding the chair as far away from his dad as possible when he did.

It hurt to see his son so afraid of him, but Judd understood. It wasn't the first time he'd been through something like this. "I hope you know I would never do anything to hurt you."

There was no response. Jackson barely moved except for his chest heaving up and down in response to his breaths which were shallow and fast. The uncontrollable shaking of his hands convulsed hard enough to wobble the entire table they rested upon.

"Son," Judd said soothingly. "Take a deep breath, and look at me."

Jackson continued to panic.

"Look at me. I promise there will be nothing frightening this time," Judd requested again.

He was tentative, and he cast a couple quick glances before lifting his head to look at his father.

Once he had eye contact, Judd spoke slowly and deliberately. Only he could hear the resonance echo of his voice that would seep into Jackson's subconscious and allow him to control his son's state of mind. "You are not afraid of me; you are only surprised."

His boy sat there staring at him frozen like a statue. His eyes never blinked. All that was noticeable was the rapid rise and fall of Jackson's chest from his heavy breathing as it slowly began to return to normal. Jackson managed a weak nod, and asked in a whisper, "What are you?"

"I'm what the humans call a vampire."

"That's not possible," Jackson said, shaking his head. "Vampires don't exist."

"Well, that's half true. Vampires in the way humans tell the tales don't exist, but nonetheless, it's the box where I fit."

"No," Jackson shook his head violently. "It's not possible. You're my dad. Vampires can't have children." A look crossed Jackson's face as though he realized something important. "It's recent then. You just became a vampire. How?"

Judd smiled at him. His son was talking normally again. He was happy the echo command worked. Jackson was much more calm and thinking more clearly now. He took a deep breath. "Like I said, vampires in the way humans tell it don't exist."

He rose from the table and grabbed a towel to clean up the spilled drink. The glass had been almost empty except for some ice when it was knocked over, so there wasn't much of a mess. He brushed the ice cubes into his hand and tossed them in the sink. It was difficult to know exactly what was going through Jackson's mind, but not hard to wager a guess. His son was still in shock from seeing the change on his face. Echo commands can take time to rewire the brain, so he decided to give him a few minutes to collect his thoughts.

Taking his son's glass to the counter, he refilled it for him and brought it over to the table. He pulled his chair out and sat down being careful not to move too fast or too close to his son until he had ample time to calm down. "Are you ready to hear about your lineage?"

Jackson nodded without taking his eyes off the table.

"Close to a century ago, the Elements existed in the spiritual world as entities. Balance of the Elements on earth was maintained by them." He continued to explain how it was Water who wanted to come to earth in human form and was granted permission for the Elements to experience life for a short time. Throughout the history of the planet as they watched different species evolve, human life was like nothing they had seen. Water thought it would be better for them if they understood this species first hand.

Jackson interrupted him. "Did they all have children during that time? Is that why there are supernatural creatures around now?"

"They were sent here for one year with rules to follow," Judd continued, not answering Jackson's question right away. During that first year, the only Element who didn't break any of the rules was Air. At the end of it, only two Elements made it back for the Return. They were Air and Earth. The Return can't occur without all Elements present, so they continued on in human form to try the Return again a year later." He paused there to see where his son's mind was at and to make sure he was following along fine.

"Which Element are you? Which one did you come from?" Jackson asked.

"I'm Fire," Judd told him.

"So I'm a Fire Element? I'm a vampire."

Judd smiled and hoped his son was ready for another shock. "Not necessarily. That depends."

"What do you mean? Does it sometimes skip a generation or something?"

"No," Judd laughed. "But your mom was a wolf."

Jackson didn't seem to react at first then Judd noticed the increase of the rise of his son's chest. "Hey, breathe," he told him.

His son's breathing became more troubled, and Judd worried he may pass out. Jackson started to look all around the room for something, for an exit, for a sign he was dreaming. Judd couldn't be sure, but it worried him how badly he took the news.

"Breathe," he repeated, leaning in and making eye contact with him to allow his voice to echo. "You're at peace. You feel safe here. You are calm enough to listen and learn about your history."

It worked. It didn't take long before Jackson was becoming more in control by focusing on each breath, in and out, until his entire body limped in relaxation. "How did you do that?" Jackson asked. "I know it was you, something you did."

"It's one of the perks of my genetics," Judd said.

Once he thought his son was fine, he told him, "To my knowledge with hybrids, children usually take after their mom, but there have been exceptions. Time will tell. The day is approaching when there will be a change in you, and we'll know which way you'll go."

"I'm either a Fire Element or a..." Jackson's voice trailed off not sure what Element wolves belonged to.

"Technically, you're an Elemental. The original four are Elements. Their descendants are called Elementals."

Jackson nodded like he understood. "So you're a Fire Elemental then."

Judd shook his head no.

"But you said you were a vampire."

"I am."

Jackson's brow furrowed in confusion then his eyes widened as he began to understand what it meant. "So, that means... But you can't."

"Why can't I?"

Jackson looked puzzled, "I thought you were only supposed to be here for a year, but then it took another year to complete."

"That's partially right, but there hasn't been a Return where all four Elements have shown. And before you ask, yes, I have made my way there many times since the first one."

Jackson lifted his glass then looked at it like he wasn't sure how it got into his hands. "Why didn't you show up for the first Return?"

Judd looked off before dropping his head with a sigh. "There are so many reasons, and none of them would make sense."

"Try me."

"I had done some very bad things. I hurt a lot of people." Judd looked his son in the eye, "I killed a lot of people. Most of them deserved it." To his surprise, his son didn't even flinch hearing that confession.

Judd continued, "But most importantly, I had fallen in love with a woman."

"Mom?" Jackson asked. "Do wolves have immortality?"

"Not your mother. This woman's name was Sophie," Judd answered, looking down again at the memory of his beloved. "I think more than anything I felt like I couldn't leave her, so I hid behind the guilt of what I had done as my reason not to Return."

He waited, giving his son time to process before he continued.

"When the Return wasn't completed, punishments were handed down. They were appropriate for what each Element had done. Air followed the rules. They are psychic shapeshifters and are immortal. They can reverse aging in humans with their blood, but they don't. Earth are witches."

Jackson's head perked up. He glanced at his dad then his phone.

"Yes, that's right."

"Can you read minds?"

"No. I can't, not exactly, but I saw what flashed behind your eyes. There are witches here in Fairview. Earth's transgression was falling in love, but even so, she was willing to leave her new family for the sake of the Return. I think that's why she's a witch. The Elements are family in a way, and now Earth can manipulate to a degree of all of nature's elements. Fire are vampires. We're immortal except that we can be killed by fire. Possibly due to an incident involving my temper and a very flammable village," Judd tried to joke.

"That means werewolves are Water," Jackson thought out loud.

"That's right."

"What did Water do?"

Frown lines appeared across Judd's forehead, "What do you mean?"

"Well, are werewolves like I think they are? They transition every full moon."

"Yes," Judd said quietly, giving him the short answer, but wanting more than anything for his son not to have to endure it.

"When Water broke the rules, what happened?"

Judd pursed his lips for a minute, not sure how much of the story he should tell. "I wasn't the only Element who took a life that first year. Water is a beast when it comes to fighting enemies. A lot of damage was done by

Water's bare hands."

Jackson was still scared. His fear could be detected in his voice. The echo command can only do so much, but he'd never seen it work so poorly. It wasn't until Jackson spoke again that he realized his son's fear didn't have anything to do with his father.

"How will we know what I am? Do I just get chained up every full moon in case I turn into a wolf? Or wait to see if I attack someone at school and drink their blood? How do we know?" he asked again. "I assume there's not a DNA test for this type of thing."

Judd understood his son's fear. The unknown can be the scariest thing to face. "Nothing like that. There will be signs," Judd explained, thinking about the three sons he lost centuries ago.

The signs were never noticed for a very long time with his firstborn, Bennet, because they didn't know what to look for yet. By the time his second son came of age, he and Sophie knew more of what to expect. Mostly they were like any other human, just more enhanced. Their senses were sharper, and it was what set them apart the most. The abnormally keen hearing was always the first signal of their supernatural development.

After that, there would be some physical changes that coincided with their emotions, especially anger. Lines would appear on their face near their mouth and eyes. Lines that were noticeable if you knew what you were looking for at first, but they would become more prominent and extensive when they took the form of Fire. Their eyes may glow. The centers of their eyes would turn red and radiate.

The eyes of Jackson's mom were different. When she transitioned, her eyes were a pale amber, almost gold. Judd expected the only sign he would really have as to which parent his son took after would be the color of his eyes.

Until Camilla, he hadn't associated with a wolf for centuries. Not since that day outside of Versailles when he found his family murdered. He was rusty on his knowledge of wolves. He couldn't know what to expect when a wolf comes of age. There had never been a precedent to use for comparison in Jackson's unique situation. It's also the only reason he both thought Jackson might be the exception who took after the paternal Elemental lineage, as well as the reason he was convinced his son would take after his mother.

clear the idle chit chat was growing on her nerves. Judd was about to get down to business when a little girl around the same age as his son ran through the room with her arms out to the side, pretending to be an airplane.

"Shush now, child. There's a young'un sleeping in the other room," she told the girl.

It was too late. Those words were followed by the sound of Jackson's laughter as he poked his head around the corner.

"Everleigh, this is Jackson," the woman introduced them.

"Lee-Lee," Jackson giggled.

Everleigh crossed her arms and stomped her foot. "No. I'm Everleigh."

Jackson cocked his head to the side and nodded like he understood. "Lee-Lee," he repeated confidently.

Judd watched the smile spread on his old friend's face as she watched the children head off to play. "Finally! I wasn't sure if that sour façade of yours would ever crack, Anya."

"Around these parts, I go by Eloise."

He smiled at her and nodded. "My apologies, Eloise."

She took a deep breath and leaned back. "I still can't believe you have a child." Shaking her head, she looked at the hall where the children had disappeared just a minute before then glanced back his way. "I'm happy for you. I really am."

He lifted his glass and stared at the ice cubes floating at the top. Lifting it to his lips, he took a sip, not sure what to say to her. Jackson wasn't planned, and even he was surprised by how well he took the news. Maybe it was finally time. There had been centuries for him to heal.

"Where's his mother?" she asked.

"She's dead," he lied without hesitating.

Eloise gasped and threw her hand to her chest. "I am so sorry. I didn't know."

Judd waved his hand and looked over her shoulder, focusing on a painting behind her to keep his thoughts collected. "Like you said, you didn't know," he muttered.

"How did it happen? I mean if you don't mind telling me," she asked him.

He took another drink and contemplated how to answer. The story he had devised started to feel flimsy all of a sudden. "Drowned."

Not knowing how to really answer his son thoroughly, he told him, "There will be some changes beforehand, nothing extreme. There will be slight things that could easily be spotted by an Element, but not necessarily by everyone. Your eyes may change color when you're emotional for example," Judd told him the only clue he really had. "When those changes begin, we'll know."

Jackson wasn't satisfied with that answer, but he knew his dad well enough to know that he would only dish the information he felt necessary to share. After a moment he asked, "What if I'm a vampire? They aren't mindless killing machines then?"

"No. Well, there have been a few of those over the course of time, but no, we are not."

"You can become a vampire whenever you want? It's not blood that causes your features to change?"

"Yes and yes," Judd answered. "Soon enough I'll teach you the nuances of blood in relation to my kind, but it's not the driving force people think it is."

"And if I'm a wolf, I have to go through the change every month?"

"Yes and no," Judd told him. "That's a good question with a layered answer. Turned wolves must transform with the moon."

"What's a turned wolf," Jackson asked, reaching for his sandwich that he'd finished without noticing.

Judd rested her arms on the table and rubbed his hands together. "A bite from a Water Elemental can turn a human into a werewolf. Their bite injects a substance. Think of it like venom, but it's more of a virus. Since the virus is supernatural, the human body has no means capable of fighting it off. It's difficult, however, because when Water is in beast form, it's harder for them to stay in control. The vast majority of attacks result in death," Judd explained. "Their children are also controlled by the moon."

Jackson didn't say anything. He stared at his empty plate and toyed with his napkin.

Judd was about to continue when his son got up and went to the refrigerator. He smiled and shook his head. Jackson was certainly a teenager now, always eating.

After a few minutes, Jackson sat down with some leftover chicken and between large bites of food asked, "Are there turned vampires too?'

"Humans who become vampires are created. They're a lot like turned wolves in that there are similarities to the direct blood line, but that's where it ends."

"Are the created children like their parents too?"

Judd smirked, shyly curious to see how his son held up with the rest of what he would tell him. "Created vampires can't have children. They're dead. They don't breathe. Their hearts don't pump blood, but they appear very much alive."

Jackson gawked at his father for several long moments.

"I'm not dead," Judd laughed, holding out his arm. "You can feel my pulse. I'm very much alive. In order to become a vampire, a human must die with Fire blood in their system. True Elemental blood."

Picking up a chicken leg, Jackson cleaned it to the bone in three bites. With a mouth full of food, he said, "They need blood to function then."

"Not at all. As I've said, the human retellings are full of untruths. It took me a long time to understand how these creatures who, for all intents and purposes, were nothing more than animated corpses, could survive, and could live what resembled a normal vampire life."

"How does it work?" Jackson asked, finishing off his second snack.

"Fire's blood has healing properties. It can bring someone back from the brink of death. In instances where the blood is in someone's system, but they die very suddenly like a gunshot wound or broken neck, it doesn't seem to be powerful enough to fully heal them. It's only capable of reactivating the parts of the brain that control their senses, speech, and movement. It just can't give them their life back."

Jackson took a long time processing all the information his dad was giving him. It was a lot to take in, and it went against everything he knew about supernatural creatures, not the least of which was they don't exist. "Okay," he said with a sigh. "You said turned wolves are controlled by the moon. What about blood wolves?"

"To be honest," Judd said, twisting sideways in his chair, "I don't know enough about the Water blood line to be sure."

"Was my mom blood or turned?"

Judd smiled instinctively, thinking about Camilla and how she was before their relationship went south. "She was blood. She wasn't controlled by the moon, but it triggered an urge deep within her. Sometimes she enjoyed giving in to it."

Jackson looked relieved, "Oh, good."

"Why is that?" Judd laughed, knowing the answer.

"I'd rather not go through it if I don't have to."

"Yes, but both blood and turned can transform at other times as well. In situations where emotions are heightened such as protecting a child, it can bring out the beast in them without the moon. That's why most of them nowadays regularly take a sedative cocktail, so if they do become agitated, they don't risk outing themselves with a transformation. Your mom kept herself under control that way."

"And it's painful," Jackson said more to himself.

Judd nodded, "My understanding is the first transition is excruciatingly so. It's the type of pain that etches in your memory, never allowing you to forget it. After the first time, it's easier. Plus, you heal quickly. The pain won't last long."

It didn't do much to comfort his son. "There are tribes in the south who have been spelled by witches to not have pain during their transformation," Judd added and almost immediately regretted mentioning it.

"That's good," Jackson's eyes lit up. "Maybe Everleigh's family would be willing-"

"No, wait," Judd interrupted. "You're getting ahead of yourself. One Elemental's power doesn't have any effect on a different Elemental. The reason the witches in the south have been able to help the wolves is because both of their people have been very close for generations."

Jackson shrugged, "Yeah, Everleigh and I are close. It's worth a try."

Judd massaged his temples, letting out a low frustrated moan. "No, son. I mean they were *very* close."

"Oh," Jackson said. "Oh! I see." Jackson rubbed his forehead. His eyes were fixated on the table while his head turned toward his dad. He was visibly deep in thought. "So, couldn't you just use the sedatives to prevent the first transition from happening?"

"Unfortunately, no. I've been told the wolves who tried that suffer excessively. The pain from refusing might not be as severe as the transition, but it is agonizing. When they refuse their first full moon, they are tormented with pain until the next one. From what I've heard, it's not something I would recommend."

"A werewolf," Jackson said, getting used to the sound of the word.

Judd reached his hand behind him and rubbed the back of his shoulder. If not for echo command, Jackson would've split by now. There was so much to abandon from the legends and learn correctly from reality. He really should give his son a break for the night, but the least he could do was get that horrendous fictional image out of his head.

"Water isn't what you picture when you think of a werewolf. Think of them as a man-beast. They're larger in frame. They take on some animal characteristics, but you can recognize their human form as well," Judd tried to explain. Soon enough his son would be able to see for himself.

"And they attack?"

"Sometimes, yes. They're not the brutal carnivoristic murderers they were portrayed as for so long. If they're provoked, or if they're angry, they can attack, and it can easily be deadly."

His son sat not saying a word for a long time. The conversation and the weight of having the world, as he had always known it, change dramatically inside of one short conversation could be seen on his face while he processed everything that had been said. Without breaking his fixed gaze off the table, Jackson finally told him, "I hope I'm Fire like you."

"Me too, son," Judd told him, longing to avoid anything that might happen if Camilla found out her son was, in fact, a wolf.

JACKSON WENT OUT BACK and hesitated on the porch. He wasn't sure what he wanted to do. He wasn't sure of anything. His mind was having

a hard time focusing on a single thought.

He went down the steps and rounded the corner to the driveway, picking up his basketball. He tossed it between his hands and dribbled it a few times, but his heart wasn't in it. The ball rolled back across the driveway until it came to a stop safely alongside the garage.

Werewolves. Vampires. Witches. Psychics. When he woke up that morning, he had a few certainties he knew to be true in life.

Basketball was an awesome sport that he loved to play, and he was good at it.

Girls were weird.

Right now, the most important certainty he previously held was that mythical beings only existed in books and on television.

If that wasn't the case and those creatures did exist, it made him wonder what else he could be wrong about. He stared at the basketball and began to doubt himself which he hadn't done for quite some time. Maybe the reason he was so good wasn't because of his talent. Maybe it was because he had an added advantage from having a vampire for a father, a werewolf for a mother, or both.

'Wait a minute,' he thought. *'Does that mean girls actually aren't that bad?'*

"Nah," Jackson said out loud and laughed. "There's no way."

He walked down the drive away from the house and trees that blocked the view to the street where the sky was more open, and he looked up at the moon. Only a sliver of it was visible tonight, but he hadn't paid enough attention in science class to know if the full moon was approaching or if it had passed.

Jackson began walking with no real destination set in his mind. This might be his life now, forever looking up, fearful of the night sky and what the moon might bring. It was not the life he wanted to have. It was no life at all.

Even if he doesn't turn into a beast like what's portrayed in the movies, he would still have to transform into something distorted and not completely human. There would be nights of agonizing pain followed by exhausted days, trying to recover. He hoped his dad was right, and they could find a way to control it. He didn't want to suffer this fate every month for the rest of his life even if it was something he might be able to manage and keep at bay. It would still be there, consuming him.

Looking around, he realized he had walked about halfway to his friend's house. He reached into his jacket pocket, but it was empty. His phone was at home. Jackson considered going back, but he wasn't ready to just yet. Besides, his dad would call Everleigh if he couldn't get ahold of him.

He kept walking until he reached her house, but instead of going up to the door, he let himself through the gate in the fence. There was a shed across the yard near the back. He and Everleigh had spent many hours at a time hiding out behind it when they were little, either because they were in trouble, not wanting to be found, or because they had something they weren't supposed to like candy snuck from her grandma. Jackson walked over to it now unsure if it was the solitude he was after, or if he wanted to reclaim a piece of that childhood which held blissful ignorance to what life had in store.

When he came around the corner of the shed, he jumped. He wasn't expecting anyone to be there.

"Lee-Lee!" he cried in delight.

Everleigh put her face in her hands and muttered, "You're lucky I love you."

"I know you do," Jackson said, sitting next to her.

"Why didn't you tell me you were coming?" she asked.

"I didn't know I was."

Everleigh nodded. "I get it. My feet found their way here on their own too."

"I didn't think you'd be that surprised," Jackson said.

She lifted her head toward him. Even with very little light making its way to the corner of the backyard, he could see she looked confused.

"Of course I was surprised," she insisted.

"Yeah, but you grew up knowing witches were real, and someday you would be called to become one. I was the one who didn't believe in it. I believed you thought it was real, but I thought the witchcraft you talked about practicing was no more real magic or real witches than people who use lavender to keep bugs away."

Everleigh shook her head then pressed one side of her face into her palm. "What am I going to do with you?"

"What?" he asked.

"Of course I knew I was a witch. I was surprised to learn about you."

"Oh," Jackson muttered. "That makes more sense."

Everleigh playfully smacked his arm. "You're such a goon."

"What did your Grandma tell you?"

"She told me about your dad and your mom, and that you'd most likely take after your mom."

Jackson picked a twig off the ground and began breaking it into little pieces nervously. "That's pretty much what my dad told me too," he said, wondering if she knew exactly who his dad was.

They sat in silence for a long time. Both of them struggling to come to grips with Jackson's identity.

"You're not scared of me, are you?" Jackson asked after a while.

"No," Everleigh said softly, resting her head on his shoulder. "I know you'd never hurt me."

When their fatigue finally won out, it was too late for Jackson to walk home. Neither he nor Everleigh wanted to bother anyone for a ride at that hour. Jackson stayed with her that night and slept on the floor of her bedroom like he used to do when they were little. This was the last night he'd be able to cling to innocence. Starting tomorrow, he'd have to face what lied ahead.

THE NEXT MORNING JUDD woke up not sure how he got to bed and wondered what happened to the shirt he'd been wearing. He could remember coming down to the kitchen to see how Jackson was holding up only to discover he was gone. At the time, he assumed his boy went to

Everleigh's to discuss their newfound knowledge, and the text waiting for him when he woke up let him know he had been right. Jackson had stayed over.

That's all he remembered. Jackson was gone. He fixed a drink. That's it.

'Wait,' he thought. *'There was a knock at the door.'*

Judd rubbed his fingers across his forehead, hoping he could massage the memory out of its hiding spot. There had been a knock. He went to answer it, but no one was there. Then he went back and finished his drink. He couldn't remember going upstairs or getting into bed. And, he had absolutely no idea where the shirt he wore last night went. It unnerved him.

The mystery deepened when he made his way to the kitchen. His glass from last night was still on the counter, but next to it was an empty prescription bottle. Judd picked it up and examined it, but the label had been peeled completely off. He was certain the bottle wasn't there when he came back to finish his drink, so someone had felt kind enough to leave him a clue.

It was easy to figure out what happened. It was much harder to decipher who did it and why.

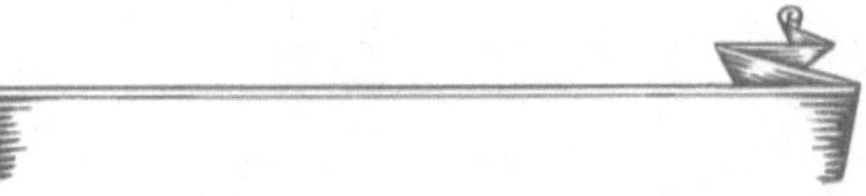

Chapter Six
Summer Plans

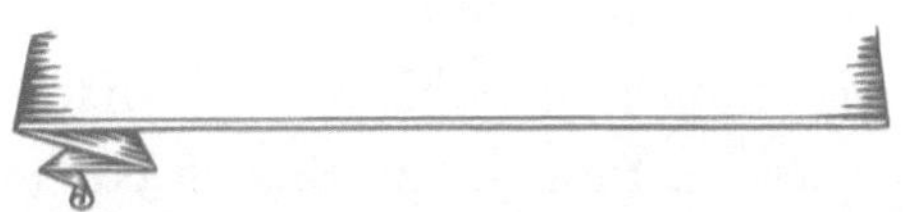

The signs were there. They'd been there for months. Judd knew what was coming, but he wasn't sure the best way to handle it. There were many people he could contact for advice, but that would be a risk. He trusted them, but people were flawed. They let things slip sometimes, not aware of the repercussions their words might bring. And everyone has a price. If Camilla ever had an interest in finding her son, she wouldn't know what name to use to find them unless he slipped up.

In all other circles besides Fairview, he was still Ulric Larsen, Fire Element. No one outside of Marcus and Anya, and yes more than likely Leena, knew of Judd Montgomery's real position and name. Most people only saw him as a family man. They thought it tragic what happened to his wife. As far as the supernatural world goes, he was nothing more than one of many Fire Elementals. He was simply a face in the crowd where vampires were concerned. If Judd started seeking assistance for his coming of age wolf son, it might raise some eyebrows. Something like that isn't easily forgotten. If anyone were to come around asking the right questions, they might be pointed in the direction of Fairview.

The Air family kept to themselves. Their abilities couldn't extend to the other Elements. And Anya? Well, she liked to keep her distance. It was a safety net, and it had been working out for her people. They wouldn't be able to provide much advice for handling a first time Water transition.

Judd sat at the table lost in thought while his coffee turned cold. There had to be someone he could trust with the delicacy of this situation. Not a single name was coming to him. Jackson was at school. It was almost the end of the year, and he rambled incessantly about his summer plans. He hadn't broke it to his son yet that this summer wasn't going to go the way he expected.

Letting out a sigh, he knew more than one life in Fairview was about to change dramatically. Everleigh had received the calling. It had always been a matter of time for her since she was an only child. Instead of nights hanging out at the mall and gossiping with friends on the phone, she would be holed up in her grandma's house learning the craft.

Those children were immersed in this world from the moment they were born. *'Witchcraft is easier,'* he thought, putting his cup in the microwave to warm it. *'Everyone fancies themselves a witch in this day and age.'*

Vampires and werewolves were a wholly different ball of wax. They're myths, legends, and scary movies. Ask anybody, and they'll tell you they're not real.

Judd laughed quietly in the empty kitchen. *'But they want it to be real,'* he thought. *'Until they find out the truth, and their entire existence gets flipped. Then the fear sets in and controls them.'* He'd seen it for himself many times since he arrived. The fantasy is always better than the reality.

It was harder making Jackson aware of his heritage. From a young age, he told his son they were more than just stories told around campfires. He approached the topic hesitantly, being careful not to scare him. Also, he didn't want him to make a fool of himself at school knowing the other children would laugh at him for believing. It was a fine line he walked trying to make sure Jackson grew up with a grain of truth.

It had been a failed plan. When he had the talk with Jackson a couple years ago, his son did not buy into a single word of his dad's chitchat about supernatural creatures until he showed his son his fangs. He had grown up believing his dad was encouraging the lore, nothing more.

All of his life that boy fantasized of being a vampire. Every Halloween Judd would run to the store for fangs and a black cape as his son had always outgrown the old one or worn it out from playing with it for months after Halloween had passed. It filled him with joy that Jackson wanted to take after him, but he knew it was a long shot.

Many other hybrids had been born throughout the past although it was rarer with vampires, and rarest with Air. Only natural members of the Fire line could have children because their bodies functioned much the same as mortals. Created vampires were dead in the clinical sense. The only thing keeping them functioning was the exponential regenerative properties of Fire's blood flowing through their veins. Very few natural vampires remained compared to where their numbers were centuries ago, and most of the ones who had managed to survive had no desire to start a family.

Almost every single hybrid child regardless of the combination of Elemental blood shared took after their mother. The maternal genes are strong. There have been a few rare instances when it went the other way, and nothing would've pleased Judd more than to have his son become like him. Either way one thing had always been definite, immortality would be guaranteed. With Judd's genes, there was no way he wouldn't be. He couldn't be certain, but his son may very well be the first born immortal wolf.

Water signs were already becoming apparent. In fits of rage, his son's eyes would softly glow. It was mellow for now, but with his first transition, it would grow stronger and more noticeable. His appetite was another sign. Most teenage boys can eat their parents out of house and home, but Jackson was never without food. The wolf metabolism is extraordinarily high due to the calories burned during transformation, and they're abnormally high body temperature. That was something else Jackson exhibited.

He would be able to control it more easily than other wolves. It was a leg up over the Water Elementals. With the natural Water blood in him, Jackson would be able to change at will. He needed to get through the initial transition. After that, it was a matter of learning how to stay in control. It would take a lot of time, and it wouldn't be easy. There were other ways to obstruct the lunar transitions until Jackson got it in hand.

Judd found his thoughts wandering to Camilla as he had the last several months. *Damn her for leaving him!* He slammed his fist on the table hard enough to put a hairline crack across the full width. She would better know how to guide their son through this, but she was the one person he couldn't turn to for help. Not ever.

The morning had already gotten away from him, and he had a laundry list of errands to accomplish. Whether Jackson liked it or not, they would be summering at the cabin on the lake. It was the one Judd used as a cover for the years he did attempt the Return. He rented one before Camilla walked out, and he enjoyed the peaceful escape so much he bought one after moving to Fairview.

"The Return," he groaned. Now more than ever, it was imperative to him to complete it. He needed to do what was best for his son which meant fixing the natural state of the world even if it meant leaving him behind to get it realized.

Judd stood from the table and left the house to do some shopping. Years of experience had shown him that the quickest way to get his son on board with a new project was to buy him new gadgets to play with while doing it. Tools brought Jackson around to fix up an old car. Athletic clothes and equipment were all that was needed for him to try out for the basketball team. All it required was something new and shiny to make the boy's interest come alive.

They'd spent weekends at the lake before, and sometimes they stayed as long as a week. If Jackson was going to be apart from his friends for the entire summer, he knew he'd have to spend a small mint on new fishing tackle and camping gear. He may just have to give in and buy a new boat.

THEY ARRIVED AT THE cabin after supper time. Judd picked them up something along the way because he knew his son wouldn't make it the whole trip without eating. It felt good to be back at the lake with him even if the circumstances for this trip were less than ideal.

Jackson walked to the back of the pickup to lower the tailgate and looked out at the lake. It was late spring, not quite summer. It hadn't had a chance to get too hot yet.

Judd could see his boy's mind racing, trying to decide what he wanted to do first: swim, fish or prep the boat for tomorrow. There wouldn't be any of that right now. They only had three full moons before school started in the fall. That's why Judd insisted they leave for the cabin the day after the school year ended. They needed to be here for the first one tonight.

The signs of his looming transformation had been increasing to the point that Judd had to pull him out of school a few times in the spring. During the days surrounding a full moon, it was becoming progressively unsafe for Jackson to be seen in public. The hint of amber in his eyes this time of the month radiated a glow that couldn't be missed. The upward turn of his mouth created a semi-permanent snarl that Jackson was unable to shake. It would've sent people running in fear.

They needed the use of all three moons. The first one would be to get through the initial transformation. It was always the most difficult to endure. Judd vowed to make sure his son didn't suffer through it alone and to make sure it didn't happen at an inconvenient time. He feared Jackson would never fully recover the emotional scars of transforming, or even beginning the change, around his friends. The next two were to help Jackson adjust to the change, to be familiar with his surroundings as well as himself when he was in wolf form.

It would still leave a few weeks to attempt a sedative regime that would prevent him from turning during the school year. Judd would keep a close eye on him. If there was any indication the sedatives weren't working and a transformation was near, he'd bring his son back to the cabin.

Of course, the plan hinged on tonight being Jackson's first transformation. Unfortunately for Jackson, Judd had discovered a way to make sure it happened.

"Why did we stop coming up here like we used to?" Jackson asked, leaning against the tailgate. His legs were crossed at the ankles, and he tilted his head back, pouring the remaining crumbs at the bottom of a bag of chips in his mouth. He crumpled the bag and stared out at the water.

"Because you grew up."

Jackson laughed and grabbed two bags from the back of the truck to carry inside the cabin. "I'm sixteen, dad. I hardly think you consider that grown."

"No, but you do."

Jackson grunted his typical hint of irritation.

It was Judd's turn to laugh. "You did grow up. You got involved with sports, made friends, got a social life. It happens. You're not the little boy who always wanted to tag along with his dad like you did when you were younger."

They unloaded the rest of their supplies while reminiscing about past trips to the lake. After everything was inside, they unloaded the groceries.

"What should we do first?" Jackson asked, opening a package of pop tarts, biting through both pastries at once as he ate them.

Judd worried he'd spend most of the summer running to the nearest grocery store to restock. He glanced at his watch. There was only about an hour before the moon rise. "I'm glad you asked," he told his son.

He grabbed the backpack he had loaded specifically for tonight. "Follow me. I want to show you something."

They hiked out behind the cabin about two miles. Judd kept a quick pace the whole way. They were running out of time. He stopped at the remnants of an old stone gate that once guarded a set of stairs into the ground. He put his foot on the first step to begin the descent.

"What's this? I don't remember this being here."

"That's because you were too busy following your dad around to go off exploring on your own," Judd smiled.

Jackson shot him a look. "But what is it?"

"Most of the older properties had something like this. It was a type of storage cellar where they'd keep their harvest and their canning."

"Cool," Jackson said, stepping toward the stairs eager to check it out.

At the bottom of the stairs was an old metal door that had been chained shut. Judd turned the key in the padlock and removed the chain, swinging the door open. He stepped inside and got out of the way to give Jackson a better view.

The cellar was large and mostly empty. There were some old shelves along the walls and a broken table on one side. What stood out the most was the ten foot by ten foot iron cage in the center of the room. It stood directly under a skylight that he had installed shortly after buying the property. It wasn't visible from the outside unless you were practically right on top of it.

"Storage cellar, huh?" Jackson scoffed.

"Hey, I was telling the truth. Part of the reason I chose this property is because of the use I could get out of this cellar. I was married to a wolf. We had a child who would likely take after her. I wasn't wrong to think some place like this could come in handy."

Jackson was upset. The amber in his eyes gave off an almost reflective glow. "So what? You're going to bring me here every month and put me in time out. Is that it?"

"No, not every month," Judd assured him, hearing his watch tick away the few remaining minutes they had. He hoped his son would forgive him by the end of the night. "We'll use it for the first one definitely. It's the hardest one, and some handle it worse than others," he said, balancing the backpack on the broken table.

He unzipped it and grabbed a granola bar, tossing it to Jackson. He hadn't ate for over thirty minutes which is a lifetime to his son when it comes to food. The poor kid was probably starving by now.

Jackson munched on his snack while walking around the cage, inspecting it. He never noticed what else his dad took from the backpack.

Judd walked over to join him. He opened and shut the door a few times showing Jackson how it automatically locked when the door closed. There was a retinal scan to open it.

"There's one inside too," Jackson noticed, peering through the bars. "Why would you need to do a retinal scan from inside the cage?"

"It's a safety precaution in case I ever get locked inside somehow," Judd explained. He pointed to Jackson's face. "Once your eyes return to normal, I'll get a retinal scan of your eyes in the system as well. That way when you're in there, you can let yourself out once you've transformed back."

Jackson nodded. His attitude was cooling down. The glow in his eyes was fading. He no longer felt tricked like he did when they first walked into the cellar. "But how's this going to work?"

"I just told you," Judd said, opening the door of the cage.

"You don't know when my first time will be. You're not going to lock me in here every month until it happens, are you? Or are you going to wait until it begins then fight to drag me all the way out here?"

"The thing is," Judd said, positioning the syringe he had hidden in his hand, "I do know when your first transition is going to occur."

"How? You always said there was no way to be absolutely sure."

"Because I figured out how to trigger it." Judd lunged at Jackson, piercing his chest with the needle. It injected him with enough ephedrine to restart his heart three times. He pushed him into the cage and slammed the door, leaving the needle in place.

There was the briefest look of betrayal on his son's face before his snarl turned up even more in a grotesque, misshapen way. His mouth and nose elongated from his face into a snout. Jackson's screams took Judd's breath away. The excruciating agony his son felt could not only be heard, but it echoed throughout every cell in Judd's body.

Vampire blood wouldn't take the pain away. It would slow the transformation, trying to heal the body. In trying to help him, he'd only cause his son more pain and suffering. There was nothing Judd could do but watch.

Jackson's wrists and ankles broke, and his feet and hands grew larger. His entire body thickened with muscle mass until his clothes ripped to make room. The cries he let out were heartbreaking.

It lasted seven minutes. It was the longest seven minutes of either of their lives. That's how long it took until Jackson was replaced with a creature who was half man, half beast. The ephedrine worked better than expected. Without an accelerant, the initial transformation typically lasted hours.

He towered over Judd, holding onto the bars, shaking them, trying to break free. If looks could kill, Jackson would've been the only one in history to figure out how to put down an Element.

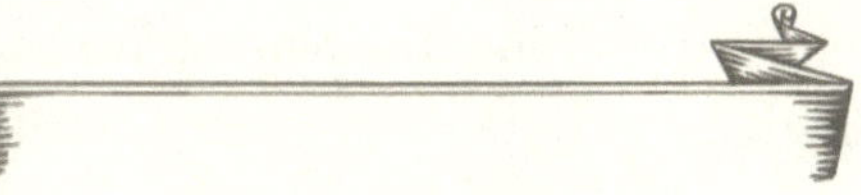

Chapter Seven
Blood Thirst

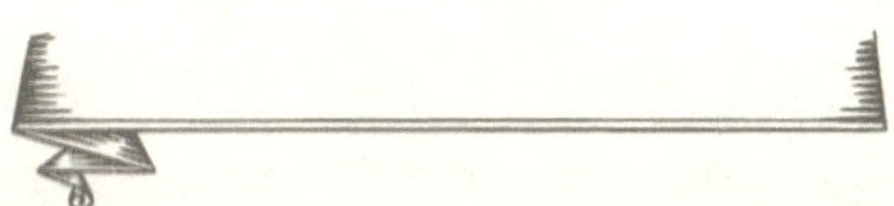

There had been so many questions in the beginning about who he was and what he was capable of doing. He had always told her the truth. He was the Fire Element who came to live on earth in human form, and in doing so, he'd retained some of his abilities. He had chosen to keep secret the part about the Return. Ulrich worried she may leave him if she felt that one day he may have to abandon her. It was a baseless fear; Sophie had nowhere else to go.

Sophie used to say he was an angel who had been sent to save her.

Ulric could never tell her he was too filled with evil to ever be anybody's savior.

He doubted she still considered him to be her protector after he was so quick to taste her blood.

The knife barely grazed her finger, but the sharp inhale of pain caused Sophie to drop it to the floor. The deafening sound of the blade bouncing on the ceramic tile as it tumbled to a halt wasn't enough to muffle the sound of her heartbeat in Ulric's ears. The beading of blood that rolled down her finger kept time with the steadily increasing beat of her heart.

He tried to convince himself of his motives. More importantly, he later persuaded Sophie that it was the threat of her injury that rushed him to her side that night, not the smell of blood that filled his nostrils with delight, overwhelming his every thought from the moment the skin on her finger broke.

It was not the first time the scent of blood had controlled his thoughts, nor would it be the last. Every street or market he ventured would send the aroma drifting back to his senses. Any cut, no matter how well concealed, could not be kept secret from him. The temptation had always been there. It was the only desire that captivated him more than the thought of lying in Sophie's arms.

The urges had always been willfully denied, of course. He had always been able to turn and walk away from the innocent bystanders who had no concept of the monster that roamed the streets beside them, but he could not walk away from Sophie.

That was simply not true. In hindsight, he could've let her be if that had been his true wish. It was the excuse that his place as her husband was to see to her well-being. That's what drove him to her side in an instant, taking her hand and placing her finger to his mouth for a gentle kiss. One small drop of blood touched his lips, and the taste sent shockwaves throughout his body. The eyes of the soldier in the forest flashed in his mind from the first, and until now only, time he had tasted this bittersweet liquid.

It was an inarguable fact that even in his first year before sanctions had been enforced upon the Elements, he was stronger, smarter, faster, and in all ways superior to any mortal. Tasting the soldier's blood, seeing the fear in the soldier's eyes while he licked the blade reaffirmed it. The two most basic conditions of human life were that the lungs need to fill with air, and the heart must pump blood. When he took away one of the two most basic fundamentals of human survival, it made him feel more powerful than anything else ever had.

At the start, it seemed a strange business the Divine Spirit would heighten all of his attributes and senses. It seemed ill thought out that having him excel even more all-around would be a fitting judgement for his wrongs. If Ulric was going to revel in his dominance over mankind, the Divine Spirit would take the ascendancy to excess, and let him drown in it.

He couldn't remember exactly what had been said to him the night of the first Return. It didn't make sense at the time, but it was becoming clearer now. "Since blood is what you lusted, it will serve you, but your weapon of fire will own you." It may not have been the exact wording the Divine Spirit used, but it was close enough.

'Ah, I may be adding my own dramatic flair to the memory of it, but blood and fire were the keys,' he thought.

This was the night when he learned how powerful human blood was to him. It was potent both in how it affected him and in the power it held over him. It would be his downfall if he let it.

He was not aware of how much time had passed since the crimson drop painted his lips. He was not aware of how long he had been unable to reenter his home. Sophie's fear and reaction to him savoring her blood was instantaneous. She ordered him to leave, demanded it. She had stood up to him in such a way as no one ever had. The shock of it moved his feet, and he did as she insisted.

The timing was perfect because the effect of her blood hadn't yet filled his being before he reached the outside of their cottage. If it had, he was certain he wouldn't have listened. Things would have gone in a completely different direction. He would never hurt his beloved Sophie. He would never harm a single hair on her head. He knew this, but he would not have left. That would've made all the difference.

The moment the door closed on his back he could hear the draw bar slam shut. It angered him. The level of his ire was still impressive all these months later. Quickly, he put his hand on the door, knowing it would be easy with his strength to bust the lock and topple the door to the ground. His hand hit with a force he didn't recognize, and he almost upended it without effort. This feat of strength was far more extreme than he was used to possessing.

He could hear the scuffing inside as Sophie struggled to barricade the door against him. *'She's frightened of me,'* he told himself. *'And for good reason. She's seen firsthand what I can do.'*

It hurt him to think she was scared of him at this moment. He kept his hand on the door, trying to will some comfort through the thick oak to her. This was his wife. He was meant to keep her from harm. The only way to do so now would be to allow her to believe she was the mastermind behind her own protection. Sophie needed to believe she could have this peace, this safety. The only way to achieve it would be if Ulric restrained from breaking through the blockage. He would have to wait until she allowed him to come back.

Gently, with the softness one would apply to a newly born babe, Ulric nudged the handle of the door. Finding it locked as expected, he delicately pushed against it. Sophie's heartbeat could still be heard, almost felt, even through the walls of the cottage. It was racing now. She doubted she had done enough to keep him out of their home. That's where he left it. He walked away from his home, leaving her to feel protected by her makeshift obstructions.

The next day, perhaps longer, was spent loitering around the home until venturing into the woods and eventually the town. He found no need for sleep while under the influence of human blood which made the time wasted longer and more unbearable.

For a few hours or so, he rather enjoyed it. He could hear the frogs croaking their nightly song near the bank of the creek which was miles from their home. Something he wasn't normally capable of doing. In the early morning hours, he tried to identify every noise in the woods for many miles. The sound echoed off his ears and painted a picture in his mind. Then the aromas wafted in from the village. The baker was preparing the day's goods. The scent was so vivid he could taste the flavors of the sticky buns.

It did amuse him for a spell, but it grew tedious and fast. Each time he checked he would find he still couldn't gain entry without force. Sophie wouldn't let him back in his house. The house he fought earnestly to acquire for them to begin their life together. *'My house!'* he screamed in his mind.

On the second full day of exile, he sat with his back rested against the door. The effects of her blood had worn off, and he was tired. He needed to eat and sleep, and he didn't necessarily have a preference for which he accomplished first. One of two things was going to happen. Sophie would eventually risk the chance that he could be trusted at home, and let him inside. If that didn't come to pass, she would ultimately need to leave the home for supplies. He was going to be here regardless of why the door was opened.

Tonight was proving to give that experience a run for the money. This woman who sought shelter in their home against him for days before finally opening the door to him was now asking for his blood. Fear froze him in place, staring into her pleading eyes. Ulric wanted to tell her no. It was uncertain the effect his blood would have on a human, and this seemed the worst possible situation to experiment with it. But, he had also never denied her anything she asked.

Sophie knew his tolerance for pain and his quick ability to heal. Many times she saw his cuts heal before her eyes in a matter of moments. He almost never took notice of them because even the deepest gash was no more bothersome than a pinch.

Her labor had been drawing on for hours now and was intensifying. They were to be blessed with their first child. A blessing that was being cast over now by her almost maddening lust to determine if his blood would help her through it.

The argument raged inside his head. If her blood could have some effect on him, it was possible his blood would provoke a response in her. There was a risk of course. His blood could do far more harm to her and their unborn son than either of them could ever imagine, but he also knew how many women lost their lives trying to bring a child into the world. The trouble she was having progressing through her labor worried him.

The midwife and maids ignored her request. It was probably not the first time they witnessed a woman in labor demanding her husband's blood, even if the request to drink it would surely be odd. There was too much at stake for them and for their life together. Sophie didn't know what he truly was. Ulric didn't know himself for that matter. She had always been aware he was different somehow even before the night he kissed her bleeding finger.

The ladies eyed him with irritation. They had instructed him to wait outside the bedroom and insisted upon it when he refused. It wasn't traditional, but neither was he. This was his child, and he was adamant he'd be there when it was born. Sophie's demand for Ulric's blood must have been viewed as a distraction to them. It was an illustration of their view that the husband has no place in the room during delivery. At least, he hoped that's all it was.

Ulric couldn't have her repeating her request. Digging his nail into his finger hard enough to break through the flesh, he slid into bed next to her. Sophie's hair clung to the sides of her head in dampened locks. The color was all but drained from her face from the hours of pain she'd endured, yet the birthing process was far from over. Reaching to remove a wasp of hair that clung to her cheek, he brushed his finger ever so lightly across her lips just enough to wipe a small smear of blood upon them. It was just enough to satisfy her demands, so she might not make the room of people even more suspicious of Ulric than he already knew them to be.

Continuing the façade of adjusting her hair, he watched as she licked her lips fighting the desire to taste her blood again as well. He could smell it. The entire room reeked with its powerful stench. If not for being fearful of harming her or their soon to be born babe, he would've given in to the urge to help himself. Her eyes rolled back, and her head that she had been straining to keep righted fell against the pillow.

"Sophie! Oh, no!" Ulric shouted.

'I've killed her,' he cried internally. *'My beloved Sophie!'*

The midwife rushed to Sophie's side and checked her over. Afterwards, she reassured Ulric that Sophie was very much alive, but had passed out, likely from the pain.

Ulric slowly lifted his body off the edge of the bed to the chair nearby. *'It wasn't from the pain; it was because of me.'* He watched carefully for any sign of anything unusal. It wouldn't be long.

She felt Sophie's forehead, "She's warm. Fetch some fresh water," she ordered the maid.

Before the maid returned, Sophie started coming around. Her laughter was eerie. It wasn't the sound of someone in dire agony from impending childbirth who might laugh for lack of else to do. It was the cackle of a madwoman, of someone with no root in sanity.

"Look at us. Look at this place," she told Ulric while her focus held on something across the room only she could see. The invisible fascination brought her hysterics back for a moment.

It unnerved him. He shouldn't have given her a taste no matter how unbearable her pain or how much she had pleaded. Not now. Not with witnesses to whatever effects she'd suffer.

"Who would believe I was born into wealth like I've known from the sight of this ramshackle of a house?"

The midwife and the nurse looked on intently. Ulric feared they may take her words to heart and look into who Sophie might really be.

Their interest waned quickly. The midwife checked on Sophie's progress. "It's time, missus. You need to push."

Ulric was relieved. He was ecstatic to become a father, but wanted his child born now more so than ever. Once this was over, these ladies wouldn't have to be near Sophie quite as much. It would give him what he hoped would be enough space for the blood to run its course.

To his horror, he watched as Sophie placed her hands flat on the bed and pushed against them, slowly raising her torso.

"Push," the midwife repeated.

"I am!" she shouted, putting more effort into lifting off her hands.

The midwife stifled a smirk, but not before it was noticed by Ulric. "No, missus. You need to push like you're using the facilities."

Sophie chortled and looked at Ulric. "I would have married you anyway."

The thoughts these women must be forming about them would surely be horrendous. "I know you're in a lot of pain, my love. It's taking a toll on you. Let's get through this. You're almost there," he told her, stroking her sweat streaked hair from her face.

"I know I didn't have a choice after what my father did and what you did to him, but I would've married you anyway," she insisted before passing out again.

Ulric looked at the midwife, pleading to know if his wife was alright with his eyes.

"What's she on about?" the stout woman asked.

He shook his head and muttered, "I don't know." An idea came to him. "I only gave her one drink to calm her nerves." It was the truth, but he knew a different conclusion would be gathered from it.

"A drink?" she scoffed. "Are you sure it wasn't the whole bottle?"

Sophie stirred again and erupted in a fit of laughter. "It was a drop! It was just a drop of-"

"You need to concentrate now. You need to push," Ulric interrupted before she could say more.

"You want me to relieve myself on the bed? I shall not!"

Ulric smiled softly, "I will forgive you this one time. Now, push."

She propped herself on her elbows and pushed. In minutes, the child was born.

The midwife wiped off the baby and wrapped it in a blanket. Sophie had laid back on the bed, concentrating on whatever it was across the room that held her attention. If you paid her too much mind, you could see her eyes dart to and fro, trying to stay atop of the action.

"Here's your son," the midwife said, cutting through Ulric's thoughts.

'My son,' he thought. His heart burst with pride.

For a moment, he was caught up in the wonder of this tiny little being he had helped create. Sophie's giggles brought him back to the gravity of the situation in the room. The maid was taking an armful of linens out while the midwife was attending to Sophie, cleaning her up.

"Tell me what needs to be done, and I'll do it," Ulric offered.

His words fell on her ears no better than Sophie's gibberish. "That's not how things are done."

"Do not bother me with what is traditional. She's not in her right mind, and I want to save her further embarrassment," he explained. The truth was far more sinister. He feared Sophie may say something that would leave him with no choice but to make sure these ladies never had a chance to repeat it.

Reluctantly, the midwife gave Ulric orders. She warned him that she would see to the maid in case she needed a hand, but she would be back soon to check on his wife.

When the midwife returned, Sophie was once again laughing at the corner of the room. Ulric watched the midwife's gaze as she tried to fathom what Sophie could be seeing. She walked to the edge of the bed and felt Sophie's head. "There's no fever now. That's a good sign. She's just lost so much blood. Give her plenty of water and broth, and she will come through it," she told Ulric, trying to convince herself everything was normal.

Ulric was confident his wife would pull through. The effect human blood had on him lasted about a day. He thought the same would be true for her with his blood. If they could survive the night without giving the midwife any more reason for her to wonder, they'd be fine.

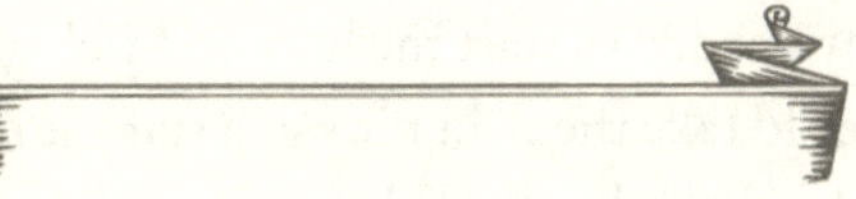

Chapter Eight
Questionable Circumstances

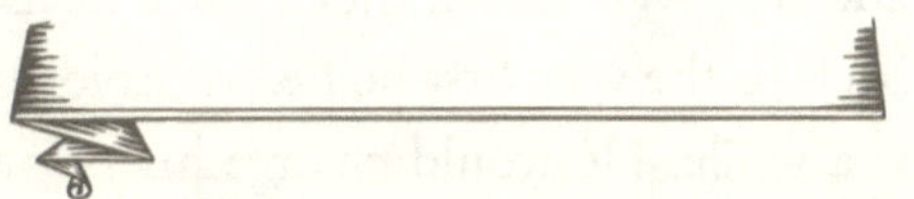

Driving home from the hunting cabin he'd bought after moving to Fairview, Judd contemplated last night's events. It had been a good Return even if it wasn't successful. Water was missing as always. Judd, himself, hadn't been sure if he was going to attend this year, but at the last minute decided to show. He had made a silly promise to himself a couple decades ago to attend every one until they hit their thousandth attempt. Then he'd take a few years off from the hassle. One more year after this, and he would fulfill that undertaking.

That might not be the right word. Most years he just didn't care. This world was now his home. His presence spanned back millennia before they took their human forms, but time was different here. On the other side of the veil, time doesn't exist. Human years flash by in seconds. It can be slowed down if you desired to pierce through the veil for a closer look, but time is definitely a human construct.

The years spent here dragged on and on until it felt like most of his existence had been spent in this body. That was definitely not true, but living out and experiencing each moment of every day has made this chapter longer than the previous one. This was the existence he knew the most now. His former life was a distant memory, and he wasn't entirely certain he wanted to give this one up.

He scolded himself again. It was past time to Return, and he knew it. The more comfortable he became here, the more he found himself thinking and feeling mortal, the more he became aware he needed to go back. It was shameful to ever think otherwise.

Marcus and Anya were on their way to search for Water. He'd given them the information they needed to start the hunt in Michigan. It was hard to say where the search would take them, but it was a start. It may be hard for them to trust him, but what he'd divulged about where Water was living was the most recent and honest details he had. He hadn't lied, at least not about that.

It was possible they suspected he had lied about something else or rather withheld information. He couldn't blame them. He'd been living a lie for the past twenty years, and they were still in shock when he left them. Judd tilted his head thinking back to the very first lie he ever told: Ulric Larsen. It was a name he used for a while. He would change his name whenever he had to start over somewhere new, but he could never drop his original name for good. Ulric Larsen was what he used from time to time over the centuries when he needed an alias, before coming back to it a century ago. It was the name his people, and all manner of supernatural beings, knew him by.

He thought he had settled on that name for good until Jackson's mother forced his hand, and he had to finally assume the name he'd refused since the beginning. It was a name she had never learned. After the first lie, the rest rolled off his tongue easily. Most days, he found he was even lying to himself.

Telling the other Elements over the years that he had seen Water in medieval times was the truth. Their paths used to cross quite often. When they'd run into each other, they would spend time together to catch up and discuss their mortal life. Any mention of anything about before they came here or the Divine Spirit would send Water running. He learned long ago not to bring up the heavy topics.

They didn't see each other again until around fifty years ago. It was a different era, and the times were alive with electricity. The events that kicked off that one fateful New York weekend left behind seismic repercussions that Judd was still dealing with today. That is something no one, not even the other Elements, needed to know until it had to come to light. They didn't need to know the truth until tonight.

The plan was that Marcus and Anya will go in search of Water on their own. More than likely Leena will join them. Marcus is rarely seen without her by his side. There were no pressing matters in their line to tend to before they left. In fact, they often went long periods without visiting their descendants. The entire Air family had lost very few members over the years because of the strict rules they followed for their own survival. It was no way to live as far as he was concerned, but very few people suspected their existence while witches and vampires couldn't stay out of pop culture for anything.

Anya had her ward, Everleigh. The thought caused a mischievous smile to form on his lips. Even alone in the truck, he could imagine the reaction from Anya if he referred to her granddaughter as simply a ward to her face. *'I know better than that,'* he chuckled. *'Anya's good side is the only one I ever want to be on. I learned that the hard way after many run-ins with her.'*

Still, there were plenty of family close by if Everleigh needed anything. She would not be left to her own devices if there was a problem while Anya was away. Until one of her other grandchildren received the calling, she was free to do as she pleased, wherever she wanted to do it.

Fire had one very big excuse to stay out of it, but he would soon learn his attention was needed elsewhere. His son had no one else. The world was dotted with vampires and werewolves, but he didn't keep close ties with most of them. Not since he went into hiding years ago. There were a select few that he could trust, but they contacted each other only when absolutely necessary. The number his son knew could be counted on one hand, and his son didn't have the means to contact any of them. Judd would like to keep it that way for as long as he could. No one aside from Anya, Marcus, and Leena knew he feared for his son's life and safety every single day, but even they didn't know the full reason why until this last Return attempt.

To say he feared for his son's life was a bit of a stretch. He was fearful his son would be taken from him by Jackson's mother. Even though she chose to leave, Judd had always known it would be a matter of time before she came back for him. Camilla wasn't supposed to be able to bear children, and she was aware hybrids favored their maternal heritage. Eventually, the notion that she had a son in this world to continue her bloodline would have her on Jackson's trail sniffing him out from wherever Judd chose to hide.

It was akin to it being his own life he was in fear of losing. The idea of having his family taken from him for a second time was more than he could bear. It had been several hundred years, but even a millennium wouldn't have been long enough to heal from that pain.

The next Return would mark their thousandth anniversary of human life. There was so much he felt he needed to teach Jackson before he left for good, but he knew his son was well equipped to survive. His temper was the worst of it, but they'd been working on that for years. The thought of leaving his son was terrifying and saddening, but he knew the weight of humanity would be off his shoulders once he crossed into the spirit realm. The pain would ease and cease to exist in an instant. He told himself he'd watch over Jackson, but deep down he knew it was another lie. Once restored to Element form, he wouldn't have the same emotional connections. It hurt like hell when he allowed himself to acknowledge that truth, but still, if he were to ever lose Jackson, he'd rather it be on his own terms. The Return was something he could control if the others were successful in finding Water.

Judd pulled into the driveway and let his son's truck idle. He was in no hurry to rush inside to an empty house. He had been stir crazy the whole first year Jackson was away at college. Now that his son's senior year was underway, he wondered why he hadn't just moved at the start of it. Jackson was grown now, and he recognized he couldn't guard over him forever. He could've traveled to Europe and visited all the places he yearned to see once more. The answers to why he didn't were all around him and materialized in all the things he'd tried to avoid since he lost Sophie. This was home.

All this time he had viewed Fairview as a necessity for Jackson's safety. Everything he had done since moving here was for the purpose of blending in and not seeming suspicious. While he was protecting his son and building a life for him, he found something he never expected. He found a life for himself, a community that he enjoyed, and wanted to continue relishing in it even though it was impossible to do forever.

He unloaded the truck from his trip and unpacked as quickly as possible, starting his laundry right away. The Return could be done anywhere, but he had rented a cabin to use during one Return shortly before moving to this town. He enjoyed the respite so much he decided to continue it when they moved.

Jackson had been too young to know the truth. In the years since telling his son about his heritage, Judd continued to go to the cabin every year anyway. If it was ever successful, there were two trusted companions who would've covered up his disappearance as an accidental death on the lake. More than the convenience of that explanation, Judd enjoyed the solitude. He'd spend a couple days preparing for The Return, making peace with leaving the world behind. Then he'd need a couple days to prepare for dealing with the world for yet another year.

Once the washing machine was started, he headed to the kitchen. He was famished. It was already almost eight, and he hadn't eaten a bite since before noon. He'd stopped by the store to pick up something for the morning with the intent of eating take out tonight, but the restaurant was packed. The wait for the order was too long for him to stand. Breakfast for dinner was on the menu now.

The eggs had barely been poured in the pan when his phone rang. Judd closed his eyes and cracked his neck from side to side not ready to deal with this reality again just yet, but he glanced at the screen.

'Collin?' He did the math in his head. It was three in the morning in Munich. There was no chance he was calling for a friendly chat. Something's wrong.

"Hello, old friend. What troubles you this late?"

"I have devastating news. Olav is dead."

Judd inhaled sharply. Olav was one of the longest serving members of the Council and one of the oldest living Elementals. It was strange. He'd never felt his cry. He turned the fire off on his eggs and leaned against the counter. "How did it happen?"

"It was a car wreck."

"A car wreck?" Judd laughed in spite of the gravity of the news. "Surely, you're pulling my leg. We cannot be undone by something so miniscule as a-"

"It was a bad wreck, Ulric. The car was engulfed in flames."

"No matter. He should've been able to free himself. The recovery would be long and grotesque, but he would've survived."

"During the wreck the windshield shattered, and he was decapitated."

Judd considered Collin's words carefully. It was improbable, but not impossible. He pictured Olav's car in flames, and his decapitated head burning on the back seat where it was flung after being detached from his body. Something about it didn't sit right with him. "Are you positive that's what happened?"

"Yes. The car was destroyed. There was a witness who came across the car after it was engulfed."

Judd interjected, "No, I'm not asking about the police report. Did you investigate it yourself?"

Collin stumbled to speak, "No, it... I... It was an accident, not a murder."

"Do the work. Use whatever resources you need. Take anybody with you to assist."

"But, Ulric, we only investigate in cases of murder. Are you suggesting there's more to his death?"

Judd was careful not to play his hand too soon. He didn't want to cause alarm. If a Council member of such esteem and capability as Olav could be murdered and his death made to look like an accident, the clan would panic. "I'm not suggesting anything. He is one of the oldest of my line. To have him die in a way that is so bizarrely human..." his voice trailed off. "We owe it to him, to his legacy, his memory, to put in the effort of an investigation."

Collin agreed, "I will begin first thing in the morning."

"Good," Judd rubbed his forehead and slowly walked to the stairs. "We're going to have to convene the Council. Have they been notified?"

"No, you were the first phone call I made."

"Call the others and send word to the Elementals. I'll notify Luke. It's Tuesday," Judd did a quick estimate of how much notice would be needed. They preferred to vote in replacement members quickly. "Make arrangements to meet in Brazil on Friday."

"Ulric, with all due respect, shouldn't we meet in France?"

"It's Brazil's year to host the Council, and Halloween has passed. The meeting should rightfully take place there."

"I understand, but they're not ready. Nothing has been moved."

Judd spoke sternly, taking the stairs two at a time, "When you gather up your resources for the investigation, put a team in charge of the move. We will not shun them especially with the first meeting of the Elemental year being of such importance. Mourning the loss of a dear friend. Voting in a new Council member."

"As you wish," Collin ceded.

He ended the call and shoved the phone in his pocket. The internal investigation would prove Olav's death was not an accident. There had only been a handful of his clan who had met an untimely death over the years, unfortunate circumstances that managed to lead to the demise of a vampire. To say it was difficult would be an understatement. It was damn near impossible.

Vampires could only die in one manner. They had to be decapitated, and both their body and head burned. The decapitation wasn't entirely necessary. Even the most badly burned body could be healed through a painfully slow recovery. Separating the head from the body prevented the brain from sending signals that would save it in time. It was a just to be safe, default move to decapitate a vampire before setting him ablaze.

A car accident, however, could manage it easily. Judd would have taken it as certainty had it not been for Olav's phone call last week.

There was one thing he didn't understand. The soul is not silent, but not everyone can hear it. When the body is in peril, the soul will cry out a lone, desperate plea for help as it reacts to the fear of the body it inhabits. He'd heard the souls of his people as they perished in persecutions countless times. The cry of a soul when a created was born is how no vampire could keep a play toy without the Council's knowledge. Olav's soul had been quiet. Either the death was too quick for Olav to know what might be coming, or he met his end willingly.

'And this is the second death in a row where I heard nothing.'

He walked into his room and looked at the recently emptied suitcase still on his bed, dreading packing and leaving again so soon. Plus, he still needed to talk to Luke. "Right," he said out loud. "I better get moving."

Luke answered on the second ring, and Judd set the phone on the bed, putting the call on speaker while he meticulously folded his wardrobe for the trip to the Council meeting.

"Hey, boss," Luke greeted.

Judd rolled his eyes at Luke's latest nickname for him. He was no one's boss. He didn't even officially have a seat on the Council. Instead, he presided over the meetings and only voted in the event of a tie. His presence was more theatric than necessary. It reminded those who may need it that there were consequences if rules were broken, and those consequences would be carried out without exception.

"What's going on?" Luke asked when Judd didn't respond.

"The Council's being convened. Friday. Brazil. I want you there," he told him, knowing Luke attended almost all meetings.

"So soon?"

"Friday," Judd repeated. "Brazil."

"What happened?" Luke asked, knowing it must be something serious to have an unscheduled meeting.

Judd exhaled deeply and set a pile of shirts into the suitcase. "Olav is dead."

"What? How?"

"It's been made to look like a car accident."

Luke was quiet a moment. "You don't believe it was an accident?"

"Let me ask you, Luke. A short while ago when your grandfather died-"

"You mean your grandson?" Luke countered.

Judd scowled at Luke's constant insistence of pointing out relation and dropped the pants he was carrying to the garment bag. He didn't like for any member of Fire to call him by a familial term aside from his children and his first set of grandchildren centuries ago. After a while it became mundane and unnecessary. He didn't keep tabs on his family in the way Eloise had managed. It must be exhausting to stay up to date on so many people across so many continents. Yet, she never seemed to amaze him with all the details she knew about her kin. She probably knew their favorite colors and knitted them sweaters every year on their birthday knowing her.

"I'm sorry, boss. You were saying?"

"Didn't he perish in a barn fire?"

"Yeah," Luke said sadly.

"I hate to press you for this information, but what can you tell me about the fire and how he died?"

"Just the basics. The barn went up in flames. Completely destroyed. Almost all of his horses survived thanks to him. There were two left in their stalls when a beam fell on him and pretty much obliterated his entire head."

Another death that was plausible, but too coincidental. "What was the cause of the fire?"

"Some electrical issue."

"That's what the fire department concluded in their investigation? Was it a short or what?"

Luke seemed shocked by the question. "I guess that's the official word."

"But you don't know if there was a thorough investigation?"

"No, I just assumed there was. That it was required. Are you going to tell me what's on your mind?"

Judd was prepared for this. It wouldn't have been possible to ask about Luke's grandfather without connecting the dots to the picture forming in his mind. Of all his living clan, he knew Luke to be the most trustworthy.

"I received a strange call from Olav not long ago," Judd began.

Luke quipped, "Olav was a little strange."

"He told me he believed he was being followed by a beautiful, young blonde woman." He could hear Luke's muffled laughter on the other end of the line. "Olav said she just appeared one day at a restaurant while he was dining. When he looked back in her direction, she had disappeared. After that, he saw her pretty much everywhere he went and had been seeing her for a few days."

"Olav's always been paranoid," Luke commented, "but a beautiful, young blonde?"

"That's what I told him. His paranoia was going to be," Judd paused, regretting the words he spoke during his last phone call with Olav, "the death of him one day."

"Anyway," Judd took a deep breath, "I told him she was probably new to the area, and the only reason she stuck out to him was because of her good looks. Basically, I told him not to worry about it. Lay low for a while, and I'd pay him a visit soon to check into her for him."

"You never made it, did you?"

Judd rubbed his temples, wishing he'd taken Olav more seriously. Perhaps he could've prevented it. "No," his voice filled with guilt. "The Return was close, and I thought it could wait until after it had passed. I was going to meet up with him this weekend."

Through the phone came a chorus of sound as Luke clicked his tongue in a variety of ways as he often did while he was thinking things over. "So you think this attractive woman had something to do with Olav's death?"

"The timing makes it seem it could be related. Also, and most importantly, two elder members of the clans met their end weeks apart."

"Yeah," Luke said softly. "It's not by chance."

Judd rolled his shoulders feeling physical strain from the solemnity of the conversation. "Anyway, this Friday. Brazil. I'll send you the address once I get it from Collin."

"I'll see you there," Luke ended the call.

His clothes were packed. The toiletry case was still on the edge of the bathroom sink where he placed it when he got home and was an easy grab to add to the suitcase. Judd walked to the back of his closet and squatted in front of a large safe. He turned the combination dial to unlock it and opened the door. Taking a stack of cash, he flipped through it. It shouldn't be a long trip, he thought. This will do. Then he reached for a stack of manila envelopes and grabbed the top one. He closed the safe and spun the dial.

Walking to the bed, he opened his briefcase and tossed the cash and envelope inside. Judd took one last look around, making sure he hadn't overlooked anything before grabbing his bags and dashing down the stairs. The buzzer on the washer signaled the end of the cycle as he walked out the front door, but it didn't permeate his thoughts just as the pan of uncooked eggs on the stove had been forgotten as well.

He hesitated only a moment on the porch before making a bee line for Jackson's pickup. With the recent events, it would be better if anyone was looking for him, they believed him to still be at home. More so if something, regardless of how small, happened at the house while Jackson's pickup was there, it would be hard telling what he would do. The thought of someone being after his son would invoke a rage he had only known twice before and never wanted to meet again.

Once in the cab of the pickup, he opened the briefcase and dumped the contents of the envelope onto the seat. A passport, driver's license, and several pieces of plastic fell out. He picked up the license and studied it. "I guess I'm Gregory for the next few days," he said, reaching for his phone to book a plane ticket on the drive to the airport.

COLLIN SAT OUTSIDE of the small, dreary police authority. The building was not at all foreboding. It rather resembled a place you would go to rent a car or purchase insurance, not a place where interrogations were conducted and criminals held behind bars, awaiting their trial.

The windshield wipers kept a steady beat as they cleared the rain, and it had a lulling effect on him. He yawned. There hadn't been any sleep after receiving the news about Olav's accident. He had to awaken the other ten Council members in the dead of night to inform them the entirety of the Council offices had to be moved to Brazil by Friday.

He delegated the task of overseeing the move to Isolde, putting her in charge. Ulric had requested he direct a team to do it, but he wouldn't get it accomplished in time. As it was, he would need to form his own committee for the investigation of Olav's death, but not before speaking to the police chief directly.

Collin yawned again. There would be time for sleep on the plane. He turned the key, silencing the car's engine. He got out of the car pulling his coat over his head to run into the building.

He walked through the door and approached the officer behind the desk. "I'm here to speak with the chief," he announced.

"You will need to make an appointment for that," the officer responded.

Collin looked into the man's eyes and let his voice resonate. "I have an appointment for nine o'clock. Collin Weber. I'm sure you'll find it in the system."

The officer typed something into the keyboard and looked at the computer screen. Collin knew no such appointment actually existed.

"I'm sorry, Mr. Weber. I must have overlooked this meeting when I checked his schedule at the start of my shift. Come with me."

They walked down the hall, making a right turn at the end into a second hallway. The officer continued to lead toward the back of the building before finally stopping in front of a closed door, giving it a quick knock.

"Yes," the voice from inside called out.

The desk officer opened the door and said, "Sir, you're nine o'clock, Mr. Weber, has arrived."

"Good. I've been expecting him," the chief said, standing from his seat behind the desk.

'That wasn't anticipated,' Collin thought. He entered the room, and the chief walked around the desk to greet him.

After introducing himself formally, Chief Fletcher walked back to his chair, motioning for Collin to take a seat across from him.

"You're here to inquire about the car accident, correct?" the chief asked.

"That's correct," Collin said, wondering if Ulric had made a call to the police authority before he arrived.

Chief Fletcher picked up the file that was lying in the center of his desk. "The accident that caused the death of a," he read the label on the file, "Mr. Olav Stein." He looked to Collin for confirmation.

"Yes."

"Are you a relative of his?"

Collin nodded. "Distantly, but I am his next of kin."

"Is there anything specific you'd like to know?" the chief asked, opening the file.

"There were few details given to me when the department called to notify me. I wanted to verify a few things and try to find out a little more about what happened."

"Of course," the chief agreed. "He is your family."

Collin paused while the chief flipped through the pages of the police report. He waited for him to look up. Once Chief Fletcher made eye contact, Collin told him, "You will be honest with me even if what you say may be hard to hear."

His voice echoed while he spoke. A tell-tale shimmer passed over the chief's eyes, telling Collin the echo command had worked.

"Yes, if that is what you wish. The accident occurred about half past one in the morning," the chief checked the file. "A pedestrian called to report the car in flames."

"Yet the investigation had been concluded by the time the department called me before three? That was less than an hour and a half later."

"Oh, yes," the chief responded. "It was open and shut," he stated, closing the file to emphasize his remark. "It was clearly a car accident."

"How could you be so certain?"

"Well," the chief replied. "It was an automobile, and it was on fire. Obviously, a wreck of some nature had occurred causing the car to engulf in flames."

'This is odd,' Collin thought. He knew the echo command had worked. He heard it. He saw it.

"You are saying your detectives didn't investigate the scene for evidence of an accident."

"Oh, no. You misunderstood," the chief told him. "The area was thoroughly investigated by the detectives assigned to the wreck. These are good detectives, the best in Munich."

Collin was convinced something else was at play here, but he wasn't sure what. "What other evidence might they have found that would point to an accident?"

"None."

"Nothing at all?" Collin asked, leaning closer to the desk.

The chief shook his head.

"Was there anything notable about the scene?" Collin asked, pointing to the file on the desk.

"Yes, Chief Fletcher told him. "There were no tire marks. Quite often when one tries to avoid a car accident, the driver applies the brakes with enough force to leave tire marks on the road. There were none."

"But you still concluded it was an accident?"

"These things happen," the chief told him. "No two car accidents are the same. Sometimes the driver falls asleep. Sometimes the accident is intentional."

Collin knew he had to change his tactic if he was to get anywhere with the chief. "Is there anything else you can tell me about the scene that might have been unusual for a car accident?"

"The car was in park on the side of the road. There was no indication of a collision. Very strange indeed," the chief said, narrowing his eyes as though he hadn't given it much thought until now.

Collin's mouth fell open while he tried to understand what he was hearing. He repeated what the chief said out loud, hoping that hearing the words a second time would force them to make sense. "The car didn't come into contact with anything, and Olav was able to pull the car over, putting it in park before it caught fire."

"It would appear that way, yes."

This was no car accident. Olav had been murdered.

"Is that all?" Collin asked.

The chief opened the file and flipped through a couple pages. "His head was not recovered."

"What?"

"Mr. Stein had been decapitated, but his head was not found at the scene. The detectives scoured the area even long after you had been notified of your relative's death. It was never found."

Collin breathed deeply and scratched his head. "Let me get this straight. There was no evidence he tried to avoid an accident. There was no evidence his car actually hit anything. His car was in park on the side of the road, and his head is missing. Yet your department still declared this a car accident."

"Yes," the chief nodded. "These things happen. No two accidents are the same."

Something was amiss, and he needed to find out the truth. Collin tried using his echo command again. "You believe this car accident was a cover up," he told the chief.

"No," the chief answered him growing irritated. "It was open and shut, just as I've already told you.

Collin's eyes widened in shock, in alarm. This could only mean one thing. Someone had beat him and his echo command to Chief Fletcher. Echoes are temporary. They will wear off, but their effects can easily last up to half a day if the vampire commanding it is strong. As an elder, his echo should have superseded any others. With Olav's death, there were only two vampires alive who were older than Collin. One was Ulric, and the other hadn't been heard from in over a week.

He stood and thanked the chief for his time, planning to return the next day to try again. After the details of the supposed wreck and learning someone more powerful than he had influenced the chief first, he didn't think anything else could surprise him more, but he was wrong.

The chief placed the file into the trash bin near the desk and lit it on fire.

Collin watched in disbelief, unable to say a word.

After the file burned, the chief poured a glass of water into the bin to extinguish the flames. The odor from the burning papers and smoke hung in the air.

"Why did you do that?" Collin asked dumbfounded.

The chief looked up at him and smiled, "I'm supposed to. I was told someone would be inquiring about this accident and to answer all of their questions honestly. After the conversation ends, I was ordered to burn any hard copies of the file, delete it from the system, and forget the accident or the conversation concerning it ever happened.

He turned his attention to the computer, striking a few keys before looking back at Collin. "There. Done."

His whole body slumped as if suddenly taken over by pure exhaustion, and he sank into his chair for a minute. When he sat up again, he looked genuinely surprised to see Collin standing in his office.

"I didn't see you come in," he said, standing up and extending a hand to Collin. "I'm Chief Noah Fletcher. How may I help you?"

Collin shook his hand and said, "I'm Collin Weber. A relative of mine, Olav Stein, was killed in a car accident early this morning."

"I'm so sorry," the chief offered, returning to his chair. He narrowed his eyes and sniffed the air with no apparent memory of the fire he had just started. "The accident hasn't been brought to my attention yet. What can I do for you?"

This meeting had begun peculiar, turned worrisome, and was now full blown bizarre. Collin couldn't make heads or tails of what was going on. The only possible explanation didn't make sense. Collin couldn't accept that it was true.

He went back to his seat, looked the chief in the eye, and echoed his voice. "You remember the car accident involving Olav Stein last night."

The chief pierced his eyes. "I already informed you that the accident hasn't been brought to my attention yet. Let me look at the file."

He logged back into the system. After a few keystrokes, he asked Collin to spell Olav's last name. The chief typed it into the system as Collin spoke then said, "I'm sorry. It appears my detectives haven't filed the report yet."

Collin was speechless. This couldn't be happening.

"We can set up a later meeting to discuss it when the detectives have finished their investigation," the chief offered.

"Yes," Collin told him, standing to leave.

"Very good."

"I will call this afternoon to set up a time."

The police chief smiled at him and said, "I'm sorry I couldn't be of more assistance to you, and I'm sorry about your loss."

Collin nodded and thanked him.

He left the office and slowly walked down the hallways, making his way toward the front door. *'He was ordered. Controlled,'* Collin thought. *'Impossible.'*

The echo command was a manipulation. It was a hint, a suggestion, and it only succeeded when the outcome didn't go against a person's true nature. It played with a person's mind, temporarily rewiring some of the thought processes. It could help someone access a memory or encourage them to tell the truth. The one thing the echo command could not do in any circumstance was override control of a person's actions. It couldn't force someone to steal, murder, or in this case, cover up a murder unless the person was already prone to act in that manner.

Collin knew the chief of police to be a good man who wouldn't willingly cover up a murder and destroy the evidence. He pushed open the door and walked outside. The rain was still coming down in torrents, but he barely noticed. He slowly walked to his car and was drenched by the time he folded himself in the front seat.

There was only one thing that would have the power to not only control the police chief's actions, but also erase all of his memories of it. That one thing was vampire blood. Specifically Fire's blood. Ulric's blood.

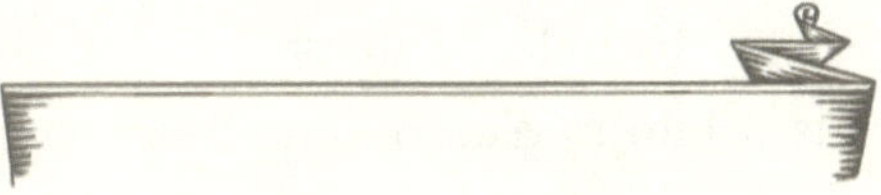

Chapter Nine
Council Meeting

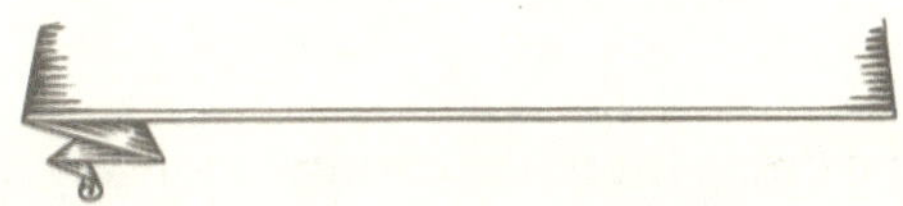

Judd lurked quietly, sipping his espresso at an outdoor table near the Mercado Modelo. Nearby, two men unloaded a moving truck into a newly rented office space. He had discovered the Council's new Salvador location a full thirty-six hours before Collin advised him of it. There were many doubts about the site.

He counted at least four men inside the building setting things up. All of the boxes coming off the truck looked brand new. They all pictured computers, desks, and office chairs, but he knew most had been packaged in France with goods dating to the era of King Louis XIV. If the movers had caught the eye of anyone else, it may raise suspicion why they were carrying in fourteen desk boxes for the office of a single lawyer.

The space was large enough. The seven-story building was divided up into multiple offices per floor. This space was the exception, encompassing the entire first story. It had formerly been rented to a modeling agency who used a studio in the back for photo shoots. The area was large enough for the Council and any clan members who chose to be in attendance at any given meeting.

It would be a lawyer's office for appearances sake. The cover was good with an actual lawyer working out of the front, claiming the studio space was perfect to put on run-throughs of mock trials for his clients. It was part of the reason why Brazil chose an office in the middle the city as the new location.

Judd hadn't been so sure. There can be safety in numbers when you're looking for anonymity, to get lost in the crowd. Yet the middle of a high traffic tourist area wouldn't have been his first choice. He had to hand it to his people in Brazil for doing their research.

The modeling agency had closed down because the owner had been charged with using his studio to record himself doing the unspeakable. He would meet women at local clubs, drug them, and bring them here where multiple cameras would document the attacks for his twisted enjoyment. When he was finished with them, he would discard them at their home or car. They would awaken the next day with little to no memory of the previous night.

'Disgusting.'

He would still be doing it too if he hadn't foolishly not recognized one of his former clients while he was on the hunt. The woman recognized the studio from the few details she could remember of what happened to her. When the police searched the business, they found the artist's home movies.

This building was one of the few old relics remaining from the modern city that was building up around it. The monster who had previously rented it had sound proofed the studio, and as argumentative as the Council meetings often became, this was advantageous.

Also, the parking lot in the rear had been covered recently with shelter. Any area security cameras would not be able to detect who, or how many, entered the rear door of the studio. It should provide just enough secrecy. They would be hiding in plain sight essentially.

It didn't matter that the culprit was behind bars. The people who lived in the area were well informed on what happened there, and they warned the tourists too. They avoided getting too close to the building, making sure to walk on the opposite side of the street out of fear that the evil that remained resonating inside might reach them. Even the businesses on the upper floors were losing clients because of it. They needn't worry about garnering attention to themselves too easily.

Judd stood up from the table, leaving a large tip before walking to his hotel a few blocks away. The meeting was in a little over three hours which gave him just enough time to retrieve Luke from the airport. He was cutting it close.

It had been a long while since he spent any time with Luke outside of Council meetings. He was looking forward to visiting with his new ally. There was much to discuss, but he feared they wouldn't have a chance before the meeting. As it turned out, the night would be full of surprises for the both of them.

"YOU BROUGHT MEREDITH?" he asked, not bothering to hide the irritation in his voice.

"It's lovely to see you too, Judd," Meredith's full bodied laugh echoed as she climbed in the back seat.

"Always a pleasure," Judd told her.

Luke grinned, "It surprises me you didn't expect her."

Judd sighed, "If I'd had a moment to think, I probably would've planned on her arrival. It's just been..."

"Hectic," Luke finished his sentence.

Silence filled the car while all occupants were reminded of the grave matter that brought them to Brazil in the first place. Judd maneuvered the car through the airport traffic and onto the road that would take them to the heart of Salvador.

"You were right about the fire," Luke shattered the quiet of the car. "It had never been fully investigated."

Judd listened intently as Luke explained the meeting with the fire chief. The file contained nothing but blank sheets of paper which the chief couldn't explain. The man insisted he had done the investigation himself, and everything was in order when he filed it.

"Who do you think would steal the real file?" Luke asked.

"I don't think anyone stole it," Judd didn't hesitate to say. "I think someone convinced the fire chief those blank pages were an actual report, and told him what to conclude in the cause of the fire."

The car pulled up to the rear of the office building barely making it in time. "Meredith, would you mind taking the car and handling the hotel check in without Luke. It is imperative he arrive on time tonight."

"Not at all," she smiled.

Leaving them to their goodbyes, Judd entered the building through the rear. People were still arriving and finding their seats, and a few were still setting up the last of the relics. He watched their progress with admiration and nostalgia until he saw Collin signaling him.

He walked to the side of the room where his old friend waited.

"I finished the internal investigation as requested," Collin whispered quietly.

Judd's head turned sharply. He had been worried about the vote and hadn't assumed Collin would be done with the investigation so soon. "And?"

Collin's face was solemn, giving away the answer before he said it. "You were right. There was a cover up."

"By who?" Luke asked, joining them.

"I don't know, but it's more than that," Collin told them, looking around to make sure no one was listening. "Whoever is behind it was able to give the chief of police a command I couldn't override," he said, not wanting to give away his suspicion just yet.

"Nonsense. There's only two of us with the power to do that," Luke pointed out, glancing at Judd. "And I'm certain you didn't do it."

Judd shook his head, "No, I did not. I don't believe Collin's older brother was behind it as well."

"They would've used a fail safe," Luke insisted. His face skewed as he tried to figure out how it had been done. "They had to know we'd investigate for ourselves. Even if they figured out a way to supersede our commands, they'd make sure that we couldn't detect it."

"Not if the person who killed Olav wanted us to find out," Collin said with an air of impending doom.

Judd didn't know who was behind it, but he had a feeling he might know how they accomplished it. "We'll have to finish this later," he said, motioning for them to take their places.

He stared at the chair behind the Council's table where he would oversee tonight's meeting. Members were already seating themselves, preparing to call the meeting to order in minutes, and he knew what he had to do. Luke had to be voted on to the Council tonight. Luke was the only Fire Elemental he trusted.

Judd barely listened as the meeting droned on. It began with the news of Olav's death, and details of the cover up. There hadn't been enough time to fill Collin in on the new information surrounding Luke's grandfather, so he gave Luke the floor to explain what had been discovered. Judd began to drone out all the official talk, focusing on the murmurs in the background.

The number in attendance was significantly lower than he expected. A good amount of his clan have never bothered with attending any of the meetings, including the ones where new members are voted onto the Council which have always had the greatest number in attendance. Some of the regulars were noticeably absent. At first, he blamed Collin for not getting the word out fast enough. Then he started hearing the whispers.

One had talked to a friend that afternoon who said she'd be here tonight. Another had breakfast with someone yesterday who was on an earlier flight, but they didn't show. It seemed almost every table had at least one story of a surprise absence. Judd worried that news of more deaths would be reaching his ears sooner than he'd hoped.

There have been very few times he had flaunted his position in front of his clan. The biggest instance being when he initiated the first Council and set the rules into place. He never wanted to be a dictator and have his clan bow down to his every whim. That's why he created the Council in the first place. Tonight would be one of those exceptions.

Collin was about to begin the process of welcoming nominees for the new member. This was a tedious process that could draw on for hours, days in some instances. Everyone in attendance had the opportunity to nominate a candidate except for the current Council. There was to be no show of favoritism or encouragement of votes from the existing members. Those present would be called on one by one to either make a nomination or pass.

At the end, it could be possible to have only one candidate although that had never happened. It could also work out that everyone in attendance had their name thrown in the hat. This was also an outcome they had never faced, but they had come close.

Once the nominations came to a close, each of them would be called on one at a time and would be asked the same question. "Do you accept the nomination to Clan Council?" A simple yes or no answer was required. That was it. There were no speeches allowed and no campaigning for the position. In a surprising twist, many people actually did decline the nomination.

The floor would then be open to questioning the nominees. They could be asked anything from the important to the mundane. Are there any issues you believe threaten our existence at this moment? Or how do you like your eggs? This is the part that would toll on endlessly.

They don't accept the nomination lightly. The ones who respond with a yes will stay the course until the vote. None have ever dropped out regardless of how long they were forced to stay awake to endure the interrogations.

'But we don't have days,' Judd thought. 'We need a Council member now.' Teams needed to be on the ground investigating not only the deaths of Olav and Luke's grandfather, but the location and safety of everyone not in attendance tonight needed to be determined.

Collin stood and addressed the room, "We will now proceed with nominations for the empty Council seat."

Judd rose from his chair. "I nominate Luke DeRossi." He barely gave them time to process what he had said. "Luke, do you accept your nomination?"

The roar of outcries was instantaneous. Not a soul in attendance kept their disdain to themselves. Judd slowly scanned the room. Within seconds, all noise had ceased. Everyone was too afraid to even fidget in their chair. No one would object any more.

He turned his attention to Luke and nodded.

Luke's voice trembled as he answered, "Y-yes."

"The voting shall begin now," Judd declared. By all means, this was not his place, and he had no technical authority to do it. He was their Element, but the Council was in charge. Any of the eleven seated in front of him could have overruled him and opened the floor to new nominations. He would love to think they didn't out of respect, but he knew it was the stories of his past self that made them feel the consequence of standing up to him would be grave.

MEREDITH LOOKED OUT the water view window of her hotel room on the beach, longing to walk the shore. Their suitcases remained packed nearby. Luke had been sure they would be spending several days in Salvador, but she didn't believe that to be the case. Her gift of sight showed them in Trinity on Monday, but the reason wasn't yet clear.

She wanted to make the most of what little time they had here, but now she couldn't shake the nagging feeling that she was needed at the law offices of Advogados Acessiveis. There was no way they would allow her inside. Created vampires were excluded, and that didn't take into consideration her Earth heritage. She smiled wryly, thinking of the scandal it would cause if she sauntered in after the meeting had started. It was something she would never do. Luke was far too important to her to ever jeopardize his standing in the clan.

Even so when she left the hotel, she turned away from the beach and walked the five blocks to a popular sidewalk café. She was unknowingly seated next to the table where Judd had drank his espresso earlier in the day. Something was wrong. She could feel it. If she couldn't join the meeting, she wanted to be as close by as possible.

The salad she ordered was more to have an alibi for being there than out of hunger. Tourists crowded the streets and noise combatted her senses. While people watching and keeping an eye on the front of the office, she nibbled at her salad. After a while, she wondered if she should've brought the car.

This feeling, an eerie premonition, a sense of something untoward coming their way was growing stronger. Meredith signaled for the check and paid it with a lofty tip. It wouldn't take more than a few minutes to walk to the hotel and drive back. As she prepared to leave, she noticed the odd woman across the street from the office building.

Everything about this woman screamed she wanted to stand out from the crowd. She wanted to be noticed. Her icy blue eyes were set in a face of sheer perfection, framed by her silky blonde hair. She stood directly in a pool of light on the street, making it easy to see her features and commit them to memory. An ugly, oversized green raincoat draped over her body, hiding whatever clothing she wore. The hood was pulled onto the top of her head, but it wasn't pulled forward to block the view of her face.

She stood there almost completely motionless, staring across the street at the front office window on the first floor where the Fire clan huddled in the back room. It was the weird juxtaposition of the woman's appearance that caught Meredith's attention, but it was the woman's fixation on the office that held it.

There was something else. Something Meredith later would not quite be able to explain. If this woman had been an Earth Elemental, she would've felt it, would've recognized the sisterhood. If this woman had been any other Elemental, created or turned, she would've been able to discover it by the lack of impression. There was a feeling emanating from this woman that was different that anything Meredith had ever felt from someone. It was cold, and it made Meredith's stomach flop. Any other day, any other place, any other person, the presence of any feeling would signify humanity, except Meredith didn't believe her to be human.

Cloaking and protection spells had been used since Anya's first lifetime, but Meredith was considerably strong. She was usually keen at detecting something. If not the exact spell, then just an air of magic.

It had been rumored the wolves were experimenting with herbs that could hide their scent. Those tales had gone back the entirety of Meredith's life. No evidence had ever been found to show they succeeded. In fact, there had never been proof they were trying. It had always simply been talk, hearsay.

Meredith slipped her phone out of her purse and held it on the table. There was only one person who might provide insight on this woman. She sent Eloise a text, "I'm going to send you a picture. Tell me what you think."

She selected the camera icon and opted to take a new photo. Tilting the top of the phone toward her just enough to get the woman in view, she zoomed in and snapped a photo secretly. It didn't take long after pressing send for Eloise to respond.

It was one word. "RUN!"

When Meredith looked back up, the woman was gone. She jumped to her feet so fast, the chair tumbled behind her. The sound of it crashing onto the pavement was barely detected over the loud din of the crowd gathered in the market. Scanning the area, she found the woman crossing the street toward the office building. Meredith grabbed her purse and hurried after her.

The woman had over a twenty yard lead, and Meredith walked briskly to shorten the gap, but also not wanting to alert the stranger she was being followed. The blonde turned into the alley that ran along the north side of the office. Meredith's heart skipped a beat. She was heading toward the rear which was where the entrance for tonight's meeting was located.

It didn't take thirty seconds, forty-five at the most, for Meredith to make the turn into the alley herself. The woman was gone. She kept walking, quickening her pace to a slow trot, eyeing the building on either side of the alley, looking for doorways the woman may have used to escape, or a place where she could have hidden. It was as though she just vanished.

The sound of a bottle being kicked, and rolling out onto the gravel of the alley from the parking area behind the building froze Meredith in her tracks. She held her breath as she waited for the guilty party to appear. From the rear corner of the building, a young man stumbled, nearly falling into the alley while pulling up and adjusting the waist line of his shorts. "So shorry," he slurred in a proper English accent when he saw her.

"I woo no," he waived his arm in front of his face, "reweaved myshelf if I knew I was't awone."

Meredith rolled her eyes, irritated by the interruption, but she continued forward down the alley, passing him as he barely made his way to the street. She surveyed the cars parked behind the building, thinking this is the only place where the woman could have disappeared. The only entrance or exit to the lot was through the alley, but it was empty. If she had paid attention to the garbage cans standing near the dumpster, she would have noticed the discarded green raincoat crumbled inside one of them.

The rear door to the studio opened and startled her. She whipped around to see Judd making his way outside, followed by Luke. As she ran toward them, she forwarded the picture of the woman to them both. Their phones dinged the notification in unison at the same time they spotted her approaching them.

"Find her!" she yelled, pointing to the picture on her screen before running out of the lot and farther down the alley. It was unlikely the woman would be found now, but she also knew, without a doubt, the woman had wanted for Meredith to discover her. She wanted Meredith to be aware she knew what went on behind these closed doors.

AFTER SPENDING OVER an hour searching first the market then the neighboring areas of the city without luck, Judd went back to the law office, leaving his two companions charged with the chore of going back to the hotel and arranging flights back to the states for all of them as early as they could manage. He believed Meredith was right. The woman wanted to be seen. If she wanted to be discovered, she would have come prepared with an escape plan.

The picture wasn't very flattering, but it was clear she was quite attractive. The blonde hair and blue eyes were just as Olav had described when detailing the woman he believed was following him. There was no doubt this was the same woman, and there was no doubt she was behind Olav's suspicious demise. He was certain she was behind the death of Luke's grandfather as well.

It was unlikely she was still in the city with the vast number of Fire congregated in it. If her plans for Brazil were to attack, she would've done so.

This woman's plans were more egotistical than that. She risked her identity being discovered because she believed she was above capture. Judd knew the woman wasn't of his line unless she was a rogue created. He didn't recognize her. He also knew she wasn't nearly as intelligent as she believed herself to be if she thought she could reveal herself without threat of centuries of supernatural creatures tracking her down and ripping her apart on sight.

There were always those who hung behind after the Council meetings came to a close to socialize with kin they hadn't seen for a while. This meeting would be an exception. After he forced their hand in electing Luke to the Council, he was positive every Fire Elemental was still in the backroom discussing their disapproval of his actions.

He pushed open the back door much to their surprise, "Pardon the interruption. I know we've adjourned, but I need a few minutes of the Council's time."

Judd waited while the members left their conversations and approached him. "We have two pressing matters at hand. Collin, I need you to survey everyone here. Draw up a list of the missing. Find out any details you can about the last time they were seen."

"I had wondered if I should bring the disappearances to your attention, or wait until I knew more. I wasn't sure you knew."

"I heard bits and pieces of the talk during the meeting tonight. Once you've devised your list, send it to me, and I'll prioritize it. Take nine Council members, including yourself. Form teams of three to probe into each one. No one investigates on their own. I don't want anyone walking into a trap."

Collin nodded. "I'll email you as soon as I've finished."

Judd turned to Isolde, "There is a woman I want you to investigate." He pulled out his phone and forwarded the picture Meredith took. "She was in the market this evening during our meeting and was paying close attention to this office. I have reason to believe she may have been stalking Olav shortly before his death. I'm afraid I don't have any more information than that."

"You believe she's connected to the disappearances?" Isolde asked.

"I do. You can take the remaining Council member here tonight to aide you in your search, but I'm afraid that's the only assistance I can offer you. I already have another task for Luke."

Collin shared a knowing glance with the Council member standing next to him. "What task is that, Ulric? If I may ask?"

"You may ask," Judd told him, "but you will not receive an answer."

Chapter Ten
Blood Drug

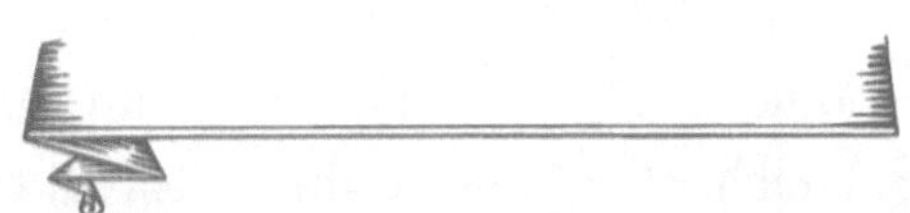

Ulric had learned his blood had a powerful hallucinogenic effect on humans, quite by accident, through Sophie. He would later learn it wasn't just his blood; the blood of any natural Fire Elemental had the same effect. The properties of his blood provided many other useful effects for humans as well. That was also knowledge he acquired through his loving wife.

After she begged him for blood during labor with their first child, he swore he would never offer his blood to her again. He kept that promise for many years. They had two more children. For both of those births, Ulric listened to the midwives and stayed away. There was always the risk Sophie might demand they fetch him because she needed his blood. If it came to that, he would make sure there would be no one left alive to tell any tales about his family.

The delirium she was in when Bennet was born had been worrisome. It didn't last long, but it had been a powerful psychosis. For a time, he worried he may have lost her for good. He feared she'd never regain her faculties.

If not for the serious threat to her health, he would have continued to keep his vow not to feed her his blood. She had injured herself quite severely. After a bad fall, she was left with a bad gash on her forearm that became infected rather nastily. The pain was intense, and Ulric feared he may lose her. The doctor had been treating her for days. He applied a fresh salve before he left and gave Ulric some powder to mix with water for her to drink.

The doctor hoped to see some improvement when he returned. They both saw the grave look on the man's face. It wasn't necessary to put into words what would happen if her recovery didn't turn a corner soon. Sophie would die an agonizing death from the infection.

There was nothing Ulric could do to help her except let her drink from his blood. He feared it was his punishment for breaking so many rules during the first year. He had interfered with the lives of humans mercilessly, and he had broken many more rules since. It didn't stop there. It was punishment for staying on earth and never attending the Return.

Sophie would pray to her God that she be spared, making promise after promise of how she would change to honor him if only she lived. Ulric could never bring himself to tell her God was turning a deaf ear to her pleas because it was what Ulric deserved. When her God didn't heal her, she began to pray for him to make her husband take away her injury and pain instead.

Late that night, she came to him with puffy, swollen eyes and tear stained cheeks. Her voice was weak, and she could barely speak above a whisper. He would have done anything for her after seeing her so frail, so when she suggested it again, there was no way he could deny her.

Ulric bit through the flesh of his forearm and held it to her mouth for her to drink. Sophie's eyes clenched shut from the taste of the bitter liquid, and she started to gag. She didn't stop. She brought her left hand up and clenched the back of his arm, holding it tightly to her mouth.

Shortly after she began to drink, he watched the reddened area slowly shrink. The pus from the infection spewed out of the wound, and the ends of the gash began to heal.

Ulric jumped upon his knees beside her and pried her mouth from his arm. "Sophie, look! It's working!"

There was no response.

"Sophie!" he exclaimed again.

When there was still no answer, he looked up to see she had sunk back into the bed, and her eyes had rolled up into her head. Her entire body had tensed.

Panic swelled deep inside just as it had the night she delivered Bennet. He had only given her a drop during labor, and she lost consciousness. This time she had guzzled from his arm. He sat by her head, lifting it into his lap, brushing the hair back off her face with his fingers. "Oh, my love," he cried. "What have I done?"

He rocked from side to side with tears streaming down his face. Silence stretched on for minutes that felt like hours. The horrible realization was settling in that he had killed the only thing that made his wretched existence on this earth bearable, until he heard her laugh.

It began as a low giggle. His eyes flew open unsure he actually heard anything at all. Then she giggled again, only louder. He looked at her face gently resting on his leg.

"Sophie, I thought I lost you."

The giggling turned into laughter.

"Are you alright?"

Without a word, she lifted her hand and pointed across the room while her laughter grew.

His eyes widened. Joy replaced the sorrow in his heart. Sophie's arm had healed completely. It had worked. Not even a scar remained. The happiness he felt was short lived.

"Why," Sophie asked slowly, "is there a cow in the house?" Her eyes were fixed on something only she could see, and she broke into a hysterical fit of laughter.

Ulric slowly took his eyes off her as he followed the direction she was pointing, knowing he would not see a cow or any other animal. There was nothing save for empty space between the foot of their bed and the wall. This was only the beginning of a very long night. A swarm of bees chased her out of the kitchen. Bats flew through the fire out of the fireplace like burning devils attacking her mercilessly.

With every new episode, he would tell her it wasn't real, and she would relax. Then the next vision would begin.

Deep into the night, his anger caused him to be forceful. "Sophie, you're hallucinating!" he growled at her. "Nothing you're seeing can hurt you."

Sophie continued to see all manner of invisible beings. She even once warned Ulric not to get out of bed because he would step on the snakes that slithered on the floor. "You're not afraid of them?" he asked her.

"No."

"How is that?" he asked, keenly aware Sophie was deathly afraid of snakes.

"You told me nothing I see can hurt me."

It made Ulric curious. "Sophie, stand up."

She did.

"Sit down."

Again, she complied.

This was too easy. He needed to try something that might be difficult for her to follow through. "Go into the kitchen and get a knife."

When she returned to their bedroom, he told her, "I want you to cut me with it."

She walked to his side and brought the knife within an inch of his arm. Her face was full of fear, but she was not hesitant in her actions.

"Why are you doing this?" Ulric asked as the blade began to scratch the surface of his skin.

"You told me to," Sophie answered.

"Drop it," Ulric told her.

The knife clanged as it bounced on the floor.

This was a startling new revelation, and it was one he'd have to explore again soon. He had now confirmed four things about his blood. Drinking it would cause expedited healing in humans. It also caused hallucinations. Too much could possibly be dangerous given how long Sophie stayed knocked out after drinking from his arm. It would appear that a person who had drank from his blood could be controlled, but he wanted to test that further.

It wasn't all good news. They would be forced to move. No logical explanation could be given to explain her sudden and complete recovery. The doctor would be paying a visit the next day to check on his patient, and Ulric knew the only way to prevent suspicion of him and his family was to be gone long before he arrived. Their abrupt departure would leave a multitude of unanswered questions, but it would be less likely a hunt would be formed.

The worst result of this experiment was learning how highly addictive his blood was to humans. Once Sophie had a taste during childbirth, she asked for it often. Now it seemed she couldn't get enough. Her cravings consumed her. She would throw literal tantrums ordering him to let her have a taste, accusing her of not loving her when he refused. There were times where she even went to the extent of injuring herself, demanding he heal her again.

Over the course of decades, he learned much more about his blood. Smaller doses would be enough to satisfy the addiction with a bonus side effect. He could control anyone who drank his blood, but only for so long as the blood remained in their system. Because of this, he didn't have to worry about what Sophie might do while under the influence. It varied, but it typically lasted up to a day. Everything would be remembered, so he was careful not to do anything that would draw unwanted attention to his family. Larger amounts were necessary to facilitate human healing which he always doled out with the apprehension that too much might bring about death, an overdose.

They also discovered it slowed the aging process in humans. It was evident in their sons who never aged a day after reaching manhood. But Sophie, his human wife, looked just as young and fresh as the day he first saw her over thirty years ago. Their appearance caused their family to resettle every two or three years to keep their unending youth from drawing inquiring eyes. Already their sons had to pass as Ulric's younger brothers because they looked so close in age.

In time, he learned that a few drops mixed in her glass would satisfy her cravings without the intense hallucinations a larger dose would bring. An agreement was forged between them. Sophie was allowed to imbibe during special occasions or events. If those times fell few and far between, she'd try to put her tiny foot down to convince him to indulge her. As amused as he was to see her so small in stature, so weak in form, attempt to order him, it worried him twice as much. The addiction was overpowering her.

By now, she fully, freely, and without hesitation used the word vampire to describe him. Yet he hoped it was how secure she was in his love for her that allowed her to be so impertinent to speak to him in that manner and not the addiction fueling her. His life became a constant supervision of his wife and managing her demons.

It all came to an end the night their butler, Henry, entered the room as Ulric squeezed a few drops of blood into a glass of wine for Sophie to drink. He saw the movement from the corner of his eye when Henry tried to slink away as quietly as he entered. It was long enough to see the terror in his eyes.

Ulric moved with super human speed and was in front of him in the hall in the blink of an eye. Henry's terror intensified, and Ulric could hear the increasing heartbeat and the sound of his butler sucking in air to scream.

Rumors of blood sucking beasts prefaced him, and he always knew he would one day face the eventuality of being accused. Today would not be that day. The punctures on his finger had already healed. He tore into it again with his teeth, and forced it between Henry's lips, smearing the blood across them and into his mouth before his butler had time to vocalize his scream. The effect would take hold almost immediately.

"You are not afraid," Ulric told him. He watched Henry's body relax. "You saw nothing out of the ordinary."

Henry smiled at him. "How are you this evening, sir?"

"I am well. Did you need me?"

"Your guests have arrived, sir. They are in the drawing room."

Their company that evening were their eldest and his beautiful bride to be. The butler would have to wait. Ulric knew once the effects of the blood was out of his system the butler's panic would return, but there would be enough time to get through the meal before having to find a long term solution. Regrettably, he knew what that solution would have to be.

Ulric returned to the bedroom. Sophie had already finished off her glass. He brought her downstairs to greet their guests before moving to the dining room for dinner. No one would have ever guessed anything else was on Ulric's mind.

ONCE THE DINNER HAD ended, Ulric found the butler in the pantry. There was an odd look on his face, a look that worried Ulric. If his blood was out of the butler's system so soon, his family would be forced to flee. There would be no time to spare.

"Stand on one foot," Ulric ordered him.

The butler complied.

He was still unsure if the butler did it out of fear, or if it was because his blood left Henry with no choice.

Ulric asked him, "Why do you look so afraid?"

Henry opened his hand to reveal one of Sophie's most exquisite brooches garnished with rubies. "I stole this while you dined."

He nodded and paced the pantry, telling his butler to standby while he decided how to handle the situation. Henry had no idea what predicament Ulric was actually trying to solve. There simply was one lone solution, but he dreaded it. Henry had been a faithful and trusted servant, until the brooch tonight, since they moved there barely a year ago. They could never take the help with them when they left, and it took time for new staff to settle in to their needs. Henry's had been a most seamless transition to their household.

Glancing once again at the brooch in Henry's hand, it made the decision easier. Death would be a severe punishment for thievery alone, but it meant Henry needed to be removed from their employ even without what he had witnessed. Plus, it wouldn't be long before they would replace their entire staff again anyway.

Ulric stopped and came round to his butler. "You have nothing to fear," he said, reaching out to take the brooch. Depositing it in his pocket, he pivoted on his heel. "Come with me."

He walked Henry under the cover of darkness into the woods on the east side of the property. It would be easy to take his butler's life with a blow to his head, breaking his neck, or any other manner of serious injury. A new and different idea formed as they walked. The only blood he had ever known was his wife's, and it had been a long time since he had so much as a drop. He had been using his refrain from blood to try to encourage her to quell how much she partakes as well. This opportunity was too good to pass up.

"Stand perfectly still," he ordered. "You are not afraid."

He could sense Henry's heartbeat. It called to him in that steady rhythm. He could follow the path Henry's blood flowed throughout his body. By scent he knew where the largest amounts of blood flow centered. He approached his butler slowly, tilted his head, bit into the beating vessel on the side of his neck, and drank until he was empty.

Henry's lifeless body fell to the ground as soon as Ulric lifted his head away. The thud his body made when it hit would have been audible for a moment had anyone else been standing nearby. To Ulric, the sound echoed off the trees deep into the woods and vibrated within his own body.

A glowing warmth ran through him as he drank. It was almost astonishing that his body didn't radiate a soft glow along with the heat. His body temperature rose enough to combat the chilly night air and would keep anyone close to him comfortable as well.

He could hear every noise for miles in all directions: conversations, people moving through the streets of the nearby village or in their homes, dogs barking, animals scurrying through the woods. All of the sounds circled like a wheel, landing on each one distinctly, letting him choose where to place his focus. With an almost radaresque hearing, it allowed him to see the scene that caused the sound instead of only merely hearing it. Visions of everything he heard from the rabbit that scurried away when Henry fell, to his wife who was changing into her nightdress, to the man taking liberties with his mistress as his footman drove the team farther away played in his mind.

Ulric could even hear the absence of sound. The kitchen of his home was quiet and empty in part due to the man who lay on the ground not even a foot away, but also because his cook's affair with one of his groundskeepers was keeping her away from her nightly duties. The wheel permitted him to hear the quiet of Henry's heart, the stillness, the lack of a pulse.

Throwing his head back, he opened his eyes and could see the light of the moon filtering through the canopy of the trees, sparkling like diamonds. It illuminated everything it touched with a halo of light making everything appear to be lit by lanterns.

The body would require disposal. It would be buried in a shallow grave in the woods where animals would hide the evidence of his crime while his family fled somewhere new. It would have to wait.

He mindlessly walked to the edge of the trees distracted by the sweet music the blades of grass played as they rubbed together in the breeze. He was still swaying to the sound of the symphony nature created all around him when a voice brought him crashing back.

"What have you done?"

Ulric froze. Surely, it was a trick. His mind was intoxicated by the amount of blood he had consumed, so much more than he had previously tasted on any one occasion. This was a byproduct. It was a hallucination similar to what his wife experiences when she overindulges. It must be.

"I do not feel well, sir," the voice continued.

He closed his eyes for a moment then opened them before turning around, expecting to see no one. His mind must be deceiving him, but he had to know for sure. When he rotated toward the woods he had just left, he saw Henry standing before him. The man was as pale as if he had seen a ghost. There were bits of leaves clinging to his hair. Henry's hand gripped his abdomen as if he were in pain.

Ulric looked over his butler's shoulder curious if he would see the body still laying there, proving the man before him was nothing more than a vision produced from his own guilt and aided by blood. There was no body. He reached out and poked Henry's shoulder with his finger then grabbed him first with one hand before gripping him with both. He placed his hands on either side of Henry's face and turned his head to the side, revealing the puncture wounds on his neck that were slowly healing.

'Impossible,' Ulric thought.

"Sir, what did you do?" Henry groaned in agony.

"I...I..." Ulric didn't know how to respond. He had been desperately listening for Henry's heartbeat, but there wasn't one. This man was dead.

"My gut churns as if I'm suffering a terrible ailment, but at the same time, I'm so ravenous I could eat for days." Henry no sooner got the words from his mouth when he began vomiting the entire contents of his stomach.

Ulric stood in shock unsure of how this was happening.

"Ahoy!" Another voice called out in the darkness.

Without taking his eyes off of Henry, Ulric saw a man approach them out of the corner of his eye. It was his groundskeeper who had stepped outside after his evening tryst.

"Is everything in order?" he asked. His eyes fell to the figure crippled over in distress. "Henry?" The name rolled off his tongue like a question when he spied him.

Hearing his name, Henry's attention swung to the groundskeeper.

Ulric watched in utter disillusion as Henry's teeth sharpened. Henry leapt higher than he had ever witnessed any mortal man being capable of doing. His feet fell at the groundskeeper's side, and he tore into his neck like an insatiable animal. Still in disbelief from watching his hallucination attack another person, he was delayed by seconds in stopping it. He finally pulled

Henry off the groundskeeper and shattered his skull with one blow. Henry fell dead for the second time in less than an hour.

Maxwell lay bleeding profusely, but Ulric could still hear the slow, declining beat of his heart. He tore into his arm and fed him the blood, hoping to save him. He pulled back quickly, but it was too late.

'What am I doing?' he thought. *'Maxwell can't survive this. He mustn't be given the opportunity to tell his tale of what happened this evening.'*

The groundskeeper began coughing. Ulric listened to his heartbeat increase as he watched the wound on his neck disappear. In less than two minutes, Maxwell crawled to his feet. The terror that rocked through his body rendered him speechless. Before he had a chance to dart away, Ulric snapped his neck.

Ulric squatted and hugged his knees, rocking back and forth. He tried to process the mess he created. There were now two bodies he would need to bury in the woods. Two missing persons that would cause rumors to speculate in the area after his family left. They would have to travel a great distance this time to outrun the events of this evening.

While he dwelled on his mistakes and what he must do, he also considered how to break the news to Sophie that their time in this place would be short lived. He was so lost in his worries he didn't notice the movement in Henry's body until he was sitting up, rubbing his head where Ulric had struck him. "I know not what came over me, sir. I mean it. It was almost like a primal urge. Even as I did it, I was terrified. I didn't know myself anymore. It frightened me because I did not wish Maxwell death, but I also was not bothered by taking his life," Henry told him softly.

Ulric watched him speak, not hearing a word that was uttered. His hallucinations were becoming unmanageable. He held up his hand to silence him. If it wasn't a big enough problem to face that Henry was once again in the world of the living, Maxwell began to stir as well, clutching his stomach in misery just as Henry had done a short while ago.

It was hard to stay focused. Ulric felt his sanity slipping through his fingers still unsure how much was reality and how much was blood induced delusions. Both of them stared at him with a quiet trepidation. He needn't look at them to see it. Their fear could be heard in the sound of their trembling thoughts.

He quickly assessed the situation. Henry had originally been drained of blood while Maxwell's spine had been severed when his neck snapped. The manner of death wasn't the connection; it was his blood. They both had his blood in their system when they died, and that was the only explanation he could ascertain. His blood continued to heal them after their hearts stopped.

It wasn't as certain what brought Henry back a second time. It could be his blood was still potent enough to cure death, but Ulric wasn't so sure. His own children could not know death. They had survived every illness in infancy and childhood, every accident and fall. His oldest survived a fatal wound by his body slowly spitting the steel of the blade out as it healed. Ulric assumed dying with his blood in their system is what caused their formulation as creatures of his nature.

Before the groundskeeper was on his feet, Ulric reached out and snapped his neck again. When Maxwell repeated his feat of surviving death, it would prove what Ulric already believed. The questions of what to do with them still remained.

Henry was a proven servant apart from the admittance of theft earlier. It seemed like ages had passed since Ulric saw the brooch in his hand. There was a powerful attraction to the notion of bringing at least one member of their staff with them when they moved who was knowledgeable, not only of their family and how they wanted their household to be run, but of their family's secret as well. He believed there wouldn't be a risk of more theft from Henry now that he knew who Ulric was and what he was capable of doing. Maxwell wasn't as invaluable, but having two with that insight might prove useful.

"How are you feeling now?" Ulric asked his butler, more to keep his sanity from wavering any farther in the ticking quiet than it already had.

"Great. I've never felt better in my life to be honest," Henry answered.

Henry had sat nearby watching as Ulric killed the groundskeeper, and he couldn't tear his eyes from Maxwell's body. With a terrified voice, he asked, "Are you going to kill me too?"

"I already did," Ulric replied. "Twice."

That revelation stopped Henry in his tracks. He sunk back into the base of a tree, trying to make himself as small as possible, too afraid of Ulric and of himself to attempt to flee.

Ulric waited for Maxwell to come around again while pondering the differences of all the Elements. Air was severely limited in their ability to reproduce. They couldn't bring any new Elementals into their family except hereditarily. Their numbers were few, and their family was close. Meanwhile, Earth could have as many children as they wished, but only one child from every other generation received the calling. It limited the number of actual Earth Elementals, but as generations passed, it would increase significantly. Many would claim to be a witch, and some even had limited abilities in witchcraft. It was nothing compared to what a member of Earth could do especially with the power of their coven behind them.

He had been aware Water could turn humans into wolves. Their bite was very toxic, but their appetite was powerful. Attacks in wolf form almost always ended in annihilation. The bites couldn't be made when Water was in human form which proved turning more wolves to be difficult. Most packs were supplemented with turned wolves if they could manage the feat.

It had never occurred to him that he could possibly be able to create more of his kind, or how it would work for him to do so. As he sat there while Henry whimpered and Maxwell lay lifeless, it began to make perfect sense. Balance was always necessary. If two Elements were limited in numbers and only able to produce more of their kind naturally, then it would stand to reason that both he and Water could add to their numbers in an unnatural way. Earth's crime that first year was quite normal. She fell in love while Water committed the most twisted acts of savage murder. It wasn't much different than he had done himself.

The noises of the night filled the air around them. Owls screeched warnings to other owls. Animals scurried through the woods looking for food. Each sound echoed in the butler's ears and caused him panic.

Ulric took his focus off of Maxwell and steadied the butler. "Are you sure you're fine?"

"It all sounds so very different now," he told him. "They're talking about us."

"And what are they saying?" Ulric asked aware Henry was now sounding like Sophie when under the effect of his own blood.

Henry looked around as if to see if any of the nearby creatures were listening. "They're watching us. They know we're not who we appear to be."

'Interesting,' Ulric thought. He had long presumed the only animal in

nature who would be able to see he was not as he appeared were the humans, but they were too wrapped up in their own affairs to notice.

Ulric sat on the ground and gave Henry's current state of mind some consideration. Maxwell was human when Henry drank his blood, but having come back from the dead twice, Henry was definitely not. His wife was human, but had the same effects from drinking his blood. The temptation to drink from Henry again suddenly became almost overwhelming. He knew drinking human blood enhanced all of his abilities, but he'd never had an opportunity to drink from a vampire. Actually, he'd never considered trying it until now and wasn't sure he'd have ever drank from his children if he had.

There were too many unknowns. Too many factors to consider. It made his head hurt. He placed his hands on either side of his head and pressed on his temples. It was becoming clear that Maxwell wasn't going to revive a second time, and the starkest difference between the two was the butler had drank human blood while Maxwell had not.

Ulric walked inside the tree line and quickly dug a shallow grave. He dragged Maxwell to it and laid him down, covering him with the loose dirt. It didn't matter that he would be found soon. The family would be long gone by then.

He returned to the butler who was still half giddy and half delirious. Every woodland creature who made themselves known would be met with a reply from Henry who was eagerly trying to communicate with them by imitating their sound.

Ulric lifted Henry easily and brought him to the cellar. His butler barely noticed that he was being carried away. He continued his conversation attempts over Ulric's shoulder.

"Stay here," Ulric ordered. "I'll be back for you in the morning."

Even as he closed the cellar door and locked Henry inside, he could still hear his butler's chittering. It was late. Most of the servants had already retired for the night. The butler would be safe there until Ulric retrieved him when he might have a better idea of what to do.

Then he went inside to the bedroom he shared with his wife. Her accusations flew at him in a rage. The butler's blood could still be felt throughout his body, and it radiated off of his skin in a way his wife had been able to recognize from when he imbibed off her. It wasn't enough that she should be limited to a few drops when he felt like indulging her if he could help himself whenever he wanted. Sophie continued her rant, demanding Ulric allow her even more blood this evening.

There was enough on his plate trying to understand the events that had transpired outside. Something would need to be done about Henry. He didn't have the time or patience to deal with the rantings of his angry wife, so he did the only thing he could think to do in that moment.

He killed her.

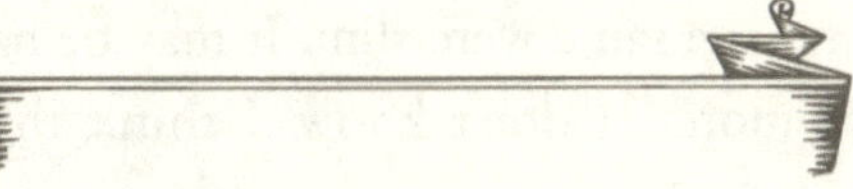

Chapter Eleven
Surprise Visitors

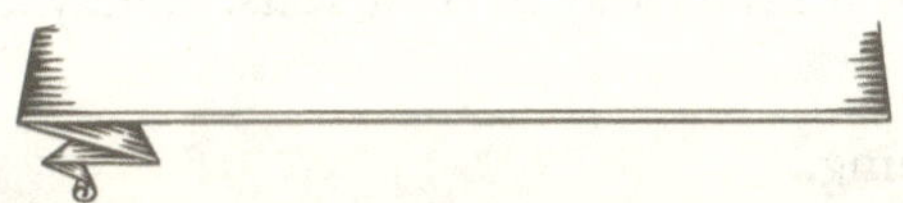

The trio slowly trudged along like cattle in the line boarding the plane back to the states. "You knew Luke would be voted in?" Judd asked.

Meredith smiled and nodded her head. It was the same response she had given him every time he had asked her since last night.

"How did you know?"

"I could see it."

"You saw the meeting?" Judd asked alarmed.

"No," she laughed. "I could see him telling me about it."

"I didn't believe her," Luke hung his head. "I know better. I do. This time though, I thought she had to have it wrong."

Judd shoved his suitcase in the overhead compartment and gentlemanly reached for the bag Meredith was holding. "Like I told you last night," he said to Luke, "you are officially the only person I can trust."

He side stepped across the row to take his seat by the window. "Outside of present company, of course," he nodded at Meredith, "my son, and a smattering of others who live in Fairview."

Luke rested his head on the back of his seat and closed his eyes. "You really think it's the same woman Olav was worried about?" he asked quietly. "Just because he said she was blonde."

Judd chuckled, "Do you know how many blonde women there are?"

"It's a strange coincidence. A pretty blonde woman outside the meeting last night, and one stalking Olav."

"You think she's pretty?" Meredith side eyed Luke then melted into a smile to show she was teasing.

It had crossed his mind many times that the probability of the two women being one and the same were slim. It may be happenstance, but his gut told him it was more. "I don't know. I think there's more than one person involved. The logistics, the planning, the tracking of our locations and activities..." Judd thought out loud. "It can't be a one person job even if this blonde is the face of it."

They buckled in for the flight home, and Judd waited for the last few stragglers to pass by on their way to their seats. "Did you ever get ahold of Eloise?"

"Yes, this morning."

"Well," he said, raising one eyebrow. "Details?"

"Eloise said she doesn't know the woman. She claimed she's never seen the woman before in her lifetime. Any of them," she added.

"Then why did she tell you to run?" Judd asked.

Meredith inhaled deeply then exhaled noisily, pursing her lips, "Eloise believes the woman in the picture to be pure evil. There was an aura of darkness around her."

Judd waited for the plane to get in the air and the okay given to use electronic devices before pulling the list up on his phone. Collin had sent it to him in the early hours of the morning, and he downloaded it to make it easier to check while in flight. It made his heart sink seeing how many of his clan may be in trouble.

At the start of the seventeenth century, there had been almost fifty thousand of his kind roaming around Europe with more scattered across the world. That number increased dramatically if you tallied created vampires with it. By the time King Louis XIV finished his reign of terror on them, there were only a couple thousand remaining. Most of them weren't from his bloodline. They were created and could be virtually impossible to control. By the beginning of the eighteenth century, they totaled less than five hundred, blood and created combined.

Fire's reproduction slowed almost to a halt. The vast majority of the surviving members were elders who had no wish to begin again with a young family. The younger vampires feared the next persecution. With Olav's recent death, they were at just over six hundred and almost a third of those were created. They had two confirmed dead of suspicious causes and over eighty were missing.

He studied the list for most of the flight, paying little attention to the created ones. They easily and often went rogue and had to be put down. Their fates were left to the hands of their creators unless they stepped out of line. If that's what happened, the Council would soon be notified of their deaths.

There were several who jumped off the page at him. These were elders who had never gone off grid a day in their lives. As he scoured the details surrounding each individual, he found a few who were more worrisome than others. People who had always been in close contact, or who had seemingly walked away from family. Some were young and wild cards. They would save those for last because he felt they'd most likely resurface on their own.

From the list Collin sent, he cut it down to thirty names. Each team could take ten and determine if they were truly missing, or worse, discover if anything unfortunate had befallen them. There was one more name that concerned him. Something made it stand out every time Judd's eyes scanned across it. He had planned to take Luke to Michigan to aide Marcus and Anya when they returned home, but he wondered if they shouldn't be going to California instead.

When the plane landed, he emailed Collin the short list with instructions to give to the teams. They walked through the airport together, retrieving their luggage.

"Are you sticking around or moving on?" Judd asked.

Meredith grinned. "Why, Judd, are you inviting us over?"

Judd was too exhausted from the trip to play along. "I was hoping Luke could help me with something."

"Sure thing, boss. What do you need?"

"Right now, I need sleep. I'm going home, but I'll call you tomorrow."

They headed their separate ways, and Judd made the hour drive back to Fairview alone. He was too tired to think about unpacking when he'd be leaving again so soon, but he knew if he didn't do it, he'd kick himself in the morning. Pulling into the drive, he was surprised to see the kitchen light shining through the window. It was always the stair and hallway lights he left on when he traveled.

'I left in a hurry,' he thought. He couldn't remember what lights he paid attention to as he ran out of the house days ago.

The memory of the eggs came rushing back. He had turned the pan off, but left it on the stove. As he thought about it, he realized he had left the half gallon of milk sitting on the counter as well. He had almost convinced himself to go straight to bed when he got inside and leave everything until the morning, but the smell that would assault him when he walked in the door would prevent that from happening.

He walked into the living room and noticed a laundry basket on the sofa. It hadn't been left there by him. The clothes it contained were neatly folded and easily recognizable. They were what he'd taken with him to the cabin.

'I never took them out of the washer,' he thought.

As he neared the kitchen, there was no foul odor. He walked into the room and saw no evidence of the eggs he had begun to cook. No milk was curdled on the counter waiting for him to dispose of it. After a quick check, the pan was discovered clean and in the cabinet where it belonged.

"I must be losing my mind,' he reasoned. He had no memory of doing any of this.

Judd turned to head back to the hall to grab his suitcase when he froze in place. Without looking directly at it, he noticed the note on the front of the refrigerator. Swallowing hard, he turned to look at it. "We're out of milk," the note read with a little heart drawn underneath. It was Camilla's handwriting.

It took no time for him to react. He ran upstairs, searching the entire house, but found no one. Nothing was out of place. He went through the downstairs checking the remaining rooms including the basement. Back in the kitchen, his paranoia grew. He paced the first floor of his house frantically with his hands clasped behind his head.

His mind was a blur, and he had trouble focusing on a single thought. He picked up a lamp and threw it against the wall, shattering it. "Damn you!" he yelled to the empty room.

'Okay,' Ulric told himself. *'You need to calm down.'*

Jackson was fine. They'd talked since his plane landed. Judd had always known the dangers his son faced because of his heritage. His blood and the echo command could control people to an extent, but it was short lived. The person being influenced is always aware something else is directing them. They just don't know what or how, and they can't say it. They can't say this is not me doing this. The controls prevented it.

For that reason, he gave him a code word a long time ago. It began as the stranger danger password, making sure no one picked him up without permission. Judd had hoped if he was ever under a vampire's command, his son would be smart enough to use it. After telling his son the truth about his parents, he tested it. Jackson was able to work it into normal conversation while under echo command, but he didn't say the word on the phone tonight. There was no way Camilla could know what the word was or that they had one to prevent Jackson from saying it.

Camilla wasn't after Jackson; she was after Judd. If she could figure out where Ulric was and who he was living as, she would easily be able to find their son at his college in Trinity.

She came to Judd's home, not Trinity. It was a mind trick. She was messing with him to put him off guard, hoping he made a mistake. It was a long con, and eventually she would show herself to him. Until then, she would continue to break in and mess with his mind to prove she had the upper hand.

'But she doesn't. I know her games and what she's trying to do. I'm ready for her.'

He picked up his suitcase and headed out to the truck. As he tore down the road out of Fairview back the way he just came to Trinity, he called Luke. The plans for Michigan were scratched. He needed Luke to keep an eye on Jackson, and he needed a favor from Meredith as well. He was sure he was leading Camilla farther away from their son, but if he was wrong, he needed Luke to be there and Meredith to hide them.

JUDD BECAME INCREASINGLY frustrated on the winding road through the redwoods. There were one hundred eighty degree turns almost every twenty yards making it difficult to drive more than thirty miles an hour at his fastest. Every couple turns would land him behind a big truck that would slow him down even more until it could move over in the next turnout lane.

Even still, it was a beautiful area. He could see why Taylor chose to live there. The view was breathtaking, and it had to offer a deep level of privacy. Not many would choose to drive this ridiculous stretch of twists and turns without good cause.

The concern for her safety increased the closer he got to her address. Collin had sent teams of three to investigate the disappearance of the Fire Elementals believed to be most at risk of harm. Judd's mind kept wandering back to Taylor.

She was young, not much older than Jackson. That's why Judd didn't place priority on her. She had no one special in her life, no children. It allowed her the freedom of being spontaneous and just taking off on a whim. Her disappearance wouldn't have even registered on his radar as an actual disappearance a month ago. He would've chalked it up to her taking a last minute, spur of the moment vacation.

Taylor's friend had been adamant something must have happened to her. They were going to travel to the last Council meeting together, but Taylor never arrived at the airport leaving her friend holding an extra paid ticket. She tried repeatedly, but couldn't get ahold of her to see what had held her up.

There were so many possibilities that went through Judd's mind. They could've had a falling out that the friend kept to herself when talking to the Council. There could have been a young man involved in Taylor's decision to stand her friend up, or a young woman for that matter.

Judd barely slept last night because he had Camilla's visit on his mind. His thoughts kept going back to Taylor while he lay restless. Once he gave up the notion of sleep, he decided he would probe into her disappearance himself instead of waiting for one of the teams to finish their investigations. He booked the first flight out of Trinity in the morning. Now he drove this winding road regretting not leaving last night.

After almost three long hours since leaving the rental desk at the airport in Mendocino, the GPS signaled that his destination was ahead. He drove down the long driveway to her house that was set back from the road. The first thing he noticed was the open garage door and car parked inside it. That wasn't a good omen.

He rolled down the front two windows of his rental car and listened. Birds sung out to each other. Squirrels clambered in the trees. He could even hear the sounds of what were most likely elk in the far distance. There was nothing coming from inside the house, not even the white noise of a fan. There was a foul odor, but it wasn't reminiscent of charred flesh. It was rank like the way the bin would smell when your trash had been sitting in it out in the hot sun for a week. He couldn't sense anything that told him someone was in the house. He also didn't detect anyone hidden in the shadows on the property, waiting for him to walk into a trap.

Judd walked to the front door keeping keenly aware of every flutter of wings, every movement of a leaf blowing in the breeze, staying alert for anything. He knocked, but as he expected, there was no movement inside. The door swung open easily when he tried the knob. It was left unlocked. That was another bad sign.

The door frame was completely intact. There was no damage visible. He eyed the keyhole for scratch marks that might indicate someone had picked the lock. Nothing looked unusual. He pushed the door through a pile of mail that had been collecting on the floor after being dropped through the slot and locked the door behind him. If there was anyone waiting in the wings, a locked door wouldn't stop them from gaining entry. The sound of a break-in would at least give him warning.

A couple lights were unnecessarily on, making no headway over the bright California sunshine pouring through the windows. He walked through the home going room by room, saving the kitchen for last. He checked under every piece of furniture, inside every closet, anywhere a body might fit while calling her name. The backdoor was locked securely. Everything was neat and orderly. There was no sign of a struggle.

Nothing looked amiss until he entered her bedroom. The two suitcases standing upright by her dresser were a clear sign that she had intended on traveling, but never made it. He lifted them, and they were very light. She didn't get a chance to pack.

Going downstairs, he readied himself to enter the noxious smells coming from the kitchen. On the table were two empty coffee cups. The liquid that had remained in them sat long enough to evaporate leaving a stain that marked the amount the cups had contained. One appeared to have been left full while the other was short only a couple drinks with several stains from the mug on the table underneath it.

The coffee carafe on the counter had the same stains on the inside of the glass. He pulled out the filter basket. The used coffee grounds remained in it covered in mold. Next to the coffee maker was a bottle of household cleaner and an unopened package of kitchen gloves. Dishes had been left in the sink with traces of food on them that had attracted a swarm of fruit flies. He knocked off the lid of the trash can with his foot. It was teeming with maggots crawling on top of each other, fighting for nourishment.

He walked into the hall where the air was fresher and easier to breathe. In his mind, he formulated an idea of what happened. Taylor was preparing for her trip to Brazil. The suitcases were pulled out from wherever they were normally stored and were waiting to be packed. She was in the process of cleaning, making sure everything was in order before going away.

There had been a knock on the door. It must have been someone she recognized. At the very least, it was someone she didn't feel posed a threat to her because she let them inside. There was no sign that anyone forced their way into the home.

The coffee pot had been left half full judging by the stains, and the rings on the table showed it was not her first cup. Taylor had fresh coffee made, so she offered her visitor a cup and topped off her own.

'It would've only taken a couple drops,' he thought. *Just a couple drops of my blood slipped into her cup when her head was turned or while she had been coaxed out of the room for some reason. After that, it would only take one drink for her to be completely under her guest's command.'*

The visitor had ordered Taylor to leave the house with them. It appeared she wasn't normally one to leave any part of her house in such disarray, but she had no choice. She was forced to leave immediately. He thought about the eggs that were on the stove and the laundry still sitting in the washer when he left for Brazil. *'Only no one was kind enough to clean up for her,'* he thought sarcastically.

Judd walked back to the counter and tore open the package of gloves, shoving the wrapping in his back pocket. They were too small. It was a struggle, but he managed to pull them on his hands.

He searched the drawers until he found a clean kitchen rag and small container. Fingerprints were a form of body fat transferred to surfaces, so he added water and grease cutting dish soap to the container. He retraced his steps through the house, wiping down everything he touched.

Eventually Taylor's disappearance would be noticed by others, and she would officially become a missing person. He didn't want to leave any evidence of his own visit behind. He took it all with him, wiping the front door down on his way out. He dumped the container along the edge of the driveway and tossed the rag in it. The gloves painfully peeled off his hands, and he threw them on the rag along with the package from his pocket. He picked it up and sat it on the floorboard of the passenger side of the car, planning to dispose of it later somewhere far from Taylor's house.

He had suspected Camilla was behind the attacks on Fire from the beginning, and she may very well have a part to play in them. There was no way she was working alone. A wolf couldn't use his blood like this. It would take a vampire. Only a Fire Elemental, a natural born, would be able to control someone with his blood in their system.

The disappearances were occurring all over the world. The timing was too close together for the same person to be behind all of them. It was a team of them working together, coordinating hits. A team of vampires were attacking their own kin. Everyone was a suspect, everyone except Luke.

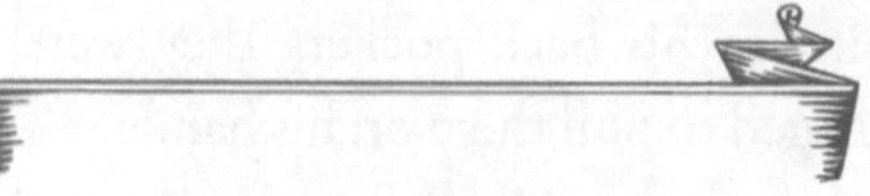

Chapter Twelve
Investigations

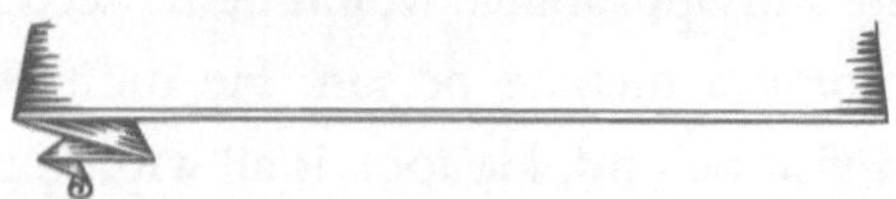

Every time she thought she couldn't become any more irate, Ulric would open his mouth and prove her wrong. It wasn't even anything he necessarily said or did by this point. Her disgust of him had grown so deep over the years that the mere sight of him would put her in a bad mood.

Isolde was young when the Council was formed, but she had believed in it. Their people had just come through the deadliest slaughter they had ever endured. They needed structure. They needed laws. They needed plans put into place that would protect them. She liked the idea of a Council, twelve equal members to oversee them with Ulric presiding over the whole affair.

She looked up to Ulric back then. He was their creator. Their people began with him. He was the reason for their existence. In her opinion, he had always been their leader even if he refused to take on that title.

No one would ever challenge him. It wasn't simply because of the stories of his savagery that were regaled. The village he destroyed using no more than his mind was legend among her kin. Just before the Council was established, there were rumors of wolves he dismembered with his bare hands. No, it was Ulric's true immortality that kept anyone from opposing him. No one could ever defeat him because he was incapable of death.

Over the years, her opinion of him tarnished until she despised him. Ulric would claim he wasn't their leader, that the power was in the Council's hands, but if he wanted something done, the Council would snap to attention. There was always special treatment for him.

The Council collected information on every single Fire Elemental including the created. They had names, addresses, phone numbers, and aliases. They had this information, so the Council could find you if it was ever necessary. If you refused to provide it or gave them incorrect details, the punishment was death. Law seven stated if a member of the Fire clan wanted to live, they could have no secrecy.

'Okay,' she thought. *'Maybe that isn't the exact wording.'*

That was, of course, unless you were Ulric Larsen. The only information the Council had for him was his phone number. If you did any work, if you checked into it, you would easily discover it was listed to a fake name at an address that didn't physically exist. Luke probably knew Ulric's identity and location. She was almost certain he did although she couldn't prove it to be true.

It irritated her that he put on this act, making them believe the Council had any form of power over the clan. He acted like he didn't abuse his position as their Element, but he did. Isolde wasn't the only one who felt this way either. There were several others. None of them had the nerve to do anything about it. Their lack of action was only because they couldn't kill him.

They didn't understand that killing him wasn't their only option. There were other ways to subdue him. She had spent many a daydream fantasizing about how to trap him, to cage him, to limit his power until he was helpless against them. There were ways it could be done. The only reason she had never acted upon it was because she knew the Council would turn on her. Even though most of them felt as she did, they were so afraid of him and what he would do if he ever got free. They would capture her, release Ulric, and allow her to meet her fate at Ulric's hands.

This wild goose chase she was on only increased her hatred of him. All he gave her was a picture of a woman who had recently been seen in Brazil with no indication of how she could be connected to the vampire deaths. In all probability, the woman, aside from her horrible fashion sense, wasn't guilty of anything other than being on Olav's radar. She questioned at first how Ulric could be certain the woman seen in Salvador was the same woman Olav spoke of in Munich.

It felt like some detail had been left out. Had Ulric seen the woman for himself? Was there another picture of the woman that had been taken by Olav to know they were the same person? As always, Ulric couldn't be bothered with further explanations. He left the law office after giving his orders. It was as it had always been. He barked, and the Council jumped.

There was some basis to his claims she discovered. Greta accompanied her in Munich, and they spent days in the neighborhood where Olav had lived. They showed the picture to business owners and townsfolk alike. Many of them recognized her. She had been seen in the area quite often shortly before Olav's death. None of them knew who she was, and none of them had seen her for at least a week.

That is what eventually led her to this little café in New Orleans eating a po'boy while waiting for DJ to arrive. She came early to scout the place, and now he was late. Isolde had located a nineteen year old hacker who could break into any computer system, specifically security, surveillance, and ones dealing with facial recognition software. It was always the young ones who could manipulate a computer the best.

Isolde had told him the woman was her sister. They had been adopted into separate families when they were toddlers. Not that he cared about why she wanted to find her. He only cared about the pile of money she placed in front of him.

They'd been in touch several times in the last two weeks. He had been facing some difficulty tracking the woman down. Isolde's patience was growing thin. She demanded a meeting to see what progress had been made.

Greta was on a bench across the street, keeping surveillance of the little café. Collin's teams had discovered too much for anyone to believe they were safe.

The sandy haired teenager walked through the door and looked around until he saw her. DJ walked to the table and sat down, setting his book bag on the floor between his feet. He took the laptop from his bag and placed it on the table.

"Sorry I'm late," he told her. "There was a second line, so I had to detour."

"That's fine," she said, waving the waitress over.

DJ opened his laptop and went straight to work.

The waitress stopped by their table.

"Just a sweet tea," he said, not taking his eyes off the screen.

Isolde listened as his fingers danced across the laptop, amazed he could work so fast.

"Okay," he began. "I found her in Munich around the time you said she'd be there. Nothing significant. Most of the time," his eyes darted off trying to find the right word, "it was like she was watching someone."

"Watching?" Isolde asked.

"Yes, she would be on a street corner staring at a home, or sitting in a café looking at the people on the street. Prior to Munich, she was in Lancaster, Pennsylvania. Same behavior. But I haven't been able to find anything before that."

The waitress brought the glass of sweet tea and set it down along with Isolde's check. "Can I get you anything else?" she asked.

Isolde shook her head no and waited for her to leave. "What about the date I gave you for Salvador?" she asked DJ.

"It's very strange. She was in the market like you said when the picture was taken, but she disappeared."

"What do you mean disappeared?"

"I have no explanation for it. I wasn't able to pick her up on any network until she boarded a plane to Sao Paulo, but when the plane landed, the security cameras didn't record her getting off the plane."

Isolde didn't follow. "Do you mean there were no cameras, or do you mean they malfunctioned?"

He took a drink from his glass, "No, I watched as everyone came off the plane, but she wasn't with the rest of the passengers."

"Then were did she go?" Isolde asked trying to understand.

DJ shook his head. "I don't know what happened on the flight, but the same thing happened before she arrived in Salvador. She was in California. It was the same scenario, only in reverse. A security camera detected her face getting off the plane, but when I hacked into the cameras at the airport in Houston where it boarded, she wasn't there."

'Air,' Isolde thought. *'I would have never believed it was Air.'*

"Where did she go in California?"

"I only got one hit outside the airport, and that was a bank," DJ said, going back to typing fervently on the laptop.

"A bank?" Isolde asked excitedly. There would be a name, an account number, something that would help them trace her.

"She didn't do anything while she was there," DJ informed her.

"What do you mean?"

"This woman," he said, "your sister walked into the bank and left." Isolde leaned forward, "Show me."

DJ typed a few commands into the computer then turned it at an angle to allow them both to see the screen. He clicked the play arrow on the video, and the mystery woman walked into the bank. "There," he said, pointing to another woman at the teller window. "It almost appears as though she's following her."

The mystery woman did seem to be keeping a close eye on the long, dark haired woman who was making a transaction. As soon as the bank customer left, the blonde from the picture walked out the door behind her.

"That's it," he told her. "That's all I could find. Two blocks away, the dark haired woman can be seen entering a nail salon, but the woman you're looking for vanished on the street."

'Of course,' Isolde thought. 'Air are shapeshifters.'

"That's how it's been since she left Brazil. I can get a hit on her then she's gone. I can spot her going into a building she never leaves, getting off a plane she never boarded, or leaving a restaurant she never went into. I get one hit then she's gone without a trace. She travels a lot. In the last two weeks, she's been in Massachusetts, Florida, London, Paris, and a small town in Greece. Most recently, she boarded a plane to Michigan."

'There are wolves in Michigan,' Isolde thought. It's a relatively new pack, but it's grown quite large. They've been turning new members at a speed alarming enough to catch the Council's attention. She wondered if they were being targeted too.

"I see," she said more to herself than DJ. "And nothing that could give us a name?"

"I'm afraid not. I've only seen her making cash purchases. I tried the flight manifests, comparing the ones I know she was on, but it would appear she hasn't used the same name twice."

Isolde nodded. Air are good at privacy. They've been practicing it since their time began.

The young man closed his laptop and folded his arms across it. "I believe I know who she is."

Isolde looked up. 'This should be interesting.'

DJ inhaled deeply, "Your sister is a spy."

"A spy!"

"I know it comes as a shock, but it's the only explanation. She travels the world. She's capable of multiple disguises. She's made some slip ups, but she knows how to keep her presence hidden. She is a spy."

Isolde nodded in agreement. "That would make sense, wouldn't it?"

"Do you want me to continue tracking her down?"

"No," Isolde replied quickly, playing into the pretense. "If she is a spy, I'm sure the government is already on to the work you've been doing. I wouldn't want you to get into any legal trouble. Besides," Isolde smiled, "she could be working on something really important."

The kid looked relieved and nodded. "I've got a class to get to," he said, putting his laptop back into his bag and standing up.

She reached out her hand to shake his before he left. Once he had gone passed the front windows, she slapped enough bills on the table to cover her check and his drink. She slowly walked across the street to join Greta.

This is huge. She'd have to check into some of the locations he provided, comparing them to where the disappearances had been reported, but she knew Greece had been a target. *'Air,'* she shook her head in disbelief. *'It's always the ones you least expect.'*

REGGIE SAT IN THE CAR, slurping his soda a half block from the fourth name on the list. It was the third day of watching to see if anyone went in or out of the little row house, and the boredom was getting to him. As bad as it was, he was thankful it was Vonnie's shift to canvass the area, looking for Elias or anyone suspicious and listening for neighborhood gossip. The temperature had dropped severely yesterday, and he wouldn't trade places with her for anything.

A couple weeks ago when Collin divided the teams, giving each a list of names, he laid out clear directions to handle the search. He didn't want anyone busting into a home blindly in case it was a set up. That's why each address had to be watched for a few days before any of them made a move to get inside. Collin was insistent on it.

As one of the younger Council members, Reggie didn't protest, but he certainly didn't agree with Collin's overly cautious approach. Collin was the senior Council member, and Ulric had commissioned him with overseeing the investigations. It was Collin's project, Collin's rules that had to be followed. Even with his objections, Reggie knew better than to rebel against the way things were supposed to be done.

It was a waste of time and resources in Reggie's mind. Someone could overtake a vampire. He was not too proud to accept his kind weren't invincible, but not three vampires. They would be hard pressed to find a match up that could overtake all of them.

They had gone to the first address in the county near Winchester. They staked out the old farm and the nearby city for three days. After they put in the time watching in case someone was waiting for them, he searched the house, looking for any clue of where they might have gone or what might have happened if there had been foul play. He hadn't finished two rooms before Alexander called him outside.

The bodies were found about forty yards from the house inside the barn. Phillip and Hannah Sergent were both in the hayloft. Their charred bodies had been staged, dangling their legs over the side of a hay bale with their arms resting on the rail. Only their bodies were discovered. They continued to search the entire farm for days, but their skulls were never found.

Phillip wasn't blood. Hannah created him long before Reggie had been born because they were in love, and she wanted him to spend her life with her. Finding their bodies in that manner made all three of them pause. Not only did something win a fight against two vampires, but two vampires who'd been together close to two centuries and were still very much in love. Each of them would have given up their life for the other, but they lost. Whoever their attacker was took the time to present them for the benefit of the search they expected was coming.

They were dealing with somebody who was powerful and sadistic. It was a combination you didn't want against you in a fight.

The next two homes they search upturned nothing. There was no sign of a burglary, no signs of forced entry. Purses and wallets were left behind. The jewelry was untouched. Cars parked on the streets. It looked like they just left for a walk one day and hadn't been back since.

The one thing he couldn't figure out was how they gained entry. These people either voluntarily left their homes and everything behind, or invited a guest inside who forced them to somehow. He thought about salesmen, meter readers, or someone collecting donations for charity. It had to be a believable con to gain access.

As he sat here parked outside this house in Boston with Alexander monitoring the back, Reggie didn't only watch Elias' house, but his neighbors as well. It would be easy to cut through the walls of an adjoining home to gain entry. It was easier still to overpower a human to get inside of the neighboring house, much easier than defeating a vampire. He began to wonder if they should be doing more than checking the doors and windows for signs of a break-in.

Reggie waited as long as he could tolerate on the side of the street before calling the team over to head inside. They walked the three steps up the stoop in front of the house and tried the door. It was unlocked, same as the other three places they'd checked. He took the downstairs while Alexander combed through the second floor. Vonnie searched the outside of the property which consisted of a few feet of fenced bare yard and a small shed.

He walked through the living room looking for anything out of sorts such as scratch marks on the floor where a struggle may have occurred. Nothing was out of the ordinary.

Vonnie was back inside quickly having little to examine and went into the kitchen to help. "Hey, look at this," she called out.

Reggie walked through the doorway and saw her holding a piece of mail from a small pile on the counter. She handed it to him.

"It's a credit card bill," he said, not seeing the significance.

"Yes," Vonnie said. "Look at the postmark. The date is a week after he went missing, and it's been opened."

He did the math in his head. "Someone was still here at least what? Ten days after his brother last heard from him?"

Alexander came down the stairs.

"Anything to report?" Reggie asked.

"Nothing new. Same as everywhere else. Everything looks natural. The bedroom is a bit of a mess, but that could just be Elias. There's a Rolex on the dresser in plain sight, and the suitcase is in the closet."

Reggie tapped the letter in his hand while he considered what it could mean. "The kitchen's a bit tidier too."

"How so?" Vonnie asked, eyeing the string of mail and other papers on the counter.

"The Sergent's had a pork roast in the crock pot that had never been cooked. There were vegetables on a cutting board, waiting to be chopped. The last house had groceries only half put away. This kitchen is clean. No dishes." He hit the flap in the top of the trash bin lid and checked inside. "It's not empty, but it's not old enough to smell."

Reggie walked to the refrigerator and pulled out a half gallon of milk. He unscrewed the lid and smelled it. "Still fresh."

"You don't think he's actually missing, then?" Alexander asked.

"I wouldn't say that," Reggie told him. "I wouldn't walk out of my house leaving a Rolex on the dresser."

He rummaged through the rest of the pile of mail and found a small planner at the bottom. He opened it to the month. "The dates have been crossed off until five days ago."

Reggie continued to fidget with the bill he was holding while he thought. "He has been here at some point since his brother last spoke with him. I don't know if anything's happened to him in the last five days, but it doesn't quite fit the pattern. Of all the houses we've searched, I think Elias is the best candidate so far to be found alive."

Vonnie asked, "Should we stick around then and case the place longer?"

"No," Reggie said. "We've already spent enough extra time at the Sergent's farm. I'll report it to Collin as inconclusive. If no one has heard from him when we finish our list, we will come back."

THEY HADN'T BEEN IN Yonkers very long. They found Ruth's apartment building and cruised the neighborhood scouting the best locations to set up. The building was secure, so they needed a place to keep an eye on the apartment windows from the outside as well as the main door. The bus stop in front of the building would allow Reggie to stay near the doors for a long time without anyone noticing him. It was only a couple hours after they were in place when the delivery car pulled up out front.

The button to buzz Ruth's apartment was on the bottom left of the two columns of names. He saw the pizza delivery guy push it easily from where he stood against the bus stop shelter.

Reggie approached him just as Ruth answered. *'Where was she when we tried?'* he wondered. He shrugged it off quickly aware there were many possibilities why she hadn't answered them.

"Pizza," the man said, lowering his voice to the speaker.

"Oh, come right up," Ruth told him. The door buzzed and the sound of the lock unlatching could be heard.

Reggie opened the door for the guy. "Is that for Ruth Young?" he asked.

"Uh, yeah," he said.

"That's my grandma," Reggie told him. Ruth didn't look more than a few years older than he did, but no one would guess that by her name. "Let me pay for it. I'm on my way up to see her."

The guy handed him the box. "It was paid online," he said glad to have part of his job done for him.

Reggie fished some money from his pocket for a tip and went inside. He sent messages to Alexander and Vonnie to join him. Ruth was home.

He waited by the door to let them in then they went up the elevator together to the fourth floor. Reggie went to the apartment while the rest of his team hung back in the hallway.

Ruth answered as soon as he knocked expecting the delivery guy to be coming. She reached for the box then noticed who was holding it. "Reggie!" she said when she saw who he was. She looked over his shoulder and asked. "Where's everyone else?"

"You're expecting us," he asked.

"Yes. Didn't Collin get ahold of you?" She pushed the door open wide, so he could step inside.

"No," he said, motioning to the team to follow him.

"Just set it there," she said, pointing to the dining table by the balcony door. "If I had known you'd be here so soon, I would've ordered more pizza."

The team stood nearby, watching her as she stacked glasses on top of plates and carried them to the table. "Sit," she insisted, heading back for more.

"When did you speak with Collin?" Reggie asked.

"Oh," she said from the next room. "Shortly after I got home. It couldn't have been more than an hour ago."

I was outside an hour ago, but I never saw her,' he thought. He quickly sent Collin a text asking if he had heard from Ruth.

Ruth went back to the kitchen for a bottle of cherry cola and returned with it tucked under her arm while typing onto her phone. "Help yourselves," she said as she sat down.

"Who was that?" Reggie asked, pointing to her phone.

She slipped her phone in her pocket. "I was ordering another pizza," she said. "I hope you like pepperoni."

"You didn't need to do that," Vonnie told her.

"No, it's fine. No trouble at all."

Ruth poured a glass of soda and passed the bottle to Alexander who served everyone else. She put a slice on her plate, and said, "Collin told me you would be in the area soon and might be showing up." She took a bite of her pizza. "And he told me why."

"Where have you been?" Alexander asked. "No one's been able to get in contact with you."

"A friend of mine was ill," she said, tapping the box encouraging her guests to eat. "I went out of state to see her before she passed and attend her services."

Vonnie put a slice on her plate and began to eat. "Why didn't you say anything to anybody," she asked between bites.

"I did," Ruth said. "I left a message with my oldest daughter that I would be out of town for a while."

"Yes," Reggie told her, remembering the message was mentioned in the notes of Ruth's disappearance. "But she hasn't heard from you since." He took a drink from his glass.

Ruth smiled, "That's because my friend was a witch. It's a touchy subject with my family. My friendship with her has always caused my daughters to give me grief, and I wanted to say goodbye without any drama."

She grabbed the empty pizza box and took it to the kitchen then returned with another bottle of soda. "I thought I had lived long enough to be able to go away and have some privacy. I was wrong."

"We understand," Reggie told her. "We're just glad you're okay."

"Don't worry," she said. "I talked to my children before I called Collin. That's how I knew to get ahold of him."

Reggie's phone vibrated, and he reached for it.

` "Could you please hand me a napkin?' Ruth asked.

He left the phone alone and moved the napkin holder within closer reach of her.

"Thank you," she said.

There was a knock on the door, and Reggie shot upright. His fangs emerged, and the lines around his eyes and mouth deepened and pulled back.

"It's just the pizza," she said, getting up to get the door.

He watched her back as she walked away and slowly moved around the table to be guarded from view of the door. "I don't know how it works here, but I've never had a pizza delivered that fast," he whispered.

"No one buzzed at the door," Vonnie said, scooting her chair sideways to be able to move faster if she needed to.

They heard her open the door and greet someone. From the front room, a voice called out, "Sit down and shut up unless I'm talking to you."

Reggie's legs carried him back to his seat even as he begged them not to move. Something was terribly wrong.

A strikingly beautiful blonde woman followed Ruth to the dining room. "Finally," she said. "I've been hoping to catch you for weeks."

Reggie's phone vibrated again, reminding him that he hadn't checked his messages.

"Who is it?" the blonde asked him. "And be honest."

He picked up his phone and checked the message. "Collin," he answered even though he wanted to lie and give her a different name.

"Ugh," she sighed disgustedly. "Good ol' Collin. What does the message say?"

Reggie read the text out loud. "No, I haven't."

"Haven't what? What did you ask?"

He read the text he sent to Collin out loud.

She scratched her head and noisily blew air out of her mouth. "I'm sure you've deduced by now your free will is gone," the blonde said, and picked up the soda. "It's been spiked with Fire's blood."

She looked at the Council trio and cackled. "Oh, the looks on your faces! To learn that your sacred leader has set you up."

The blond regained her composure, and she checked her watch. "It's a good day. I'm feeling generous." She put her hands on the table and leaned down. "Fire didn't have anything to do with this. You give credit where credit is due," she said, standing up and pointing theatrically to her chest.

"Don't blame poor Ruthie here either," she said. "She's only following orders same as all of you are now."

She glanced at Reggie's phone. "Collin won't waste any time when you don't respond to that text."

"Alright," she said, clapping her hands together and walking around the table. "We have a lot of work to do and very little time to do it. We need to move this party elsewhere. Does anyone have any questions?"

Reggie asked, "Are you going to kill us?"

"No," she chuckled. "Not today."

THEY MADE THEIR WAY through LaGuardia growing irritated by all the passengers who couldn't stay out of their way. *'We're in a hurry here!'* Isolde screamed internally.

If Collin had waited five more minutes before calling, it would've been too late. They would've been on their way to Atlanta for the first leg of their flight back to Germany. They were already in their seats and took the call real quick before takeoff. As it happened, they had to echo the whole plane to be able to leave without security getting involved.

Instead of going to Munich, they were now trying to get outside to hail a taxi to Ruth Young's apartment building. It had been eight hours since anyone heard from Reggie's team. If they were still knee deep in staking out her building, they might have their phones silenced and not use them. It was something about the way Reggie worded the question.

"Did Ruth get ahold of you?"

It didn't sound like he was trying to verify she was still missing. It sounded like he was trying to confirm what he already knew, like he had spoken to Ruth who told him she'd been in contact with the Council.

They stepped through the airport doors and got into an awaiting taxi. There should be little traffic this late at night. It shouldn't take more than twenty minutes to get there.

Twenty minutes that felt like it dragged on for two hours.

Isolde and Greta walked up to the door and buzzed Ruth's apartment. As they feared, there was no answer. Greta gave the door a try with no luck and stepped back. It was securely locked which they expected.

"What do you think?" Greta asked. "Silent alarm?"

"It's a nice complex," Isolde commented. "I'd be surprised if there wasn't one."

Greta put her hand back on the door and glanced at Isolde to make sure she didn't object before applying a little force to bust the lock. A noise from behind them caught their attention.

They looked back to find a man walking up from the street, fumbling his keys. They moved over to let him by. He unlocked it and asked, "Do you live here? I haven't seen you around."

"No, our aunt does," Greta lied. "She must be asleep because she didn't answer when we buzzed."

"Who's your aunt?" he asked.

"Ruth Young."

The man appeared surprised. "She's your aunt? I didn't think she was that old."

Isolde hadn't expected him to know Ruth. "She was the youngest of eight, so she's not much older than us," she quickly said to explain why the three of them looked close enough in age to pass as sisters.

He nodded like he understood. "She's a sweet woman."

"Thank you," Greta told him.

"It's against policy here to let people in who aren't your guests," he explained.

Isolde prepared to echo her voice. "I understand."

"But Ruth mentioned some family coming to visit when I spoke to her earlier," he pushed the door wide to let them enter.

They walked inside, and the three of them got on the same elevator together. The man went up to the seventh floor, so they had to wait until the doors closed behind them in the hall to say anything. Neither of them moved right away.

"Family visiting," Greta repeated.

Isolde anxiously chewed her nails and stood quietly.

"He spoke to her earlier," Greta added. "Do you think she knows we're coming?" she asked.

"No," Isolde answered, grabbing the handle of her suitcase with her free hand, but still unwilling to walk.

"Do you think its coincidence?"

Isolde dropped the hand from her mouth and looked at Greta. "No."

She began pulling her suitcase down the hallway toward Ruth's apartment. They got to the door and knocked. There was no answer, and they couldn't hear anything coming from inside. Light poured into the hallway from under the door, and the faint smell of burnt flesh assaulted their senses.

Greta turned the handle of the door, and it easily gave way.

Every light had been left on. They could easily see the dining room table directly across from them at the back of the apartment. Staring back at them from the table were two charred skulls with bits of flesh still clinging to them.

Isolde knew it was a parting message. She knew whoever had put them there was already gone.

She left her suitcase in the hall and walked to the table. It was littered with cups, plates and remnants of pizza. It looked like a party had been thrown.

On the table near the skulls was a cell phone she would later discover belonged to Reggie. She picked it up hesitantly and pressed the home button. The lock screen appeared wanting a password she didn't have. She cried out and dropped the phone.

Greta came up behind her, "What is it?"

Isolde leaned on the table for support, crying hard and couldn't give an answer.

Greta picked up the phone and saw for herself. The lock screen image was a picture of the Council team and Ruth standing behind the table smiling. Reggie and Vonnie each held a skull in their hands.

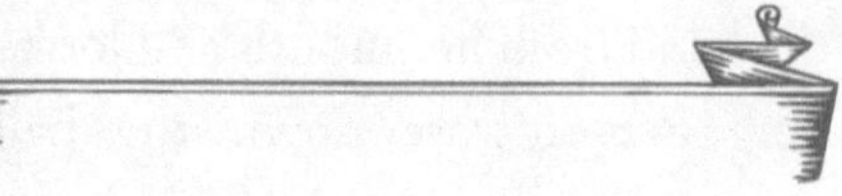

Chapter Thirteen
Versailles

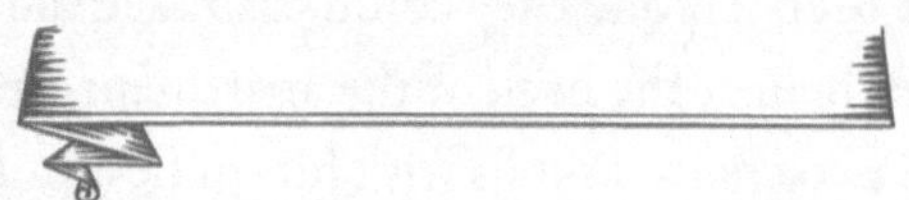

'*Sophie is safe.*'

That was the one thought guiding him as he and Collin pushed their horses faster away from her.

'*Sophie and our children are safe.*'

Without that comforting knowledge, he would not have left their home in Brussels to travel to Versailles to save as many of their people as he could.

Louis XIV's rise to power brought with it many advancements for France, but vast poverty lay strewn in its wake. Everyone knew, at least everyone in his circles knew, that Louis XIV's achievements could not have been accomplished without the help of a witch.

This was nothing new. Leaders had been buying into tales told to them by soothsayers, witches and warlocks for centuries. Many of them had no more power than that of a drunkard you might pass on the city street at night. Some managed to have a few hits before they ran out of luck. Death was typically the price paid by any of these so called fortune tellers when they let those in power down.

The witch aiding Louis XIV, however, was real.

A rogue descendant of Anya, she never understood why her kind wouldn't want to use their power to turn their favor. Many of our kinds struggle with the idea of staying in the dark, living a normal life, when they could obtain so much. Usually, they learn to accept why our bloodlines should be kept hidden. It would be disastrous for any of us if the truth got out.

And now, the truth had been unleashed. All of them were in peril.

This witch who had been behind Louis' every move for the last decade was once a fond ally as he always had a soft spot for the rebels. The ones who stood their ground, who took charge of their life and their destiny at the risk of alienating their own kind were the ones he gathered around him. None had ever risked so much until her.

Her name would be erased from his memory. It would never be learned in history books. It would never be spoken in polite company. She doesn't warrant the recognition or the friendly honor repeating her name would bestow. Her treachery was far too severe.

All of her advice, all of her sage warnings had been precise. They aided the king in his quest for power at the expense of the peasants who suffered mercilessly.

She had been living quite a fairy tale. Her husband was rather handsome and admired by many. Louis had arranged for her to have her pick of suitors. They raised a family in a country estate with servants paid for exclusively by the King of France as payment for her services. Her only downfall was refusing to sleep with her king.

Monarchs tend to take it personally when you slight them in such a manner.

It was too late to save her family, but in an attempt to save her own skin, she sold the rest of them out. Vampires, werewolves and witches had been fleeing, running for their lives. Most of them had not made it.

To add to the crimes against the Elementals, she had detailed how to kill them all. Until she opened her mouth, most of the world was unknowing to the truth of their kind. They believed a simple stake through the heart of anyone they felt was a threat would suffice, but now vampires were being burned. Ulric's people were being decapitated and burned alive. Witches were being drugged and taken below ground where their powers would be neutralized, preventing them from escaping death. Werewolves were being drowned in daylight, unable to turn without the light of the moon to transform themselves.

Many of his lineage were scattered all over Europe saving anyone they found alive. Many had already been lost. There had been too many of his family murdered to count and no time to grieve.

Bennet, his firstborn, came back home for his mother, to help keep her safe. He had taken Sophie and their other two children into the country side northeast of Versailles to hide out.

Meanwhile, Ulric rode on toward the city where a great number of his kind, lineage and created, have taken up residence over the last century. It had been a bloodbath for vampires and all Elemental creatures there for days, and the carnage was far from over. The city was secretly under siege by Louis' order, and vampires had difficulty making it out.

While he had no way to know everything the witch confessed, it was obvious she wrongly proclaimed that only Fire Elementals can change humans. They could create new vampires, but a werewolf bite could turn a human as well. The only locations being purged were the cities where his family thrived. Any other creatures living in those areas were poor souls caught in the cross fire.

Once a friend, her death did not sadden him. He only wished he could have been there when she awoke from her drugged stupor below the castle floors. He would like to have seen the panic stricken look on her face when she realized the mounds of earth that surrounded the dungeon walls left her powerless to stop whatever the king had ordered done to her.

Digging his heel into the horse's flank, a grin turned up the corner of his mouth as Ulric, for the first time, understood that she wouldn't have power enough to foresee what was coming when she awoke in the dungeon. The fear, the sheer and utter terror she must have felt was an energy that could satiate him for the entirety of this trip.

Ulric knew how her death came. Anya, herself, told him, and as it very rarely happens, they were in agreement that her demise was too quick, too easy. She was strung up by her wrists overhead until her shoulders dislocated. Then ever so slowly, she was lowered into a vat of boiling oil.

The punishment by this time, of course, wasn't for refusing the king's bed. Her death would've been swift and much more painless if that were her only crime. When the King learned of all the evil around him and that she knew without alerting him or trying to stop the darkness from spreading throughout his kingdom, it made matters much worse. It was an offense deserving a more severe punishment.

Beginning with her toes, she was slowly immersed into the vat. When she would pass out, and she did often, the executioners woke her by whatever means necessary. They prodded her with the tip of their swords, held stirring drugs to her nose, and sliced her flesh with daggers. While she was dead long before the oil reached her head, it is important to note that she was alive for a very long time while the flesh boiled off her bones. It's more important to note that she died with the smell of her cooked flesh wafting into her nostrils, smelling the rancid odor of the wrongs she had committed to her people.

IT TOOK HOURS TO FALL asleep. Collin and Ulric sat with their backs braced to each other beneath the shelter of a tree. A fire was too risky. Neither of them wanted to risk the deep slumber of laying out on the ground so close to Versailles.

They were searching everywhere, but the nearer they arrived to their destination, the more alert they became. It was something unspoken between them. They both felt it, and they were both aware the other one felt it as well. Words weren't necessary.

The horses rested nearby. They were the reason for their uncomfortable camp this evening. They were close. Ulric wanted to ride on till they reached the city, but Collin insisted on stopping for the night for fear of running them too hard. Leaving at first light would put them in Versailles around tomorrow evening, giving them the benefit of darkness when they arrived. That was what convinced him to wait. Horses be damned.

Even with their keen hearing, there was very little noise to detect, save for the occasional scampering of a night time creature hunting for food. There was no sound to keep him awake, and it wasn't the unnatural sleeping position they took either. It was his eagerness to arrive.

They were alive for now, but they were extremely frightened. Ulric could sense his kin's terror. He knew where they were, and he knew the moment their life force had been snuffed out. So far, his people in Versailles had remained hid. Some of the created lot had managed to survive thus far. The fear in their thoughts was so loud that even across all these miles, some of them had been able to penetrate his mind.

Because they were still alive, he felt the sense of urgency. He needed to get to them while he still had the opportunity to save them. Anya had assured him they were safe for now and had given him a pendant that would allow him to see her visions which remained darkened and dull.

'Anya,' his thoughts drifted. '*The contempt I have for that woman has attained heights I wasn't aware I was capable of reaching. When that witch of hers first rose aside the king, she should have done her duty to the rest of us and eliminated her.*'

Ulric hadn't cared back then. He never cared about her abuse of her Elemental powers until the day she betrayed them. Still, he did ask Anya what her plans were as soon as he learned of that witch's role to the king. He had assumed Anya would be the first in line to want to eradicate the problem. Instead, she looked him in the eye that night over ten years ago and assured him that no harm would come to any of them through that witch.

It was the witch's pride that led to her downfall. The matter could have been handled so easily. Even without their power, he knew the spells they were capable of casting. He knew the charms they used to toy with men and women alike. The king could have easily been spelled to believe that any woman in his bed was his witch.

In turn, she could have used anyone she wanted to take her place. An enemy. A servant she didn't particularly like. A passerby on the street. It would have made no difference. A coercion spell would be able to guild the woman into sleeping with the king. Not that one would be needed. Many women of loose morals would have seized the opportunity in the hopes that gifts would be bestowed upon them in exchange of favor. Afterwards, it would only take a simple memory spell to erase the deed, and no one would be the wiser.

No, not that witch. Her refusal to use a substitute wasn't even based in the idea of not wanting to violate a woman in such a way. That, at least, Ulric would have respected. She couldn't bear the thought of the king believing he had actually had his way with her. Even if it wasn't her body he was taking, she didn't want him to have the memory as false as it might be.

As far as Anya was concerned, he knew the future could change with each passing moment. Nothing is set in stone. The outcome she would have seen in her visions that night so many years ago could have changed a thousand times over since then.

'But why hadn't she stayed on top of it?' That was where his anger lied. This was a matter that required constant scrutiny, and no one, least of all him, should have had to make Anya aware of that truth. If she wasn't going to keep a constant eye on her rogue witch, then she should have handled the situation when it was brought to light.

Thinking about it then, it was his anger toward Anya that kept him awake longer than the lack of comfort or listening to the distressed cries of his family.

ULRIC JUMPED TO HIS feet in the still of the night acutely aware that Collin had done the same. "You felt it too?" he asked.

He barely saw the nod through the black darkness as Collin stared off in the same direction as he did. It was the direction of Versailles.

"We should go," Ulric barked, reaching for his bag before he even saw the red glow emanating from within.

He glanced toward Collin. His eye was on the bag as well.

Ulric ran to his horse and mounted her. They'd arrive much earlier now, but the threat to his kin was far greater than the threat of them being discovered.

"Are you going to examine it?" Collin asked.

"There's no need; I already know," was Ulric's reply.

They rode full speed until they neared the outskirts of the city before slowing down to not raise as much suspicion. Strangers arriving during this upheaval would be judged to determine if they were one of two sorts: the hunters or the hunted. As their horses trotted through the streets, the city felt almost empty. People were hoarded inside their homes having been warned to stay out of sight for their safety. Nothing blocked their thoughts however. The city was still very much alive with chatter.

The fires were still smoldering, and the scent of burnt flesh hung in the air. Not everyone had been lost. Ulric could sense the fear of the survivors.

A familiar face appeared on the street who nodded slowly, inclining him to follow. Ulric motioned to Collin to dismount. They walked their horses, not losing sight of the woman until she entered a home.

They tied their horses and approached the door which swung open before they reached it. The man who opened the door was older, in his late sixties at the youngest. "She's expecting you," he said, standing to the side to allow both men to enter.

Ulric and Collin went inside and held back until the man could lead them down the hall to a private study where Anya waited. Her back was to them when they entered, but it did not matter. Ulric had recognized her on the street instantly. She was older than when they first met, but he had seen her even older many times.

The man introduced them by name as if he knew them. "Ulric Larsen and Collin Weber," he announced.

Anya pivoted when he began to speak, and Ulric bowed to his old friend with the term friend applied very loosely at that moment.

Collin bowed as well, but being one who had never suffered propriety well, he did not wait long to ask, "And you are, Ma'am?"

Her eyes sparkled with amusement, playfully glancing at Ulric. "My apologies for assuming your companion had mentioned me. I am Lady Gillian Ward."

"Pleased to meet you, Lady Gillian," Ulric said in jest.

Anya turned to the man who had brought them to her, "Thank you," she said. "That will be all."

He hesitated, eyeing the two strangers who stood before him.

"I will be fine, Thomas," she assured him.

With that, the man begrudgingly left the room.

Ulric watched him until he disappeared then asked, "Are we safe in your home?"

"My husband," Anya sneered through clenched teeth, "is out assisting with the hunt. This is my grandson's home. We are free to discuss matters openly here."

"Your grandson, ma'am, is he assisting with the hunt as well?" Collin once again spoke out of turn. The tone of his voice implied both that he was attempting to be threatening with his words, and that he knew not who he threatened.

"My grandson?" Anya pointed to the door where the man had departed. "Heavens, no. He is among the hunted."

Ulric needn't look at Collin's face behind him to be able to see the lack jaw expression of confusion. Lady Gillian Ward appeared to be many years younger than her grandson. He held up his finger to Collin to silence him and directed his attention to Anya. "Is there anyone else left?"

Thomas returned to the room with a tray bearing glasses of wine for all.

Anya took a glass and sipped, "A few," she murmured. "Very few managed to scatter. The king's men had help finding us."

Holding the glass with little interest, Ulric waited for Thomas to leave the room once again before continuing. "Yes. That witch. Your witch provided them with everything they needed."

"No, you fool," Anya scolded him. "It was someone other than Sylvia. She gave the instructions on how to kill us, our secrets, our weaknesses, and where some may be, but she did not know all of our locations. She certainly did not know my family's whereabouts, given our spells that can shield us. Someone," Anya drawled out, "or something else aided them."

Taking another sip, Anya walked to the desk and stared at the portrait on the wall behind it. The name plate read John Ward.

"Your husband?" Ulric asked.

Ignoring him, she continued, "They did not search all the homes in Versailles. They mainly went to the homes where they knew your kind would be found."

"Water," Ulric said without hesitation. It was the only remaining option. Marcus would never interfere in such a way if for no other reason than he'd have to come out of hiding to do so.

"Many wolves were taken today as well. What reason would Water have to turn on them?"

"What of your family?" he asked, nodding in the direction of her grandson's absence. "How are you safe?"

"Thomas returned for me. His family and my children left late last night. This house was searched this morning and cleared. It's safe. They won't be through again. I made sure of it."

Collin moved to the open chaise, stumbling once on his feet as he moved. He sat down, pale and shaky, when Ulric finally took notice of him.

"Are you well?" Anya asked.

"Yes," he replied quickly, finishing his drink in one gulp. He appeared more nervous with each second that passed.

Anya approached him, studying him intently. "You have questions."

Collin did not acknowledge her. Beads of sweat had formed along his hairline and slowly forged their course down his forehead, tattling on his growing nerves.

She reached out and touched one of Collin's temples lightly with her fingertips. Nodding, she told him, "Yes, I am she. You are safe here."

"What of your husband?" Ulric asked, growing impatient. "He is on the hunt. Surely he would know to find you here. How can you be sure this home is safe?"

"My husband," Anya spat the word as if it caused pain to speak it, "dragged me from our bed this morning and brought me to the crypt beneath the abbey believing I would be stripped of my powers underground."

She walked behind the desk, standing directly in front of the painting. "He chained me to the wall, accusing me of ridiculous crimes such as slaughtering for spell casting, sacrificing newborns for their youthful properties, and then had the audacity to drive a dagger into my heart believing it would kill me." Anya took a drink and sprayed the wine from her mouth on the painting then threw the glass as well with such force it shattered.

The anger within her rose and radiated from her, creating a warm draft of air in the room that circled around her. "If that was not enough," she said, returning to the front of the desk to stand near Ulric, "I had to listen to that babbling traitor carry on for an hour about how sorry he was and professing his unending love to me, the wife he had just murdered, before he finally left, so I could free myself."

Anya's face revealed her sadness, and she delicately took her seat near Collin who continued to sit frozen in astonishment. "Thomas and I are leaving tonight. I'm thinking England this time. It's been far too long since I've been back."

He had many more questions to ask her about who was participating in the hunt and how many of each of the blood lines may still be alive, but he didn't have the time to voice any of them. A sharp pain rocked through his chest and dropped him to the floor as Anya jumped to her feet.

"Sophie!" he cried.

"Go to her," Anya demanded. "Go now."

ULRIC RODE OUT ALONE until the terrain became impassable. His hidden kingdom, as he called it, was only known to five people, and four of them had taken shelter there. It was impossible they had been found, but he felt it.

He had sensed it the moment his family's lives had been extinguished, and he could feel it still. The absence of their lives echoed through his being. Their essence had been a part of him, and the void left behind was louder than anything he'd ever heard.

'No, it's preposterous,' he thought, climbing the rocky landscape in the forest. He had stumbled upon this remote location by accident in his early days as Ulric. It was hidden deep in the forest in an area that would be inaccessible to get to by humans who knew where they were going, let alone

ones who were simply searching the area for any stragglers trying to flee.

The base of the mountain that hid his private sanctuary loomed larger and larger before him until he had finally reached it. Ulric sprinted up the mountain side until he approached the jagged rocky wall covered in vines. He hugged it, shuffling horizontally as fast as he could, hoping to find his family alive even if they had befallen some terrible predicament. His mind blessed him by ignoring the messages from his heightened sense of hearing and smell, giving him the blissful ignorance to not acknowledge the crackling scent of burnt flesh that grew with each step he took.

Each time they had come to this place his family had been a target. Vampires were being hunted or some other form of suspicion fell on them. No matter how far away their home may have been, this was the one place they all felt safe. No one could find them because no one could reach it. It had protected him and his family several times over the centuries when they needed to stay out of sight during times of amplified vampire fears. They would come here and regroup, staying for weeks maybe months, however long it took for them to feel confident that when they emerged from the forest, they could travel on to a new home without anyone recognizing them for what they truly were.

Ulric continued along the wall, clinging to hope that the feeling sickening his gut must be caused by something other than what he knew as truth deep down. He climbed sideways until his hand fumbled through the vines in an opening in the rock. He stepped through the shroud into his secluded realm. Past the opening was a small clearing just large enough for him to build a small hut centuries ago. The hut had been rebuilt every time he returned to this place because it had never been strong enough to withstand the damage from exposure to the elements. The number of times he had been back since he discovered it accidentally could be counted on one hand.

This time it proved not to be a safe haven any longer. He emerged from the vines and dropped to his knees. The scream that formulated from deep within growled out of him more beast than man and loud enough to scare off birds and small forest creatures for miles. Any human hearing it would tell the tales of the beast that lived on the mountain, and those stories would be passed on for generations with the details ever changing and growing into legend.

They were strategically placed directly in front of him. Only a few feet from the entrance were the badly burned skulls of his family placed atop spears. They were positioned to be at eye level and the first thing he saw when he manifested through the vines. Their charred bodies lay in a pile a few feet behind their skulls. Sophie, Bennet, Gregor, and Peter, all four of them. Dead. This wasn't a vampire hunt ordered by the king.

This was personal.

THE EVENING HOURS MADE way to dusk which turned to darkness, and the moon rose. Ulric remained kneeling in front of his family's remains. Time no longer held meaning. He no longer had purpose. His thoughts, if he had any, flittered through his mind not stopping, unable to find a stable place to settle.

The howling had almost ended before the sound penetrated his lost shell. Once he realized what he was hearing, he concentrated on it. They were near.

Ulric tore away from his family's former oasis that would forever now be a graveyard and sprinted down the face of the mountain. He jumped and slid at frighteningly dangerous speeds, not caring what happened to him. He was cursed to live.

Even in his hysteria fueled state, he knew the blood of his family wasn't on the king's decree. Whoever did this was sending a message. They knew who his family truly were, and they hid under the cover of the king's purge to take them out.

His sadness and grief energized his rage, and his rage demanded retribution. Ulric raced through the forest toward the sound of the wolves without a concern for the hazards in his way. His foot landed in a hole and twisted, snapping a bone directly above the ankle. He continued running not noticing the pain of his fast healing injury. He tripped over a fallen tree, rolled several yards downhill, and jumped to his feet, continuing his trek in one swift motion. It appeared effortlessly planned.

The two wolves didn't know what hit them. Ulric ran between them, grabbing the shorter one's arm as he sped by and ripped it from the socket. He spun in circles screaming like a madman, waving the arm like a mace in front of him. The larger of the two wolves came into view as he charged an assault. With one last spin, he hit the wolf in the head with his companion's arm and knocked him to the ground unconscious.

Ulric eyed the first wolf on his side on the ground bleeding profusely, using his good arm to drag him to safety. He walked to the wolf's side and gently kicked him onto his back. The wolf plead for mercy, plead for his life to be spared, plead for Ulric to stop, but all of his pleas fell on haunted ears. He put his foot on the wolf's chest, and grabbed the other arm with both hands. It came off with one solid yank.

He stood, straddling the body. The blood spray from the newly severed arm soaked the leg of his trousers and his shoe. He watched while the blood spray began to wane and the color of the beast's face turned pale. The wolf didn't have much time before he succumbed to his weakened state, but he continued to mutter. "Please. Please, no."

Ulric squatted over his body and lifted a finger to his lips. "Shh. It's almost over."

He straightened and walked away, hearing the wolf say, "Thank you."

A thrill electrified his entire being that this beast thought him capable of mercy. He felt it surge through his veins. After he walked several feet, he darted back full speed toward the wolf and jumped through the air, landing square on his shoulders. The wolf emitted a blood curdling scream. Ulric grabbed the wolf's head with both hands and effortlessly removed it from the body. To his malevolent delight, the wolf's scream continued even after Ulric was holding his head six feet above its body.

Ulric carried the severed head by its hair. Humans can be easily killed. That was not true of werewolves. Their saliva held properties much like that of Fire's blood. In wolf form, they could come back from almost anything.

He knelt by the head of the second wolf wondering how long until he would awaken. Turning the head around in his hands, he tickled the wolf's face with the hair of his fallen companion. The wolf's eyes burst open, and he sprang to his feet, sending Ulric sprawling backward on the ground. The head he'd been carrying rolled just out of his reach.

The wolf clenched his inhumanely large fists and sucked a deep gust of air into his chest while Ulric laughed.

'The puppy thinks he's intimidating,' his mind cackled.

A long, eerie howl pierced the night.

Ulric got to his feet and turned away from the beast to retrieve the head.

The wolf leapt at him, attacking from behind. Ulric reached back, grabbing the wolf's face, lifting him off the ground, and propelled the wolf over his shoulder. Only the beast's body hit the ground, and the spray of his blood splattered across Ulric's face adding to his delight.

The wolf's face stared up at him upside down in his hands. "Boo!" Ulric snickered.

He set their heads on the ground, positioning them carefully so they could watch as he continued to rip their limbs from their bodies as easily as one might tear a piece of paper. He was almost done with his handiwork when a low growl interrupted him.

Ulric looked up to see a third wolf who had come, answering the call. This wolf towered over the previous two and him as well.

'The Alpha,' Ulric relished in the satisfaction this would bring.

He dropped the leg he had just ripped from one of the wolves' bodies and closed the gap to the Alpha by a few feet. He cracked his neck and waved the fingers of both hands, motioning the beast to make his move.

The wolf lunged, and Ulric went for his head. The swing from the wolf's lengthy arm landed on Ulric's side, cracking three ribs, and forcefully smashed him into a tree. He fell to the ground and raised up on all fours. His ears were ringing, and his eyes were unable to focus. The last time he suffered this much injury from another was his first day in the realm when he was barely more than human. As soon as he was on two feet, the wolf hit him with another blow that knocked Ulric through the air, landing on the first wolf's dismembered body.

Ulric laughed. It was a laugh that started low and carried on, growing shriller until it was near crippling.

*'Who does this wolf think he is? Who does he think I am? I can't be stopped.
I can't be killed.'*

He stumbled to his feet again and saw the wolf prepare to charge from
the corner of his eye. Ulric grabbed a bodiless leg laying at his feet. When the
wolf pounced, he jumped using the wolf's hip as a stepping stone. He shoved
the shoed foot into the wolf's mouth with enough force to lodge it tightly in
the throat. His feet climbed the wolf's chest to his shoulders and jumped to
the ground behind the beast. He grabbed the leg, pulling it down as he fell
with enough force to rip the wolf's head off backwards. The lower jaw was
still attached to the body.

"Whoo!" Ulric screamed into the night, watching blood shoot out of
the Alpha's head like a fountain. "That was exhilarating," he said, picking up
turning the Alpha's head around to face him. "We should do this more often.
Does Tuesday work for you?"

Using the wolves' hair, he tied the severed heads to his belt and made his
way through the forest to his horse, talking to his new friends the whole way.
He threw the heads into a bag and secured it to his mare. The faces would
be human again by morning, and he knew how to properly dispose of them
to ensure they didn't make a comeback. He readied his horse and rode off to
gather Collin from Versailles.

Ulric hadn't ridden very far when he heard someone talking. Thinking
it was other wolves looking for the missing members of their pack, he
dismounted and carefully stole through the trees. The sun was only breaking
over the horizon, and the light barely flitted through the tree tops. He could
see well enough to find the man digging a hole while talking to himself.

He inched closer. It wasn't a hole. It was a shallow grave.

"I know you're scared, son, and you should be. You should have
renounced the devil when he came to you with his lies of magic," the grave
digger said.

The man's face was turned away from him. He scanned the area for who
he may be speaking to. The low light made him miss the dark as night shade
of Thomas' skin twice before Ulric noticed the whites of his eyes.

This man knew Thomas was a witch and was preparing to bury him alive.
*'This is the fault of that wretched piece of work, Sylvia. She apprised the king a
witch's powers could only be subdued if they were placed underground.'*

Ulric walked up to the man who didn't take notice of him until it was too late. He grabbed the shovel from the man's hands and drove the cutting edge of the blade into the man's throat clear through the back of his head. It wasn't until he picked up his fourth severed head that he realized the man he just killed was John Ward.

He chuckled and asked Thomas, "Do you suppose Miss Gillian will be irate over this?"

He freed Thomas and led him back to the horse. The bag of trophies was filled and was hard to close after his fourth prize. Thomas eyed the bag, wondering what else was in there besides the head of his grandmother's husband, but he was too afraid of the answer to pose the question. Ulric allowed Thomas to ride, figuring he would need a rest after his ordeal.

As they slowly trudged along the banks of the Seine, Ulric removed the bag from the horse. He took one last look inside, savoring the memory, before tying it off.

"What is that?" Thomas finally raised the nerve to ask.

Ulric shrugged. "Trash," he said, tossing the bag into the river.

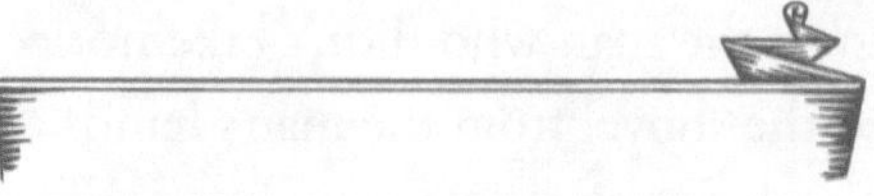

Chapter Fourteen
Secret Meeting

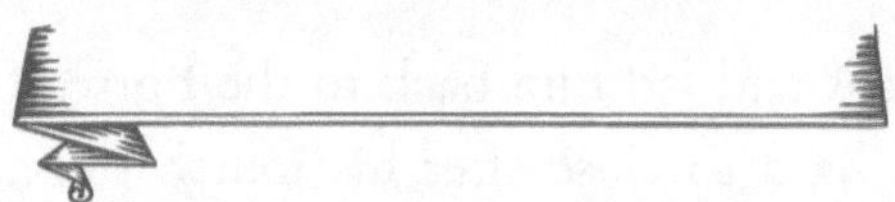

"What is going on?" Ulric asked.

Collin squared his shoulders in a failed attempt to present himself as anything more intimidating than Ulric's grandson. "Have a seat," he said, motioning to one of the empty chairs near him.

Ulric looked at the Council table which normally consisted of twelve chairs lined up at one side facing the meeting room. The chairs were now split six and six on either side of the table with several of them empty from the members absent. The table was properly laid out with goblets and decanters. It appeared as though they decided to convene a hushed meeting of the Council which was a violation of the second clan law.

All Council meetings were to be public. Nothing was to be done behind closed doors. All members of his blood line were to be allowed to attend if they chose. The only Fire Elementals forbidden from attending were the created ones. There weren't near as many of them as there used to be as very few had been allowed to be created since King Louis XIV's reign. They were often little better than mindless zombies unless properly and painstakingly trained, and they had no business in how the clan was overseen.

"I will not ask you again," Ulric said sternly. "What is the meaning of this?"

"Recent events have proved we are all in peril. I would hope you would be understanding of that. I know this is not tradition, but," Collin began to explain.

"Not tradition!" Ulric bellowed, slamming his fist onto the table hard enough to split it in half, spilling everything onto the floor and sending most of the present Council members scrambling away. "This is a direct violation of the Council Laws, and I am sure you are all aware the punishment for breaking our laws is death!"

"Well, Ulric," Isolde spat his name as if she was expelling poison from her mouth. She had barely flinched when the table crashed to her feet and continued to hold her ground. "We didn't feel we had enough time to give the proper notice to convene a law abiding meeting because it is imperative this business be conducted immediately. Also, we," she stressed, showing he was excluded from what she was about to say next, "actually concern ourselves with how many more of our clan would be dead before the meeting adjourned. Besides," she sat back, folding her arms across her chest and staring Ulric in the eye, "this might not be something you want to go any further than the Council's ears."

Ulric's curiosity was piqued. "Fine," he said with a smirk. He took the empty chair across from her and sat down, returning her spiteful gaze. There was nothing between them but the ruins of broken wood and a soiled table cloth. "I'll play your game. I will withhold punishment for your insolent violation until I've heard what you have to say. We'll begin the meeting when all the Council members have arrived."

Collin stepped forward and opened his mouth, but Ulric raised a hand to stop him. "I do not mean the team that went missing during the investigations," Ulric said.

"Yes, but-," Collin tried to speak.

"I already know you haven't invited Luke. I know this because he is still set on a task for me. If he had been called to this meeting, he would've mentioned it."

"And what task is that?" asked Richard.

Without taking his eyes off Isolde, he said, "That is none of your concern."

Greta joined the few who had retaken their seats. "You sit there preaching of laws and violations, but you are one to talk," she said disgustedly. "All Council members are to be nominated and voted on by the members of the meeting. That is the first law of the Council. You violated your own rule. You are not to make nominations, and you saw to it that no one else was given the opportunity."

"Yes," Ulric tore his eyes away from Isolde. "But what are you going to do about it? Kill me?" he chuckled. "I'd like to see you try."

The room remained silent. The eight members challenging Ulric exchanged glances, giving knowing signs they believed this would be his reaction.

"I'm the one you can do nothing about. I'm the wild card, the loose cannon, and it terrifies you," he bragged about his position, taunting them they were powerless against him.

"It might help," Collin said, positioning a chair to sit facing Ulric on his left, "if you told us why you accomplished putting Luke on the Council at the expense of the laws."

"I had recently learned of two suspicious Fire deaths that appeared to be murders. I needed someone I trust on the Council."

"You don't trust us!" Collin shouted.

"Was I wrong?" Ulric asked, waving his hands across the people in the room. "This! This right here proves I was correct to think I could not."

"Oh, enough," Isolde said frustrated. "We did not invite Luke because we do not trust him. We do not trust him because of the underhanded way you set about getting him on the Council." Isolde took a deep breath, "We don't trust him because we don't trust you."

"That's fair," Ulric said. He knew why they excluded Luke and was shocked for any of them to admit it. "It's honest. Begin your meeting. Convince me why it was necessary to violate the oath you took when you joined the Council. Convince me why you should all not be put to death."

Collin turned to Giles, "Tell Ulric about your sister."

Giles took a moment to ready himself. "We were on the phone. It was a normal conversation. There was nothing to make me feel anything was out of the ordinary going on while we spoke. We were discussing a visit we had been planning. She was going to stay with me in the spring, and," he took a breath. "She told me she had to go. 'They're telling me it's time,' she said."

"They?" Ulric asked.

He shook his head. "I don't know. She never said. I didn't know anyone else was there. I asked time for what? Her response was so normal. Her voice was unchanged from the rest of the call. 'It's time for me to die,' she said," his voice cracked. He took several slow, deliberate breaths to regain his composure. "Then she said, 'They've already lit the fire.' The line went dead after that."

"I tried calling back repeatedly, but I never got an answer. Word had already reached us about the Council team who had gone missing. I told Collin and Richard that I needed to leave now. I had to go to Greece. They came with me. When we landed in Athens, I had a voice mail from the local authorities."

Giles' eyes clouded over in grief. "It was as I feared when I returned the call," he said softly. "There had been a house fire, and my sister perished in it."

"Another death," Ulric sadly said. "This makes nine confirmed dead with countless more missing."

The clan wasn't very large. At this rate, they'd be exterminated by the next Return. They needed to find the person responsible and end them before the vampires were eradicated.

"I'm sorry to hear about your sister," Ulric offered his condolences.

"But are you really?" Giles asked.

Ulric tilted his head side to side, cracking his neck. "Yes, I am. It pains me you would think otherwise."

"There are thirteen confirmed dead," Collin corrected him. "I was planning on updating you before the meeting, but..." his voice trailed off, remembering how Ulric reacted when he arrived. "Over two hundred are unaccounted for currently, but we believe most of the new missing vampires have gone into hiding to save themselves."

"You have some of our members searching for a mystery woman. A woman we know nothing about. We do not know her name or Elemental status if she has one. The only lead we have is a photograph taken in a crowd on the street right outside these doors," Richard said.

Isolde darted her eyes away. She had not yet informed the Council of what she had discovered. It would be easy to determine which Air Elemental had been doing so much traveling, and she was working on tracking them down, one by one. She didn't want to update the Council until her and Greta had a name. The news of Giles' sister Eda meant that Air wasn't working alone.

"The rest of us, save for your precious Luke," Richard continued, "have been sent to investigate the missing clan members. Three of us are now missing as well! Vampires sent to a specific location given by you, and we now fear their fate."

Giles' head had been drooped to his chest since speaking about his sister. He didn't lift it when he said, "And we also know they are somehow being controlled into willingly going to their death."

"Thanks for the recap," Ulric said dryly. Their charade was growing tiresome. He knew the accusation that was coming. "You have not told me anything I did not already know."

"After I investigated Olav's death, I had questions," Collin said.

"Questions?" Ulric asked surprised. "I believe the word you're looking for is suspicions."

Collin nodded slightly. "With the news of Giles' sister, my suspicions have deepened. I am sure you believe I shared them with the Council and swayed their minds, but I didn't have to. After learning of the manner Eda perished, we all found ourselves on the same page."

"There is only one thing that would cause a vampire to willingly be murdered," Greta added.

"In that, you are wrong," Ulric said, thinking about the clues at his house that caused his concern for Jackson. "There is more than one thing. If I was capable of dying and I had a child, a wife, someone who was the center of my existence, I would easily trade my life to keep them safe."

"We have considered that possibility," Richard told him.

Ulric looked at the faces around the room. Some were still standing too fearful to come close to him. "You don't believe that is what's happening. You believe it is my blood that is controlling our kin, and if it is my blood, it must be myself or someone I trust who is committing these murders. The exclusion of Luke tells me you suspect him of being a part of it."

He stood and paced the floor, "I've told you Luke is the only person I trust which I'm sure confirmed all of your suspicions." He walked back to his chair and rested his hands on the back of it. "I would tell you it's not me. I'm not behind it, and aside from the mystery woman, I have no leads as to who it might be, but you won't believe me."

"We have suspicions," Collin confirmed, "but not all of us are convinced you are guilty."

"There are doubts as to your motive," Giles added. "There is no reason for you to want to eliminate your kind, whether it's all of us or just particular members of the clan."

Isolde looked up at Ulric. It was clear by the look on her face she believed he was behind it. She believed he was working with Air even if she didn't know his motive. "But we don't know how anyone could have the use of your blood without your knowledge."

"We called you here to discuss this civilly with an open mind, but" Collin said, pointing to the broken table, "you did not give us the chance."

Ulric closed his eyes and ran his hand through his hair. He couldn't tell them the whole truth, not where Camilla was concerned, but they deserved to know the rest. "It is possible for someone to have my blood without my knowledge, or rather without my permission."

Everyone's eyes were on him, intently listening to what he had to say.

"Many years ago, I was friends with a wolf who was facing difficulties growing her pack. You'd be hard pressed to find a bred wolf who wasn't an unplanned conception. No one wants to curse a child in this manner. When you find a human willing, some wayward soul so lost they would choose this dastardly existence, it's hard for a wolf to control their bite to turn them."

Ulric thought back to the night Camilla asked him if he'd be willing to experiment. It seemed like lifetimes had passed since then, but it wasn't long before Jackson came along. They had been so happy then, a perfect pair.

"After a night of one too many drinks, we decided to perform an experiment. I allowed her a vial of my blood to see if it would control a wolf."

"But it couldn't." Greta said more to herself than Ulric.

It took several minutes for him to answer. This revelation would infuriate the Council. "It worked, but only when the blood was ingested in human form."

"What?" Isolde asked in disbelief.

"This can't be," Collin said.

Richard shook his head as though he thought Ulric were lying. "Our powers hold no affect over other Elements."

"You're right," Ulric told him. "Your powers do not. We tested it with Luke's blood, but it didn't work. When Water drinks my blood, they can be controlled even after transformation as long as my blood is in their system. Their metabolism is extremely high, so the window is small."

He waited, but no one said anything. They were still too shocked to speak.

"With my help, she was able to pad out her numbers," Ulric added.

"Why have you never mentioned this?" Collin's voice was nearly a shout.

"Why do you think?" Ulric retorted. "If you knew my blood could control the other Elements..." he stopped when he realized what he let slip.

The Council members' eyes widened, and they murmured amongst themselves.

He nodded, "Yes, Air and Earth as well because their form is human. If this got out, then every dispute, no matter how small, that someone had with another faction, my blood would be requested to solve it."

"Still don't you think it's worth noting we have an upper hand?" Isolde asked.

"No."

"And why not?" she scoffed. Her hatred of him was increasing by the second.

"Because I don't believe we do," he told her. "If we are allowed this, then the other three Elements obviously have some trump card they can play on us as well." He didn't fill them in that he already knew what they were capable of doing.

"How long ago was this?" Greta asked.

Ulric waved her off. "No matter. I don't think it stems from that. Several years ago, I woke up one morning with no memory of the night before and missing the shirt I had been wearing. I had reason to believe someone drugged me, and that night when I went to bed, I found a single rust colored drop on the sheet. It was dried blood."

"Why didn't you tell us this before?" Collin asked.

Giles didn't wait for Ulric to answer. "What makes you believe you were drugged?"

"Six years ago?" Isolde wasn't convinced. "Would the blood still be good?"

"Maybe not for a transfusion," Richard thought out loud.

Collin added, "If it had been stored well, it may still be potent enough to control us."

"Why wait so long?" Isolde asked. "If someone had a nefarious plan to use Fire's blood against his own kind, why did it take them six years to use it?"

The Council members began arguing amongst themselves. They were angry and not all of them thought he was being truthful.

"It happened again," Ulric said above the din.

A hush fell over the Council members.

"It was a very loose suspicion based on minimal circumstantial evidence until it happened a second time," he continued.

"When was this?" Collin asked.

Ulric looked down and pulled his chair away from the mess. He sat and rested his head in his hands. "Two days before Luke's grandfather died," he spoke into his palms.

"Why didn't you tell us?" Giles' eyes watered, wondering if his sister's life could have been spared.

"I didn't know who was behind it or why they wanted my blood. My friend and I had a falling out. I thought maybe she needed it for her pack again, but couldn't swallow her pride to ask. It could've been a created with an addiction. To be honest, I was more concerned with how anyone had figured out who I really was then why it had happened. The list of why's is endless, but using my blood against my own people didn't make the list."

"When did you realize your blood was being used to attack us?" Isolde asked, unwavering in her belief of his guilt and wanting others to see it for themselves.

"It was after Collin checked into Olav's death. That is when I first suspected it."

"And you chose not to tell us?" Richard asked, doubting Ulric's explanation.

Ulric stood up again. "You don't think I know how preposterous this sounds? Someone broke into my house. MY house! Someone knows who I am, where I live, and they were able to drug me and draw my blood. TWICE!" He rubbed his palms over his face. "I didn't tell you because I thought it too fantastic to believe, and you would suspect me of having a part in it. As each new death was discovered, I knew you'd eventually point your finger at me. I had hoped to find the person responsible before that happened."

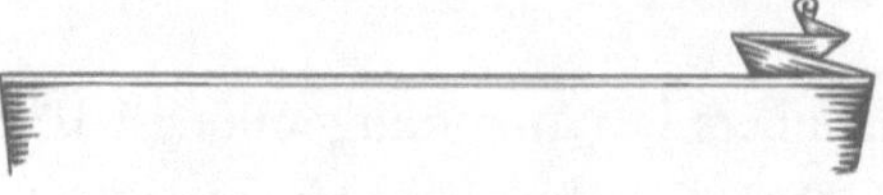

Chapter Fifteen
Saving Everleigh

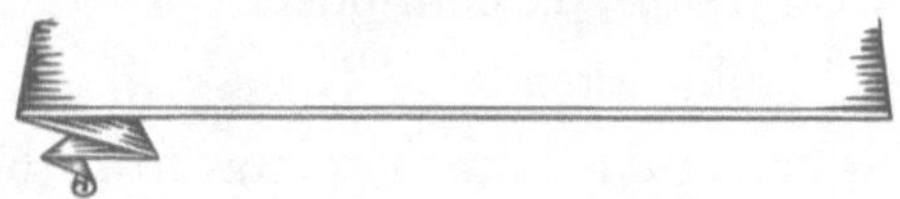

He didn't miss.

Centuries of practice had offered him the opportunity to become an excellent shot. He often reminisced about the estate days of the nineteenth century when wealthy land owners would invite you to a hunt, provide you an immaculate room for your stay, and all meals were fit for a king. No one provides hospitality like that any longer. It was one of the few changes in society he missed.

When he bought the tranquilizer gun around the time Jackson started showing signs of his Water genetics, he knew he could use it. He knew he had the capacity to render the dose accurately and timely. It was always a matter of if he would be able to when the time came.

Anyone who saw him would fear him mostly for the unknown about him: a wild animal, a beast, a demented creature from an old fairytale. They wouldn't hesitate to fill him with bullet holes unaware of how little good it would do for anything except angering him more. But Jackson was his son. Even the thought of shooting him with a tranquilizer made him wonder if he could aim the gun at his son accurately.

When the time came, he didn't see his son. He only saw a creature who was half man and half beast, but becoming more animal by the second. This beast was a threat to the life they had built in this small town, and like all threats, it needed to be handled.

As soon as he pulled in the drive, he saw his son, half changed, clawing into the shed. There was not a moment's hesitation. He grabbed the gun from his bag he always carried with him and fired one shot. Jackson's eyes were glowing and not the soft, bright blue he inherited from his mother when he spun around surprised. Those eyes held one burning question. Why?

Judd helped his son to the ground, watching the medication in the darts take effect. Jackson's growls became lower and shorter until they were a mere whimper. He opened the door to the garage to pull his son inside in the hopes of avoiding a neighbor witnessing him carrying Jackson's limp body to the house. The sight waiting for him caught his breath and stopped his heart.

Everleigh lay on the floor of the garage in a heap. Judd's mind went blank. He couldn't think of what to do or even the young girl's name. The only coherent thought he had was, *'Please not Anya's granddaughter.'*

She moaned, and he closed his eyes in relief that she wasn't dead. Not yet anyway.

There were sirens in the distance. Sirens that were drawing closer. He feared they hadn't gone unwitnessed after all.

Squatting down near Jackson's head, he hooked an arm around each of his son's shoulders and pulled him to the old Firebird hidden beneath a drop cloth. He opened one door and lifted his son onto the seat, both trying to be careful and trying to beat the nearing sirens at the same time. Once he closed the car door and covered it with the drop cloth again, he went to Everleigh's side just as the doors of the squad cars began opening and shutting, and footsteps approached the shed. Judd barely managed to check her body for bite marks before the cops got to them.

"FPD!" an officer shouted as he rounded the open doorway.

The officer saw Judd bent over Everleigh's body, cradling her bleeding head in his lap.

"One of the neighbors heard screaming," he explained, holstering his gun.

"She fell." Judd told him, pointing to the loft. It was as good an explanation as any. "I need help."

The two patrolmen assessed her quickly and radioed for an ambulance. Fairview EMT's were on a call, so help would have to arrive from the next town.

"No, I'll drive her. It'll be faster," Judd insisted.

One cop carried Everleigh to the pickup truck while the other instructed Judd to follow him.

Once on the highway, a smirk slowly drove the corners of his mouth upward. *'Oh, what a story this would be to tell,'* he thought. *'My son attacked Anya's daughter. I tranqued him. But now I'm getting a police escort to the hospital with no questions to answer about the circumstances.'* There was just no one he could share the story with because Anya must never know.

'Of course, she'll know,' his smirk quickly faded. *'She always knows everything.'*

The thought of Jackson laying in the garage unconscious worried him. The tranquillizer he used would knock him out most of the evening. There'd be no way he could defend himself if anything happened. By anything, he meant Camilla, but accidents happen too. He tortured his mind with thoughts of fires and cars that drove off the road through houses just to convince himself his only paranoia wasn't Jackson's mom.

He called Luke. "Hey, you wouldn't happen to be around by chance?"

"You always have perfect timing. I'm bored from hiding out while Meredith tries to stock up on a few supplies without Eloise finding out."

Judd almost choked on his laughter. "Good luck to her with that."

"Yep," Luke said. "It's going to be a long night for me because you know I'll be waiting till the screaming and lecturing stops."

"I might have something for you to do to pass the time. Would you mind hanging out at the house for a few hours?"

"Anything is better than sitting in this car. What's going on?"

There was no time to explain, and he didn't want Eloise finding out about Everleigh for as long as possible. Now he knew she'd be distracted which was an unbelievably stroke of good fortune. "I'll fill you in later, but Luke is in the garage."

"Yeah."

"In the car."

"Oh? He finally got that old Firebird running?"

"Unconscious. I used enough xylazine to stop a bear."

There was a long pause on the other end of the line. "I see. I'll head over there and see what I can tinker with in case he wakes up before you get home."

Luke had long been the closest he'd ever had to a friend, and Judd had never been more thankful to have him to count on than right now. "Thank you," Judd said, ending the call.

At the hospital, he pulled fake documents from his bag showing Everleigh was his daughter. Anya knew he had them. She knew they were drawn up for the specific purpose of if Jackson couldn't control his anger and true nature, but he tried to convince there could be other situations where the forged papers could be useful. There hadn't been an argument about it from her except for a warning that if Judd ever had to use them for that reason, it would be the last thing Jackson ever did.

He couldn't worry about that now; all of his thoughts were with Everleigh. Judd never wanted anything more than for Anya's granddaughter to make it through the day with minor wounds.

They wouldn't let him go back with her at first. The next twenty-five minutes were the most agonizing of his life. The gash on her head concerned him. There could be more severe damage done from a head wound like that. The police arrived too fast for him to heal her. Plus, he wouldn't be able to explain the blood on her face and shirt to the police without a wound.

'What if I missed a bite mark?' he worried, knowing the doctors would demand an explanation he wasn't prepared to give.

'Oh, God. What if I missed a bite mark?' he thought about Anya. There would be no forgiveness if Everleigh was turned into a wolf. While Judd may not be capable of death, it was an absolute certainty Anya could devise ways to torture him the rest of his years in this body, making him beg for death to release him.

They finally allowed him back in the exam room. Everleigh was still unconscious. She looked so frail lying on the gurney that he wondered for the first time since moving to Fairview that maybe it had been a mistake. Fire was essentially immortal, and their wounds healed almost immediately. It was the same for Air. Water heals faster in wolf form. Any injuries sustained when they're turned will heal almost as quickly as Fire. In human form they're more susceptible, but they still heal significantly faster than non-supernatural humans. Witches, however, their bodies are no different than humans.

The doctor walked in the room and introduced himself, "I'm Dr. Morris," he said, extending a hand to Judd. "You're her father?" he raised an eyebrow.

"Yes, I adopted her when she was a toddler," Judd replied, feeling a twinge of guilt aware he had let her down if that was his true title.

"I've given her an initial examination," he began.

The nurse who retrieved Judd from the waiting room walked in and began rummaging through the drawers and cabinets. As she looked, she placed items on the tray near the gurney.

"The gash on her head isn't as bad as it looks. We're getting ready to stitch it up then I'll have her taken down to X-Ray for her ankle. It looks pretty swollen. I also want to get a scan of her head since she hasn't woken up yet."

Judd listened to the doctor speak without taking his eyes off the tray table. It would be so much easier and less painful if he could treat her himself instead of these mad scientists in white using tools not much better than medieval torture devices.

"What happened?" the doctor asked, sitting on the stool next to Everleigh.

"She fell from the loft in the shed. I think that's what happened anyway. She went into the garage to look for something. I heard her scream," he concocted the lie based on what the cops told him the neighbors had heard. "That's when I went out, and I found her on the ground."

The doctor nodded, holding a syringe in his hand. "She's lucky. It could have been much worse." Dr. Morris wheeled closer to the side of the gurney near Everleigh's head. "This is a local anesthesia I'm giving her," he explained, making several small injections near her wound. "She may wake up during this, so I'm going to have my nurse ready to hold her arms if she does. We wouldn't want her hitting my hands while I'm suturing."

He paused and looked at Judd.

"Oh," Judd cleared his throat. "Yes. Okay," he stumbled, realizing the doctor was wanting some response. Whether it was acknowledgement or verbal permission the doctor was looking for he couldn't be sure.

Dr. Morris picked up the needle holders which looked like a large pair of scissors. He placed the first suture in position and began his work. Judd looked on fascinated. It was an odd business, sewing human flesh. He wondered who the first person was to look at mended clothes and think it'd work for cuts as well.

The doctor finished up and announced to Judd, "Eight stitches. Not bad at all."

He stood up and made a few notes in the chart before telling the nurse,

"Notify X-Ray that we're ready."

"Yes, doctor."

"One of our radiology techs will be up to take her down shortly. You're welcome to wait in the room while she's gone. I'll be back in with the results later," the doctor said before leaving. The nurse followed him out.

A few minutes later, a red headed blonde woman with her hair in a ponytail appeared, pushing a wheelchair into the room. She looked at Everleigh. "Is she asleep?"

"She hit her head when she fell," Judd answered. "She's still out."

The radiology technician nodded. "I'm not going to move her from the bed then."

The tech pushed the wheelchair out into the hall. She came back and released the brakes on the bed then pushed it with Everleigh on it out of the room.

Judd had plenty of time in the room by himself to consider the weight of everything that happened. *'It might be right to move on. Fairview had served its purpose.'*

He had moved there to keep Jackson safe while he was growing up, but he was a young man now. It was time. He tried to keep a low profile in town always making the extra drive to go unnoticed, but the neighbors were probably already gossiping about the man who never appeared to age. The truth was he never stayed in the same place as long as this. He took the risk for his son's sake to keep his son out of harm's way while giving him a normal childhood.

But he had to wonder. Could he keep Fairview safe from his son?

It was time to face the fact they needed to move on. The timing couldn't be worse. His people were dying. Some had vanished without a trace, and he had to accept the reality they were probably dead too.

Investigations into who or what was behind it had turned up nothing. He originally thought it was a fight between clans. From there, he believed someone might have been on a mission to overturn the Council. Now he feared it was worse than that. Much worse.

After Camilla's visit and the night he lost consciousness which is something else he'd never experienced before in his entire existence, he had security cameras installed. He didn't think anyone was ignorant enough to come at him directly, but they might try to use his son to get to him. If the fear of what he almost did to Everleigh wasn't enough to make Jackson understand why they had to leave, then the video footage would definitely do the trick.

The move would have to wait until the attacks were under control. If he was right, the attacks wouldn't end with Fire. If he was right, it would be better for them to stay and fight alongside Anya.

The red head from radiology appeared in the doorway and wheeled the bed back in the room. Everleigh still hadn't come to.

"Is it broke?" he asked.

"The doctor will read the images soon and let you know."

Judd pressed his lips together tightly to prevent an angry outburst, or worse, a frightening show of teeth. He could taste the blood from where his fangs bit through his lips. He darted his eyes downward and partially closed his eyelids, so the tech couldn't see the red glow in his eyes before she left.

The woman could have easily seen on the images she took if there was a fracture or worse, a serious head injury. It was infuriating that you had to have at least four extra years of school and a different set of initials behind your last name to say what the results showed. *No wonder medical care costs so much.*

A few minutes later, the nurse reappeared. "The doctor will be in shortly," she told him. She picked up Everleigh's wrist with one hand and eyed the watch on her other wrist, checking her pulse. Satisfied, she started clearing the remnants left on the tray.

Everleigh moaned and began to stir.

Judd started to bolt upright then gripped the arms of the chair he sat in to keep himself in place.

"Lie still," the nurse ordered Everleigh, trying to prevent her from moving. "You shouldn't try to sit up just yet.

"Is our patient awake?" the doctor asked from the doorway.

"She's coming to," the nurse answered.

The doctor approached the gurney and took his penlight out of his pocket. He shined the light in each of her eyes, checking for any sign of head injury. "You slept through the hard part. Eight stitches," he told her, pointing to the side of her head.

Everleigh winced as if the doctor jabbed the cut with his forefinger.

Judd's anxiety began to deepen. It was obvious Everleigh wasn't completely with it yet, and he worried what she might say. "You really had us scared," he told her, hoping his voice would bring her around enough to at least not mutter something profound.

She adjusted her eyes to the light before looking his way. The gaze she gave him unnerved him even more. It was like she was studying him, or tying to remember who he was. *Please let her remember who I am.*

"You're lucky," the doctor told her. He scribbled one last note in the chart before handing it to the nurse who hurried out of the room. "A fall like that could've ended much worse."

"Fall?" Everleigh sounded confused.

"Yes," the doctor looked at her with raised eyebrows. "I was told you fell from the loft in a garage."

"Garage," she repeated.

The knuckles on Judd's hands turned white and he feared he'd soon break the arm rests of the chair if he didn't relax. She needed to get it together quickly.

"Yeah, Mr. Montgomery. I'm sorry. I wanted to see that old train set of yours stashed up there."

Judd's entire body slowly relaxed and a small smile formed on his lips. *'Thata girl,'* he thought. *'You're getting it.'*

"Nothing to be sorry about, dear," Judd told her. "I'm just glad you're alright." He hoped no one would notice the formal way she talked to him instead of calling him dad.

The nurse returned with the discharge papers and went over the care instructions with Judd. The x-rays were clear, but he was given a list of symptoms to watch for in case she had a concussion. He nodded, but barely listened. They wouldn't be necessary. Everleigh's injuries would all miraculously heal shortly after they were allowed to leave. He kept watch on her from the corner of his eye, making sure she managed alright. They were almost in the clear. The last thing he needed was for her to mention Jackson.

"I'm surprised the ankle wasn't broke," Dr. Morris interrupted Judd's thoughts. "But a sprain can hurt worse than a break sometimes. Be sure to ice it and keep it elevated."

Judd promised to do as instructed. He could see the tears welling in Everleigh's eyes. Her memories were coming back. It wouldn't be much longer before she'd be an emotional mess. They had to get out of there fast.

The nurse left and returned with a wheelchair.

"I can manage alright."

"No. You will use this and wheel her out to your vehicle," the nurse said sternly.

Judd hesitated.

"Or I can wheel her out. It's up to you."

"Fine," Judd caved, wanting to be away from the staff as quickly as possible. "I'll use the chair."

The nurse left it by the door and locked it in place before leaving the room for good.

"I'm going to lift you now and put you in this chair," Judd told Everleigh.

She kept her eyes squeezed shut and didn't say anything.

"Did you hear me, Everleigh?" Judd asked.

Everleigh opened her eyes and looked at him. "No," she croaked.

"I said it's time. I'm going to lift you into the wheelchair. The nurse insisted I not carry you all the way out."

"Okay," she nodded. "Go ahead."

Judd took a deep breath before carefully lifting her. He didn't want to cause her any more pain than she'd already experience. He carried her to the wheelchair effortlessly like he was carrying a stack of pillows. Once she was seated, he removed the brakes on the chair and began pushing her down the hall away from the emergency department.

"You really did give me a scare," he whispered when he was confident they had the privacy to talk.

Everleigh didn't say anything. It made Judd wonder if she had heard him, but that didn't matter. There would be plenty of time for talking later.

They approached the automatic doors which opened. Judd stopped, putting the brakes back on the wheelchair. He contemplated wheeling her all the way out to the truck and bringing the chair back which is probably what the nurse would've preferred. There was no one close by to stop him, so he decided to do it the easy way. He walked around the chair and lifted her again. Everleigh lay draped over his arms as he walked to the truck.

"Where's Jackson?"

Judd knew this question was coming, and he was thankful she waited till they were safely out of earshot. It was probably coincidence. She was not alert enough yet to know it might not be wise to ask inside around other people. He decided to wait to answer her. There was something else that was priority, and it would probably leave her forgetting what happened to Jackson again anyway.

He walked to the side of the pickup truck. Judd held Everleigh with one arm and opened the door with his other hand then slid her onto the seat. "Sit tight. You'll feel better in a minute," he said gently.

Once she was completely inside and comfortable, he closed the door then joined her from the driver's side. "Ready?" he asked her.

Everleigh nodded and fastened her seatbelt.

Judd bit into his wrist and extended his arm in front of her face.

When she looked up, her eyes widened in surprise, or perhaps it was fright. Everleigh clamped her mouth shut tight. She squirmed away from him, trying to escape backward through the seat of the truck. He moved his arm closer as she tried to move away. Her tears started falling again. Judd was pained from what he was putting her through, but it must be done.

"Look," he told her in a voice that came out more cross than he intended. "The only reason we came here instead of doing this from the start is because the neighbors heard you scream and called the police. I had barely hid Jackson's body before they showed up. There you still were on the floor of the garage, unconscious. Hell! They gave me an escort to the hospital!"

The wound was healing. There wasn't much time after he tore his flesh for her to be able to drink. He brought his arm back to him because he'd have to try again.

"I don't want to, but thank you for offering," she told him politely.

"For offering?" he cried out. He put both hands on the steering wheel. Yes, she was young, but she lived her entire life in Anya's household except for college. It amazed him she could think she had a choice in this. After several deep breaths in and out, his mind calmed enough to talk to her again. "I know, Everleigh. I know why you don't want to drink." He turned and looked at her as softly as he could. "But I am not sending you home in your condition. I am not facing the wrath of your grandmother."

He bit into his wrist again, and held it out to her to drink. "Please." Everleigh didn't move.

"Please don't make me do this the hard way," he warned her.

Everleigh slowly and fearfully leaned her head forward.

"That's it. You only need a few drops. It doesn't have to be much."

Her lips parted, and he brought his wrist to her mouth. She started to gag in seconds.

Judd pulled his arm back. "That's enough. You'll be healed before we get home."

He pulled out of the parking space and steered out of the hospital parking lot toward the main road. While he drove, he kept a close eye on Everleigh who stared intently at the sideview mirror before passing back into unconsciousness.

Once at his house, he carried her inside to the couch. She was in and out, and when she was awake, she was talking gibberish. It'd be awhile before she was coherent. If it was anyone else, it'd take a day or longer for his blood to leave their system, but she was an Earth. Her body would naturally fight Fire.

Luke walked into the room and saw Everleigh lying there. "Oh, man. You're lucky you're immortal. I mean truly immortal, or you'd be a dead man walking."

"Don't I know it," Judd said and headed toward the kitchen to give Everleigh some quiet to rest.

"Meredith can be scary in her own right, but Eloise is one witch I don't want to mess with," Luke said, following him.

Judd looked at him pleadingly, "Just don't say anything until I can figure something out."

"What was the worry with Jackson?" Luke asked.

The time for the discussion about Camilla was fast approaching, but he wasn't ready to delve into that chapter of his past yet. "I was worried about him waking up while I was gone and freaking out about what happened. I didn't want him to get so worked up he transformed again."

Luke made his trademark clicking noises with his teeth, illustrating he had something on his mind he was thinking over. "The thing I don't understand is it's not even a full moon. Is it the vampire blood in him?"

"Yeah, my blood changes things for him," Judd agreed. It wasn't a total lie. It did affect Jackson's wolf nature. Someday Luke would know the whole truth.

JUDD WENT UPSTAIRS after leaving Everleigh and Jackson to discuss things farther in the kitchen. It was time to face the music and call Eloise.

"I knew the moment you darkened my doorstep with that little towheaded boy in your arms there would be trouble!" she screamed into the phone when she answered.

"I'm doing well, Eloise. Thank you for asking."

"Do not try to play this off! Your son almost killed her!"

Judd sat on his bed and closed his eyes. "But he didn't. And he wouldn't. He can't kill her."

"Don't try to give me any of this nonsense about how the two of them being close will shield his inner anger from her. I think tonight proves that's a crock."

"No," he said exhaling sharply. That was what he used to think when they were growing up. Those two kids were thick as thieves, and he fully believed Jackson would recognize her even as a wolf, leaving her be. Tonight proved that theory wrong. "They're connected, Everleigh and Jackson. You know that as well as I do. Nothing will happen to either of them right now."

"What are you on about now?" Eloise asked, pretending she wasn't following.

It was Judd's turn to be indignant. "Don't bother trying to fool me, Eloise. You're the one who saw the prophecy in that stone of yours."

"What?" Eloise's surprise was genuine. "How do you know?"

JUDD HEARD HIS SON'S footsteps on the stairs. *The smell of bacon frying always wakes that boy up,'* he chuckled softly.

"How you feeling today?" he asked.

"Hungover," Jackson said, getting a glass of water.

Judd began fixing a plate for him, and said, "I can imagine. Between the transformation and the tranqs, I'm sure it took a lot out of you."

Jackson sat at the table, and Judd put the plate in front of him.

"I'm not hungry," Jackson said, pushing it away.

Judd rubbed his temples, "You have to eat."

"All I can think about is what I almost did to Everleigh, and it makes me sick. Physically sick."

"I'm glad to see the reality of the situation isn't lost on you," Judd said, sitting down. "Maybe you can see how serious this is now because you've been thinking very selfishly."

"Selfish? Why? Because I don't like the meds that dull me out."

Judd nodded, "Partly. You've been caring more about that then whether or not you might kill your best friend."

"That's not fair," Jackson said.

"It is fair!" Judd yelled, clenching his fists. "Fair and accurate."

Jackson hung his head.

He didn't mean to lose his temper with his son, but years of setting up a medical cocktail that worked perfectly were lost down the drain the moment Jackson put his social life above the concern of those around him. "It worries me that you'll slip right back to not taking the medication if you don't start putting the greater good first."

"I'm going to take it, dad. I wouldn't risk hurting Everleigh again."

"This is bigger than her," Judd explained. "Bigger than both of you. We'll need you both for what's coming. We're going to need her Grandma Eloise on our side as well. If she believes for one moment you are a continued threat to her daughter, it will be the end of her cooperation with us."

"Jackson," he said, pushing the plate back in front of his son, "you're going to play a key role in this too which means right now you need to learn how to control your inner wolf. You need to learn how to keep it at bay at all times no matter what you're dealing with, but most importantly, you need to be healthy enough to let him out when you need him. So eat," he ordered.

"What key role?" Jackson asked.

He remembered what had been discussed last night about keeping things from his son, but his role in the events ahead was known only to a few, and Judd wasn't even supposed to be one of them. "To begin with, I believe the wolves are turning against us. I don't know why, but I believe I know how." Judd told him what he felt he could.

"Why is Water suddenly and enemy to Fire?" Jackson asked.

Judd laughed madly until his eyes watered at how absurd the question would sound to anyone else. "I don't mean against us, the vampires. I mean against us, all the Elementals, including any of their own who try to stand in their way."

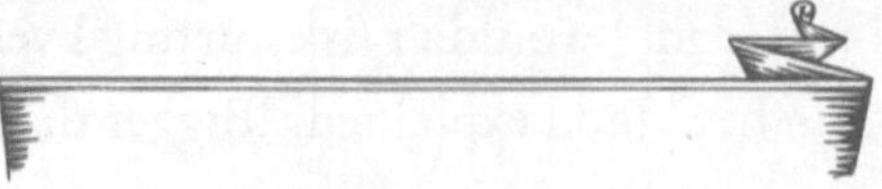

Chapter Sixteen
Council Rules

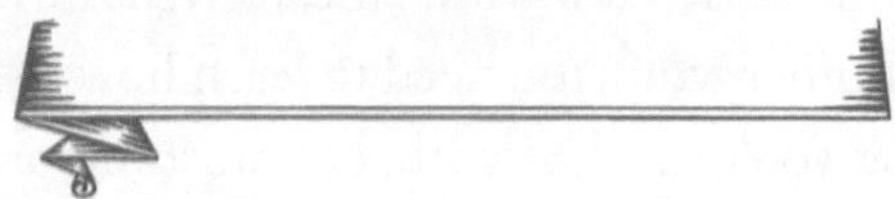

"Ulric!" Roanin greeted. "Wouldn't expect you to be late to your own party," he teased.

Fire sauntered into the room, letting the remark bounce off his chest. He had been here for quite a while. In fact, he watched as every one of them entered the castle he used to call home. It, too, would soon be abandoned along with all the rest of his estates.

The slaughtering the Elementals had occurred for weeks ended months ago. Unfortunately, Ulric knew the only way to rebuild would be to start anew. He had been hearing much about a new world that had been discovered far across the water. Except for its few natural inhabitants, the land was still virtually untouched by European settlements. He would soon leave for this place to charter a new journey.

Only two knew of his desire to do so. The closest and most trusted confidants in his family would be embarking on this adventure at his side. As for the rest of this lot, they might figure it out for themselves one day.

Before he could leave, there was one last matter to address. His people had run rampant for far too long. Ulric's disdain for humankind began the first day he inhabited this body, and it had grown ever since. It was because of this he allowed his people, his family the freedom to do as they wished. That would all end tonight.

While it was not their carelessness that brought the wrath of King Louis XIV upon them, it was their own doing that made them so easy to find. The toys they created in humans were weak. They turned vampires on a whim, for fun, as a way to cure boredom. Soon after turning, most of these loathsome creatures were brushed aside and left to their own devices.

Many of them didn't last long. Created vampires were easier to kill. The ways to dispatch them were endless. They did acquire a lot of Fire's power, but not to the same strength as natural vampires. They had a keen sense of hearing and smell. They were far faster than humans, but still slow by comparison to his family. The means to heal at an advanced rate was also passed on to them. Worst of all, they could not seem to keep any of this to themselves and were always giving away who they were, putting the naturals at risk in the process.

There were many in this room that stood as guilty, but Ulric knew that ultimately, it was the created vampires that stirred a terror in humans, far and wide. It was this terror that fueled them when the king issued the proclamation that he wanted all supernatural creatures outed and disposed. The created vampires were weak. They gave in to torture, stupidly believing their life would be spared for telling what they knew.

After giving any and all information they had to aide in the identification of others, they would be beheaded. The head and the body would both be burned at separate locations. It was the only manner with which a natural vampire could be killed. The separating of the two offered the assurance they would not reattach which was both inevitable if allowed, and a hilarity to watch unknowing humans witness it for the first time. Those who were on the hunt had not been aware these minions could be killed by much less means. Either that, or they were to take no chances with who may or may not be of natural blood.

Because of this, most of the family Ulric had left were sitting in this very room. There were less than two hundred blood Fire left to be exact. After tonight's meeting, Ulric was cognizant the number would decrease. It hurt him knowing what he had to do. It would be an unbearable pain that he would be forced to carry, but if their survival meant the sacrifice of a few, it would be worth it.

Once he announced his plans for this meeting, he would make it clear they would all have a choice. They could leave. He could not coerce them to agree to a set of rules and orders, to abide for the rest of the time they thrived on this earth. It's not anything that could be demanded.

Many of those in this room longed for order as well. He could read it in their thoughts. He could smell it in the very air they exhaled. Others, however, were too wild. They were too accustomed to living the way of life they chose. At any point this evening, those who took issue with the new structure being implemented within Fire would be aware they are welcome to walk out the door.

What they would not be savvy to is that on the other side of the door Marcus awaited them. How could they know or even suspect? Even with their fierce senses, none of them would be able to detect Marcus' presence. After all, he, too, was an Element such as Ulric.

Marcus had only agreed to assist because he lost two of his own in the spring when the hunt for the supernatural tore throughout Europe. Two. It's a remarkably low number. It pales in comparison to the tens of thousands lost by Ulric, both blood and created alike. But to Air, two was too large a percent. Their numbers had never been immense with limitations on their ability to produce offspring and lacking the ability to generate any of their kind from humans. In their entire existence, they had only ever lost one until that witch turned the eye of the kingdom onto all of them.

He was waiting for any who dared to walk through the doors, but he refused to murder. The moment anyone emerged they would be decapitated. Their heads would be withheld separately preventing reattachment to the body until Ulric was free to finish the work.

Any fires tonight would be lit by Ulric himself. He would be the one bearing the torch that extinguished the spark of life remaining in their form. He would be the last one these family members saw before their death.

Ulric stood to the side, watching his people mingle about the five rows of tables set up in the center of the banquet hall. Many of them were seated. Some of them were bored. Quite a few were ready to leave. The rest of them were lost in conversation. They were catching up with each other, commiserating over loved ones lost, and yes, even plotting their revenge.

'Imbeciles,' he thought. It was not a show of honor to kill off your entire breed to avenge the fallen. They were far too vastly outnumbered.

Rumors of supernatural creatures had spread throughout lands and time for millennia before the Elements arrived. The safety of the Elementals' survival was encased in that gossip. Foolish notions that garlic or holy water could stave off or help you detect vampires is what ultimately helped his people stay unnoticed.

There was the absurd fascination with putting a stake through the heart of any such creature. If one suspects a person of being of being a vampire, one might put a stake through his heart. It would surely kill a mortal man, leaving those who bore witness to believe they had successfully killed a vampire when in fact, they merely killed a friend, neighbor, or even a stranger on the street who happened to have some idiosyncrasy that triggered their alarm. The fact the poor human died concretes the belief he had been a creature of the night, ignoring the fact that a stake through the heart would have killed them even if they were simply human. Suspicion of vampirism had always been a death sentence.

If one suspects an Elemental of being a vampire, one might try the same tactic. However, the Elemental would not, in fact, be deceased. If the numbers of the accusers were few, the Elemental could easily rise up and eliminate all in attendance. If they chose, they could do so at the beginning without suffering the pomp and circumstance of a staking, but there's no fun in that. They derived joy in seeing the fear in their oppressor's face.

If the numbers were too great to avoid a scene, if the Elemental was not in the mood to put on a show, if the Elemental was concerned for their family or any other of a number of reasons for not wanting to play along with the humans' foolish quests, they would lie still, allowing their captors to believe they had slain another fearsome vampire. Later when the time was right and no one was around, the Elemental would depart to set up his life somewhere new.

The tables had now turned. Thanks to the witch, those in power were no longer riddled with rumors. They knew precisely the manner in which to dispose of all the creatures they saw as a threat to themselves, or their kingdom. Ulric feared it was only a matter of time until anyone you passed on the street would have learned of the newfound techniques. If his family continued on with their passion for vengeance, it would serve to fan the flames of this knowledge until it reached everyone across Europe and beyond.

They would be outraged; of this, he was well aware. But he knew none could feel more ire than he did over the loss of his beloved Sophie and their children. It was the love he had carried for them for centuries, the love he still felt even after their bodies turned to ash that gave him this novel sense of responsibility to keep the rest of his kin safe, even at the expense of a few or more losing their heads this evening.

Ulric made his way to the center of the long table at the head of the room. There were twelve open seats, six on either side of his. Tonight, what was left of his family would have several choices laid before them. The ones who chose to stay, and unknowingly save their skins, would vote in ten Council members. The other two had already been chosen by Ulric himself. They were the oldest two members of his family, and they were well respected by everyone. He felt no one would challenge Ulric appointing them. The Council would always consist of twelve members with Ulric's vote to be used only to break a tie.

They would then begin to lay down a set of laws that their people would be governed by so long as their bloodline continued. The Council would begin with a list of laws already established by Ulric which he would introduce this evening. From this point forward, any dealings with the Fire Elementals, natural and created, would be handled by the Council. This included abolishing existing laws or creating new ones. They would also be the ones to dole out the punishments for those who would betray their kind, break the laws, and in turn place the others at risk for discovery.

Ulric raised his arms to silence the room. "We are all too aware of the dark days that have plagued us. Unfortunately, I believe the reckoning of supernatural creatures is still in its infancy."

"What do you propose we do to combat the situation?" Roanin interrupted from his seat without the respect of looking at who he was addressing.

"Combat?" Ulric asked, moving closer to him. "Are you proposing we go to war? A war with the humans?"

Roanin shook his head. "No. I do not support a war, but something must be done."

Ulric waited for Roanin to offer a solution to their plight, but he didn't speak again. "Continue," Ulric urged.

"We have all lost loved ones. I feel more will be lost at the bequest of this king. We should not cower in the darkness. We need to take a stand. Those who threaten our lives need to be held accountable. The hunt wages on still in the shadows. The king may be satisfied, but there are those who haven't stopped searching for our kind in his name, hoping to earn reward or good favor. They will not stop until they believe they have eradicated us all. There must be a way to bring it to completion and punish those behind it."

Murmurs of agreement went through the banquet hall. These fools would partake in open revenge against the humans without thought to what happens next. They are like children who act impulsively without considering all possible outcomes.

Ulric clapped his hands loudly in delight, and the sound reverberated off the large stone walls. "I completely agree with you."

Roanin hooked his arm over the back of his chair and smiled, smugly pleased with himself.

"However, I fret the meanings each of us derive from your words will be entirely different."

Quick glances were shared between Roanin and the friends near him. He leaned forward looking unsure of what Ulric meant.

He took his time, walking down the length of the long table. It was a careful song and dance. There was not a soul here he did not value. Losing even one would be devastating. If he pushed too hard, the number who would walk out to their death would be debilitating to the clan. Ulric reached the end and faced the room. All eyes were on him.

"Roanin's plan is one of revenge. It would be foolhardy to take up arms against the king's army, and battling those individuals who have yet to give up the fight would draw the attention of the king to us. The combat would not cease and many more would be lost, perhaps all of you. It does not matter what label you use, it is war, and we will not be victorious."

Ulric paused and let his clan consider his words. Crossing the room again, he said, "It pains me to say Roanin has lost sight of the true enemy. Yes, the king ordered his army to search for us, to force us out of hiding, and to execute anyone suspected of supernatural powers."

His people were quiet. A few looked irritated as if being tasked with this dinner was inconvenient and irksome to their full, vivacious lives. Some listened intently. Roanin leaned forward, his arms crossed on the table. His eyes bore into the plate in front of him, and his nostrils flared. It was uncertain if he knew what Ulric meant and disagreed with what was about to be said, or if he merely did not like being wrong.

"You need to ask yourself why. Are you thinking the witch is at fault?"

More promising whispers floated to his ears with scattered nods. All of them had celebrated the news of her death.

"If she had not met the king, all of our secrets would be safe?" he paced the table.

"Yes, I too blamed the witch. She is not the reason we are being hunted. It is our own doing that endangered our lives. We create more of our kind on a whim. We understandably want our loved ones to stay youthful and by our sides forever. Has it ever stopped there?" his voice loudened.

Many hung their heads, knowing they had made rash decisions about creating vampires.

"We create vampires out of our servants, our neighbors, or other poor souls we think may enjoy the power shift, only to regrettably realize our mistake. Once created and left to their own devices, they can do whatever they please. They are careless. We sire at will, but we do not always raise our children."

"The ones we cast off are scared and alone. They do not understand the power they have been gifted. That is why we are hunted. It is because of our own carelessness. This is why I called you here tonight."

Ulric stopped in front of Roanin's table, but his friend refused to meet his eyes. "I do not want us to cower in the darkness. I want us to find a way to blend in with the rest of society."

Roanin narrowed his eyes, angry at the notion.

In a few more moments, he would discover how many would reject the structure he proposed. Ulric collected his thoughts and resumed his place in the center of the room. "Tonight, we shall create a Clan Council. Rules for our kind will be established and laid down as well as punishments for those who do not abide by them."

"A Council?" Roanin scoffed angrily. "Are you to be our king?"

"To be fair, I will not be a member, but I will preside over meetings."

"Hogwash! Do you honestly expect any of us to follow your rules?" he sneered.

"I do," Ulric said calmly. "I will not force this upon any of you. If you choose not to be a member of the clan, you may leave at any time."

Roanin's chair scraped loudly across the floor as he pushed back. He stood, throwing his napkin on the table. Then he walked to the door with two others, slowly making their way behind him.

Ulric watched as Roanin disappeared from view. *'The Council will now vote in eleven members tonight.'*

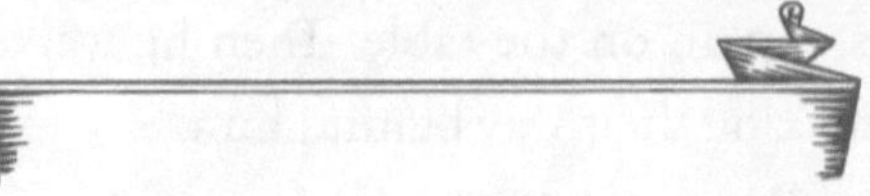

Chapter Seventeen
Club Underground

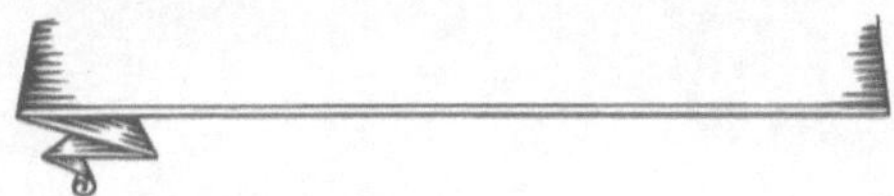

Bet paced back and forth in the bedroom, crossing the open bathroom door and sighing at her husband who splashed cologne on his hands before applying it to his face and neck. "Come on! I swear you're worse than a woman. I was ready an hour ago."

He laughed, "An hour? Try fifteen minutes at the most," he corrected over the sound of running water. "Besides, I didn't even get in the shower until you were done."

"It's been longer than fifteen minutes," she insisted.

"Hardly," he quipped.

Rolling her head toward the ceiling, she muttered under her breath, "If this man doesn't hurry, I'm going to take the invitation and leave him here."

She sucked in her breath and walked to the open doorway where Spencer could see her in the mirror. "Since you've been out of the shower, I decided against the heels I had on in case I wind up on my feet a lot tonight, so I had to change my entire outfit, last minute, to match the boots I am now wearing with the wider heel. Thanks for noticing."

There was no response aside from his snickering.

The water turned off, and he emerged, drying his hands on a towel. "You changed your entire outfit over a pair of shoes?"

With her back to him, she slowly drawled, "You plan the entire outfit around the shoes." Bet turned toward him, and her mouth dropped in dismay. "Where's your shirt?"

He playfully smacked his abs. "Is there a problem with what you see? Most people wouldn't mind if this isn't covered."

"You know you can't get in topless, and you had a shirt on when you went into that bathroom for the seventh time to check your appearance."

He shrugged and walked across the room toward the closet, tossing the used towel on the floor as he went.

Bet eyed the towel angrily. Decades. That's how long she'd been after him not to leave wet towels on the floor, but there was no time for this argument tonight. It was already later than she had planned on leaving.

"I spilled some cologne on it and was afraid of it staining. I want to look good tonight," he said, rifling through his shirts.

She rolled her eyes and tapped her foot.

"Don't," he warned.

"I didn't say anything."

He pulled a shirt off a hanger and replied, "I can sense your attitude, Bet. I want to look my best."

"Oh yes," she mocked, her voice dripping with disdain. "I forgot. You're hoping to be the chosen one."

Spencer walked out of the closet, sliding his arm through the sleeve of a sharp, black button up. With mild irritation, he said, "I never said the chosen one. You know how important this night is to me."

She inhaled deeply and softened slightly as she regretted her demeanor. This night was important to both of them and everyone who would be in attendance. "Do you really think tonight is about the Council? Are you sure it's not just an invite to the concert the club is hosting tonight?"

"What else could it be? When have you ever heard of Ulric calling so many of us together?"

"But a nightclub?" she narrowed her eyes. "It just doesn't seem like the type of place you would gather for anything important."

He half shrugged, tucking his shirt into his pants. It had crossed his mind more than once. Club Underground was a surprising choice. Versions of it existed all over the states and most countries. It was a vampire themed club, but most of the regulars were anything but Fire Elementals. They believed in vampires, but none of them actually knew vampires existed in some form.

They dressed the part. They were goth before goth had a name. Some of them drank blood from willing donors, or wore vials of their partner's blood around their necks. Spencer had even seen more than one who had their teeth filed. It still amazed him the fan base Fire had without having any proof of their existence.

When these clubs first began popping up, it was a hot spot for Fire Elementals. The curiosity wore off quickly. The humans parading around styled in the manner of what they believed vamps to be was taxing. They still came out from time to time. When you've had to fly by night suddenly and begin again somewhere new with a fresh identity because someone came too close to the truth, it was a great place to unwind. Elementals would come to people watch and make fun of the wannabe vamps.

It was rumored Ulric wasn't too keen on the clubs. Of course, it was always alleged he wasn't thrilled about anything that drew attention to his kind even if there was no factual base to it. Still, the clubs held a great reputation. There had never been a single incident involving an actual vampire at any of them. No self-respecting Fire Elemental would ever sink their teeth into one of those fools.

"Spence?" Bet's voice interrupted his thoughts. "Did you hear me?"

"All I know is everyone invited is not currently a Council member, has been a vampire for at least a century, and is in the direct blood line. No created vamps were given an invitation," he reminded her, sitting on the edge of the bed to slip on his shoes.

Bet winced at his last point.

Without seeing her, he felt her reaction. "I'm sorry. Don't take it personally, Betty. It was nothing against you."

"That's what you say," she told him unconvinced. "Every time you mention the Council, you like to point out the members are blood line only."

Spencer stood up and gave his reflection a once over in the upright mirror in the corner of the room. "It's not my fault I was born into this life," he said. Happy with how he looked, he walked toward her. "And you chose to accompany me in it," he said, putting his hands on her shoulders and kissing her forehead. "You fell in love with me and wanted to be with me forever. It's also not been my doing that Council members must be from the direct line."

"Besides, you should be supporting me in this. If I get on the Council, maybe that's something I could help to change," he pointed out.

She sighed into his embrace then pulled away. "Are you ready?"

Spencer nodded.

"Finally?"

He laughed at her.

"Are you sure you don't need to check yourself in the mirror again?"

"What's your hurry anyway?" he asked. "Parties never start on time."

"Do you remember Club Underground? I know you're old and don't go out much anymore."

"Ouch," he snapped.

"But the VIP area isn't exactly huge unless they've done some drastic remodeling we haven't heard about, and I don't want to stand all night. I want to arrive early enough to get a table."

"Yes, I am ready," he assured her, grabbing their invitation off the dresser before headed down stairs.

They locked up the apartment and waited in the hall to take them to the lower level parking garage. Once in the car, it was only a few minutes' drive to the club. They had considered walking because the autumn weather was perfect, but Ulric was known for his unpredictability. Spencer didn't want to find himself in a position where he needed to be mobile, but couldn't because they chose to take a stroll.

As soon as he steered the car out on to the road, she asked, "Are you nervous?"

"Hmm," he muttered, distracted by traffic.

"About tonight, I mean. Are you nervous?" she asked again.

Spencer gripped the steering wheel tighter unmindful he was doing so. He had been filled with a mixture of nonstop excitement and anxiety since the invitation was first discovered outside their apartment door a month ago with Ulric's official seal on the back.

He had met Ulric once many decades ago. Spencer had tried to introduce himself to talk to him a moment, but Ulric brushed him off. His manner wasn't rude or arrogant either. He obviously was in the middle of something or had more important matters to attend to than meeting someone who was one of the newer members of his clan.

Bet didn't wait for him to answer. She answered her own question for him, "I'm nervous about meeting him. I've heard the stories."

He cocked a wry grin, "Not all of them."

"That's what makes me nervous. It's what I don't know that worries me."

Spencer pulled up to the club. "Don't worry about it. You're with me, and

I'll protect you," he teased, meaning every word.

They got out of the car, and he dropped his keys with the valet. Spencer showed the doorman their invite, and he nodded them both inside.

They headed toward the VIP room only to be escorted to the back of the club where another area had been set up into a makeshift VIP lounge. It was decorated better than the original one in the club. Lighting was low, but candles lined the walls and tables. The glow illuminating from them set the perfect ambience for an evening of the unexpected. Bet was right to want to come early, and they should've left a long time ago.

The place was already packed. One hundred invitations had been sent out with a plus one restricted to vampires only. If everyone showed, there would be two hundred in attendance. Doing a quick estimated count around the room, over half had arrived already.

It was a good mix of people he knew and people he heard about as well as some whose identity alluded him. They helped themselves to champagne and began to mingle.

Before long, a woman walked into the room. She was exquisite. Her long raven hair was soft and shiny. Her red lips perfectly matched her skin tone. Something about her, something besides her looks, commanded everyone's attention the moment she appeared. She walked to the center of the room, looking around at each of them in turn, then began to speak.

"I know you are all eagerly awaiting your host, so consider me your opening act."

Spencer's phone vibrated in his back pocket. He was thankful he had remembered to put it on silent, but it was annoying nonetheless.

"Ulric will be here soon. He is running a little late, so he has asked me to get the festivities started," the mystery woman continued. "You don't know me, so allow me to introduce myself. My name is Char," she said with a giggle. "Appropriate name, don't you think?"

A murmur of laughter traveled through the gathered guests.

His cell phone vibrated again, and he began to wish he had left it in the car.

"Who would like to start with a little appetizer?" she asked with a devilish grin.

With that, she clapped her hands, and several waiters appeared carrying trays filled with shot glasses. The liquid contained within them was not whiskey. The aroma enticed his senses before the waiters had even appeared. It was blood, but not just any blood. He could tell by the richness of it. It was aged. It was vampire blood.

His stomach flip-flopped, but he thought, "There's no way. It can't be his."

The vibration started a third time, and he reached for his phone as secretly as he could.

Char announced, "Your host has sent a gift ahead of his arrival. It's a little piece of him you could say."

Spencer's heart pounded so fast in his chest he was sure people walking along the street could hear it. The waiters toured the room, passing out shots. While waiting for one to near him, he glanced at his phone with the intention of turning it off to prevent any further distractions. That's when he noticed there were three missed calls from Luke.

It made him pause. Luke never calls. It must be something important.

He looked around, but no one else seemed too bothered by their phones. He wanted to step outside to call him back, but he didn't want to miss his chance at Ulric's blood. The heightened sense of powers the blood would provide was too alluring for anyone to turn down.

As he stood there holding his phone, Luke called yet a fourth time. This time he mouthed, "Give me a minute," to Bet as he stepped toward the back of the crowd and answered as privately as he could.

Spencer only half listened to Luke while watching for the waiter to come near. If Luke wasn't his elder, he'd have sent the call to voice mail. He had been surprised to not see Luke here tonight, but it made sense. Luke and Ulric were close. He didn't need this opportunity like the others in the room.

"Hold on," he told Luke when the waiter came close. Spencer took the shot glass and drank it slowly, savoring the taste. It was still warm and coated his throat as it went down. The energy surge swirled throughout his body, and he felt invincible. It also meant Ulric would be able to have control over him for the next twelve to twenty-four hours, but that was of no concern. Ulric was a sensible man who did not draw attention to his people. He could be trusted.

Random fits of laughter drifted through the room as the drug like effect of a vampire's blood was taking hold over those in attendance. In his blind exhilaration to have the benefits of Ulric's blood, he had temporarily forgotten that unfortunate side effect. He would fight it as hard as he could. He wanted to present himself as sensibly as possible when Ulric finally made his appearance. The most important item on his agenda this evening was to make a good impression.

Spencer had almost forgot about Luke, but he told him he needed to go. Whatever Luke needed to talk to him about seemed urgent as Luke resorted to mind control to make him go outside to continue the call. There was nothing that could be more important than an audience with Ulric this evening. Spencer hung up the phone as soon as he heard the echo before Luke could issue a command. He turned it off and shoved it in his pocket. He chuckled, imagining the expression on his Elder's face when he so blatantly defied him.

Char was making her way back to the middle of the room, so Spencer hurriedly took his place at Bet's side once more.

"Did you have any idea?" he heard Bet whisper.

He turned to her, grinning from ear to ear. "No. Not at all."

"I feel like we're the luckiest people in the world tonight."

"Definitely," he told her.

Once the waiters were finished delivering their shots, Char addressed them all a second time. "How is everybody feeling?"

Amid the cheers, laughter and clapping, he noticed a couple people near the front of the room slumped toward the floor.

"Good, good," she smiled. "I hate to be the bearer of bad news, but you won't be feeling that way for long."

A hush immediately fell over the crowd both from her words and from alarm. More and more people began to drop. Some slid out of their chairs slowly. Others collapsed in an instantaneous heap on the floor.

"I have some bad news," Char continued. "Well, it's all bad news actually. First, Ulric won't be able to make it tonight. Unfortunately, he doesn't even know about this little get together. I am the one who sent out the invitations."

Spencer could feel his legs growing weak. It was becoming harder to force them to do what he wanted them to do, and he knew they were given more than just blood. By now, over half the room was on the floor.

"However, a positive note! The blood you drank was Ulric's, but it was spiked with a little flavor of my own. Pentobarbital, Atropine, and Suxamethonium Chloride. Phew! Try saying that three times fast! Oh, that's right. You can't," she mocked as more bodies dropped.

Spencer had already realized he was unable to speak, and he was certain no one else would still have a functioning voice either.

"Luckily, Ulric's blood is potent enough to hide the taste and the smell, even from all of you and your super noses. It's a bit overkill. I admit," she continued. "I had to cover my bases. I didn't want to get this far into my plan and have something come at me out of left field to throw a kink into things. You have no idea how much time and money went into setting up this party."

He was on the floor. He collapsed in a way that spun him away from Char, but he could see Bet clearly. Her eyes were filled with terror. They had no way to know exactly what was coming, but it was safe to believe everyone in the room would meet their end tonight. That wasn't even the worst of it. He wouldn't even be able to hold Bet while they died.

Between the drug like quality of the blood and the medications that it was laced with, he started to hallucinate. The walls of the room started bending inward and outward like funhouse mirrors. Char's voice echoed behind him. The volume of her words increased then decreased, and sometimes her voice would zoom by him almost as if she were speaking out of a passing car.

"I really only needed the paralytic. The sedatives are because of your high metabolism. I needed to slow that down, so the paralytic could take effect."

"The good news is the effects will only last about ten minutes before your body manages to override it. Someone over here is already wiggling their fingers. Wait. Did I say good news?" Char placed her hand on her hip and shook her head. "I forgot there isn't any good news."

"If I'm honest, and I don't see why I shouldn't be since none of you will be able to tell my secrets. I didn't need any of the medications at all. It was for dramatic effect. I do love a good show."

"You really have no one to blame, but yourselves. Drinking an elder vampire's blood gives them control over you for a short period of time. Well, I'm no vampire, but I'm still going to use Ulric's blood," she inhaled deep, and her voice took an arcane, commanding tone, "to order all of you to stay exactly where you are without making a sound for the rest of the night. Not that you'll live that long," she added.

"Oh, look! The finger twitching stopped. Surprised?"

There was a pause before Char went on, "Ah! I keep forgetting you can't respond," she teased at their predicament. "It's a shame though because I wonder what you would do. Laugh at your hallucinations? Or just sit there with confused looks on your faces?"

Footsteps entered the room, and the smell of gasoline soon overpowered anything else. He couldn't see who they were. He assumed it was the waiters and wondered if they were under her control as well. His pants legs became wet, but he was powerless to move.

"Do you smell that?" Char asked. She gasped, "That's not gas is it? And with all these candles in this room? Boy, I'd sure hate to knock one over on my way out."

Spencer could hear the footsteps around the guests. The smell of gasoline grew stronger. It would have gagged him if he was capable of that reflex.

Char's voice boomed again. "This party started with such high aspirations, yet I know all of you must be shaking in your boots right now," she chuckled. "Figuratively speaking, of course. Now, here we are. All of you drank willingly like a little kid being offered an ice cream cone," she said mockingly.

"It was Ulric's blood, right? You trust him. That was what all of you were thinking. That is your excuse for doing something so foolish. If Ulric had given you his blood, then yes, you would be able to trust him."

"But I'm surprised all of you trusted me, someone you never met until I walked into this room and gave you a fake name. Char. It kind of has that hint of foreshadowing to it, doesn't it?"

"You don't know me. Even if I told you who I really was, I guarantee you have never heard of me. I bet it comes as a bit of a shock to learn that Ulric is not the only one who can control someone who has his blood in their system, especially someone who is not a vampire."

She laughed again. "It was a bit of a shock to me too. I found out by pure luck. Okay. I lied again. I had a theory, and I tested it."

"Anyway, it's been fun, and I'd love to stay for the rest of the show. But, I have better places to be. I would say I'll see you around, but that's not going to happen."

Her footsteps retreated from the room. Spencer waited, knowing what was coming, but hoping it was all an act. Maybe it was a show of trust or faith. Hell, he'd even take pixie dust at this point.

The temperature was rising around him. Soon in the shadows on the wall, he could see the flickering of the flames. The heat they were giving off reddened his cheeks. It was only a matter of time, and it wouldn't be much longer.

The eeriest part was the lack of screaming. They had been commanded not to move or make a sound, so they wouldn't. There were footsteps. Those helping Char tonight were still walking around the room, and what they were doing was the only noises that could be heard.

The overpowering scent of Ulric's blood had been replaced by the retching pungency of gasoline. That had quickly been overtaken by the smell of fire. Now, the room was filled with the terrifying odor of cooked flesh.

The flames engulfed his pants, but it took a few moments for the pain to begin. As soon as he had the hope that maybe the medications put into their shots would prevent the pain from being too dire, he felt it. He endured every bit of it. For eleven agonizing minutes, he lay there unable to even blink while his body was engulfed in flames, and his flesh burned off the bone.

Then one of the unknown persons still walking around the room appeared in front of him. The man's boots had already caught fire. These people were being commanded as well. Spencer couldn't move to see what he was doing, but he sensed it. The man had a blade. He looked at Bet and tried to plead with his eyes how much he loved her right before the sword came down separating his head from his body.

"SPENCER!" LUKE WAS relieved to hear his friend's voice on the other end of the line. "Glad I caught you. There's been some troubling news, and I was hoping-"

"I only have a minute," Spencer cut him off. "Mind if I call you later?"

Luke recoiled as though he'd been slapped. "What's going on?" he asked, assuming it must be important for the short tone in Spencer's voice. He worried the reckoning had reached New York.

"I'm at Club Underground. Honestly, I'm surprised you're not here."

Something was wrong. Luke could feel it.

"Hey, who's the new player?"

Luke stared into his phone half expecting to see what Spencer was talking about. "What do you mean?"

"The new vamp. She's hot," Spencer whispered, hoping Bet wouldn't overhear.

Troubling just took a turn for the worse. New vampires had to be approved before they could be created. It'd been that way since their laws were laid down by Fire himself. Violators faced death.

"I don't understand," Luke told him. "There hasn't been a new created vampire in near a century."

"That would be false. I'm looking at her right now."

Luke stood and walked to the living room where Meredith was relaxing. "And you're sure she's newly created."

"None of us ever met her before tonight."

"Where are you again?"

"Club Underground. Private party in the back. Invitation only. Looks like most of us showed up too. Not surprised. You'd be an idiot to turn this down," Spencer told him with a tone implying there was more.

Luke's eyes widened and his skin paled. Meredith leaned forward in her seat, watching and waiting to learn what was happening.

"All of who?"

"Hold on," he told Luke. There was a pause. Spencer held the phone at his side while he reached for a shot glass. "Man, you are missing out. You seriously weren't invited?" Spencer asked, deciding to hold back on telling Luke about the shot of blood. Luke had held an air of authority over him ever since the day he told Spencer about their blood line. It was his turn to have something over Luke for a change.

"Alright, friend, I've got to go," Spencer said into the phone.

Rubbing his temple, Luke pressed the phone to his other ear even harder hoping somehow it would make Spencer hear what he had to say easier. Taking a deep breath, he closed his eyes and reached back into the primal part of his mind that he avoided as much as possible. When he opened his eyes again, they glowed faintly, and his voice resonated. "Something is off. Listen to me. This doesn't feel right. I need you to leave right now."

Spencer didn't say anything.

"Hello?" Luke looked at the phone and saw the call had disconnected. He tried calling his friend back, but it went straight to voice mail. Shoving the phone in his pocket, he walked through the room aimlessly.

"What happened?" Meredith asked.

Luke shook his head and paced the floor. "I think Spencer's in trouble."

"Why? What did he say?"

"It's not that," Luke sighed. "It's what he didn't do. He ignored me like I was nothing."

"But you ordered him to leave," Meredith said confused. "I heard you."

His head slowly nodded, but he didn't take his eyes off the corner of the rug he was staring at.

"He didn't," Meredith gasped.

Luke didn't respond.

"Spencer...," Meredith sucked her breath across her teeth. "Spencer didn't leave like you instructed. How is that possible?"

"I don't know," Luke told her, turning to face her. "Either someone older than me is controlling him, or he hung up on me before I ordered him to do anything."

Meredith gasped and jumped to her feet. "No. That's not possible."

He clasped his hands behind his head. "You're right. It's not, but I'm telling you that's what he did."

A moment passed before the thought occurred to them at the same time. "Judd!" they said in unison.

"You need to call him," Meredith told Luke, heading to retrieve her phone from the kitchen. As strained as their relationship was, she needed to call her mother. Eloise might be able to shed some light on this.

Luke had already began dialing before Meredith said anything to him. "I'm already on it."

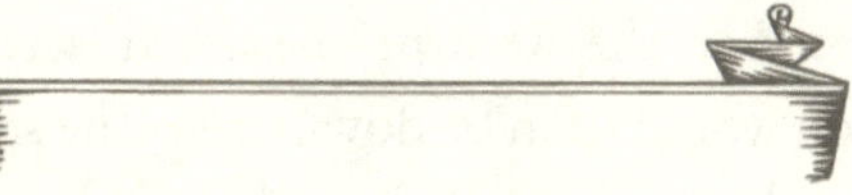

Chapter Eighteen
Time to Return

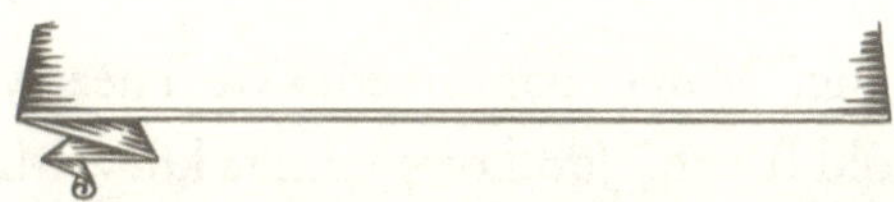

Judd stared at his phone screen. It was Marcus. This close to the Return it could go either way, but he didn't expect Marcus would call unless he found Water.

'This is it,' he exhaled deeply. *'Our time ends in under a fortnite.'*

"Hello, old friend," Judd feigned his usual taunting greeting. He balanced the phone between his chin and shoulder while he grabbed the bags off the seat of the truck.

"We found Water," Marcus told him.

There was an element of excitement in those words. Judd didn't get involved in the search until a year ago, but this was the closest they had been to completing the Return in a thousand years. It was stimulating even if it meant leaving this life behind, but the exhilaration was short lived.

They had Water. They would complete the Return. They would leave their human life and venture back beyond the veil. He would have to leave his son behind.

Judd realized Marcus was still speaking, and he shook off his pity filled thoughts to pay attention.

"...in Northern Michigan, just as you advised. How did you know?"

"I didn't," he said, unlocking the front door with one hand. "It was an educated guess. Most of the other packs have hierarchy blood lines that have been established for centuries. The Michigan wolves are newer, but their pack has grown at a concerning rate by comparison to other packs. I assumed Water found a new home."

There was a familiar voice in the background. "How is Leena doing?"

"She is well. Thank you for asking," Marcus told him.

"Has Water agreed to the Return?" he asked, setting the bags on the kitchen table. Jackson would soon be downstairs. The smell of the uncooked meat in the bags would rouse his attention easily.

"Yes," Marcus told him. "Surprisingly, there was very little argument, but I think we all know it's time."

Judd sighed. It was time. It was past time. It would've been so much easier before Jackson.

"There is one thing," Marcus continued. "We'll need your help."

"Anything, my old friend," Judd offered. He knew Marcus recoiled each time he said those words at the thought of their relationship being anything more than tepid acquaintances.

"I don't trust it," Marcus explained. "I don't trust Water not to run at the first opportunity."

"I see," Judd muttered. He didn't trust it either. Water would never come to the Return willingly. Something was amiss.

Marcus continued, "Also, Leena and I would like to say goodbye to our family."

"Of course," Judd understood.

"Anya can't assist us, not at this time of the year."

The Return was on Halloween, and it was coming up around the corner. Eloise, along with her entire bloodline across the world, would be preparing their celebrations to welcome in the witch's New Year. It was their holiest of days.

Jackson walked into the kitchen right on cue and began rummaging through the bags. Judd motioned for him to put the groceries away.

"Do you still have the farmhouse?" he asked.

"Yes, it belongs to my son. We spent time there not long ago before returning to Michigan to ready it for Eloise's coven."

That's right, Judd thought. Eloise's family celebrates at the farmhouse every year, far away from prying eyes.

"You'll have to ask Eloise if she can find somewhere else this year. We should all stay close. Have your family come to the farmhouse where you can spend time with them."

Marcus pointed out, "It's not large enough for all of us. Chloe has a property in Trinity. I could probably figure out the logistics."

Judd watched Jackson inspect each item of food he put away. His son was most likely trying to decide what to eat first. When Jackson pulled out a package of pork chops, Judd grabbed them from his hand. It was one of Jackson's favorites. They'd have that for supper tonight. It would be a special meal for a very difficult conversation.

"Okay," Judd said. "There are ten days until the Return. Give me a few days to tend to my business then I will relieve you," he said, choosing his words carefully. Jackson would have questions, but he didn't want his son to find out by overhearing a phone call.

"Thank you," Marcus' tone was heartfelt. "That will give us enough time."

"Of course," Judd told him.

"Where should we go in the meantime? To make sure Water doesn't flee? We can't stay in Michigan. The pack is too close."

"I agree. I know a place. It's safe, and you'll find it's fully equipped for handling your cargo," Judd smirked. "I'll send you the address and directions."

Jackson was leaning against the counter with a half-eaten cinnamon roll in his hand. His eyes narrowed as he listened in, wondering what his dad could be discussing and with whom.

"Go there," Judd told him. "I'll let you know when I'm on my way."

"Going where?" Jackson asked when his dad ended the call.

Judd stared at his phone. It was harder to put it into words than he expected it would be. "Marcus and Leena have Water," he told him.

MARCUS AND LEENA SAT in the front room of the cabin on loan to them from Judd. Water was pacing across the bedroom upstairs. They couldn't hear anything, but they could sense Water's presence move back and forth across the floor. The anxiety and fear Water was shedding settled into the air around them, and they couldn't escape from feeling its weight.

It was nothing like this when the three of them first arrived two days ago. There was no sign of apprehension. In fact, Water seemed relieved, almost happy, to be back amongst other Elements once again and to be going home. Water's mood started to change last night although they didn't understand what brought it on. Some form of melancholy began to set in.

Until then, Marcus and Leena had taken turns visiting their family. They felt it was safe to leave with only one person watching over Water and the cabin at a time. Neither had shown themselves to their family yet. That would wait until Judd arrived to take over the watch. They didn't want to cut their visit short, leaving their family with more questions than answers.

The melancholy had escalated to full blown agitation and panic. It distracted Marcus and Leena, draining their natural empath nature. They felt everything Water felt, and it made it difficult for them to concentrate on anything else.

"Do you suppose it was a trick?" asked Leena.

"Yes," Marcus answered, staring out the window. "All those months we spent searching without turning up a single lead then one day the clue we needed fell into Anya's lap by happenstance. It was too easy."

"I suspected that as well," Leena agreed. "Water was on to us and sent a messenger."

A howl could be heard far off in the woods, and Water began shaking in terror. They could feel it vibrate in their bodies.

"The full moon isn't until Sunday," Leena whispered.

Marcus nodded and swallowed hard. "Natural born wolves who are descendants of Water don't need the moon to transform."

"And they're stronger than turned wolves," Leena added.

They sat perfectly still using all their senses to identify those outside. There was quite a lot of them. The wolves kept moving, and they moved fast. It made it difficult for them to keep an accurate count of how many were out there.

"What did they hope to accomplish?" Leena wondered out loud. "What would they want with you? They can't kill you."

"No," Marcus told her. "It's you, my love. They can threaten me with you."

There were footsteps in the gravel, and a blur ran in front of the window. Marcus jumped up and turned off the lights, so they could peer into the darkness easier. They couldn't see anything. Whoever or whatever it was had already vanished.

The howling continued and multiplied. The cabin was surrounded by wolves in all directions except near the lake. If they had to escape, that would be the most logical.

"Why go through all the trouble?" Marcus asked. "Why come here willingly if you're going to stage an escape."

There were knocks on the outside walls. They were random and all over on all sides of the cabins. The pounding on the windows were so harsh, they were frightened the glass would break. It was hard to gauge how many were outside.

"Water didn't plan this," Leena said calmly, looking out a window for their invisible trespassers. She patted her husband's hand in reassurance, more for her sake than his.

"Who else?" Marcus was confused.

"Think about it, my dear. Whatever Water is afraid of is outside of this cabin right now. Water doesn't want them here."

It stopped in the wee hours of the morning. Their tormentors left, leaving them in peace for now. They were exhausted physically and mentally.

"They'll be back," Leena said quietly.

"I'll get ahold of Judd. There can be no more leaving the cabin with only one guard while it's under attack, and it would be beneficial to have a third person on lookout at night."

"THANK YOU FOR COMING," Marcus said, standing outside of the cabin.

"I had some affairs to get in order for what appears to be the last time. This was practically on the way."

"We had visitors last night," Marcus said, cutting directly to the point.

"Who?"

"We never got a good look."

Judd leaned against his car and kicked the gravel. He stared at the rocks moving near his feet to avoid looking anywhere else.

"Where is Leena?" Judd asked.

"She went to greet our family, but she will be back soon."

Judd tilted his head up in surprise. "I thought you were going to wait until I came out."

"After last night, we worried it may not be an option. There should be two here at all times taking shifts."

"That bad?"

Marcus pointed to the front of the cabin. "Someone ran around the house, knocking on the doors and windows. You can see where they busted the chain on the swing and knocked down some of the porch décor. There were others in the woods. We never saw them, but we heard them howling."

"Wolves," Judd muttered.

"We think its Water's people, members of her tribe, and they're here to take Water home."

"Wait," Judd said, pushing off from the car. "I thought you said Water came willingly."

"Yes."

"Then why would any wolves be doing this?"

Marcus' shoulders heaved. "Maybe Water didn't say a proper goodbye or prepare them. It has been a thousand years without a single attempt to make the Return. They probably don't believe Water wants to complete it."

It made sense. It would take a lot to convince Water's people this was by choice. "How's Water holding up?"

"It had been fine. After last night, Water's been a mess, apologizing and begging us not to let them get in."

"Them? The wolves?" Judd asked.

Marcus nodded.

"Come with me. I'll show you what I was talking about when you called," Judd said and led him to the cellar remains behind the cabin.

He showed Marcus the cage and demonstrated how the door works. "If Water goes in here, I'm the only one who can unlock the door. Don't use it unless Water agrees. I put Jackson in here during his first transition, tricked him, and I felt so guilty I almost got rid of it."

"I'm glad you didn't," Marcus told him.

They made their way back, slowly. Neither of them said much for the first part of the hike.

"It has to be done with Water's consent," Judd told him. "I hope you understand."

Marcus stopped and said, "I promise I won't put Water in the cage unless it's voluntary."

"Not just that," Judd said. "I mean the Return. We can't drag anyone to it."

"Water will be there willingly," Marcus said confidently.

Wanting to lighten the mood, Judd asked, "What's Leena doing? Having dinner with them then coming back?"

"No," Marcus said. "We're not letting them know we're there. We wouldn't want to risk putting them in danger. We are both worried about Lilah although we realize she will come through it."

"She is one of the chosen," Judd agreed.

They made their way back to the driveway, and Marcus asked, "How is Jackson taking the news?"

"Too well if you ask me. I think he's holding out hope."

Marcus patted Judd's shoulder in a rare act of kindness toward him. "That is not unexpected. He won't tell anyone?"

"No. I told him the Elements weren't giving notice to their families."

"Do you think this war is coming because we haven't made the Return yet?" Judd asked.

Marcus put his hands on his hips, looking off with his typical stoic stance he's always been notorious for when he's considering something. "Are you asking if I think it will end when we go home?"

"Yes. Is this our last chance to prevent it?"

"You call it war, but we don't yet know the enemy," Marcus side stepped the answer.

Judd was a little irritated by Marcus' refusal to be direct. "I agree we can't win a war without knowing our enemy, but that won't stop someone from getting the upper hand until we do. When we complete the Return, will it end?" he asked again.

"I'm afraid not. The war will rage whether or not we're here to do battle."

"Then shouldn't we stay?" Judd stepped around to face Marcus, pounding his fist into his palm. "Isn't it wrong to leave our people when they need us the most?"

Marcus smiled at him, "Spoken like a true father. I too have been plagued with the guilt of leaving my family at this most regrettable time, but that's why the hybrids are in place. They won't need us to secure a victory."

"And you think the four are capable? That they're strong enough?" Judd asked.

"That I can't say," Marcus said and looked at Judd sternly. "And I have tried to see it. There are too many variables, too many possible outcomes. In all of them, I can see the war, but not the victor."

"Why is that?"

"I'm not sure," Marcus admitted. "I think it's because the Return is in a few days, and I will no longer be here to have influence on it."

Judd ran his hand through his hair and massaged the back of his neck. He had always hoped Anya's visions were wrong. If not wrong, he hoped something would happen to change the course of the future to prevent this from coming. "It comes down to the four then. Our replacements?"" Judd laughed.

Marcus broke out in an uncharacteristic smile and said, "You jest, but their roots run deep. They're a part of the plan."

"The Divine Spirit's plan?" Judd asked baffled.

"What other plan is there?"

Judd straightened his posture and became very animate as he spoke. "Do you really think our kind, the destruction we've caused, and this unknown enemy we're facing who seems to somehow be more powerful than all of us is really a part of the Divine Spirit's plan? We're not even supposed to be here!"

"When the Divine Spirit sent us here, do you really think he did not know we would still be here a thousand years later?" Marcus asked, raising one eyebrow.

It wasn't like him to be rendered speechless, but he was. In all his years, he never considered this was part of the grand design. Instead, he always believed they were destroying what the Divine Spirit had built.

Judd opened the driver's side door to his car and gave the cabin a good look for the first time since arriving. He couldn't be sure, but he thought he saw movement behind one of the curtains in an upstairs window. "I'll be back tonight," he said.

"Do you have an idea of the time?"

"Late," Judd shrugged. "Jackson is out with friends. He was going to cancel, given my departure, but I insisted he go. He needs to continue as if everything is normal until after the Return, and I had a few things to get done before I left."

"Take your time, old friend," Marcus quipped. "Your family is quite young. It will be harder on you to say goodbye."

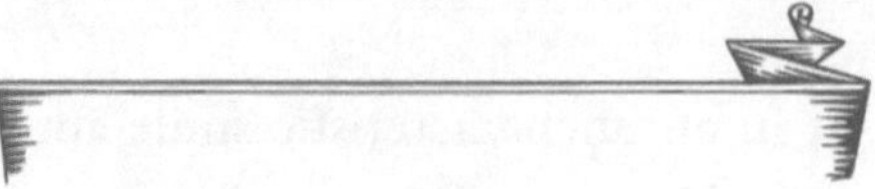

Chapter Nineteen
Serendipitous Encounter

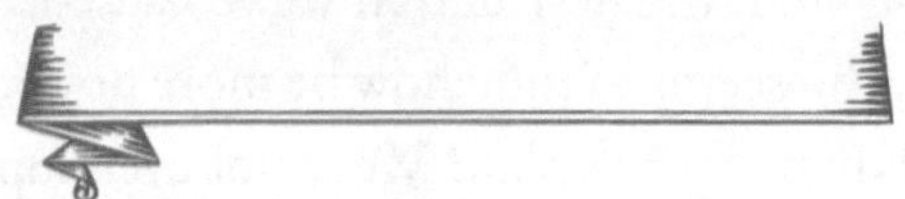

Ulric sat at the table in the club by himself. Everything about the place disgusted him. The urgency of the situation forced him to be there, and it made him all the angrier for it.

Of all the centuries he'd lived, he'd seen a lot. He'd lived through revolutions, the toppling of kingdoms, the Renaissance, and so far the twentieth century which had proven to be the time when mankind made the most advancements in history. He'd even lived through the plague which was a dirty, nasty business even without the worry of dying from it. Of all that he'd experienced, he felt that disco was the worst.

The colored lights of the ball hanging from the ceiling cascaded over the crowd of dancers making him yearn for the days when rotting corpses lined the streets. The stench of the decay and trash that filled every nook and cranny would assault his senses everywhere he roamed. It was still better than this atrocious scene.

He would go out on occasion to try to fit in, but mostly out of boredom. He loved to watch people grow more intoxicated as the night wore on before leaving with a stranger whose name they probably wouldn't remember in the morning. There was an art form to watching them, minding their mannerisms. It was a skill he quite felt he'd mastered of being able to tell who'd get the girl, who'd strike out, and who would wind up sick along the wall before the joint closed.

There was a different agenda this evening. Ulric came to New York for the sole purpose of doing his own investigation into a few missing people whose last known whereabouts had been spent at this club. This ability was what he counted on to rifle through the Fire Elementals who lacked the self-decency and self-respect to avoid this vile club in order to find the one behind the recent human disappearances.

When the place first opened, he considered intervening to shut it down entirely. A club devoted to vampires was an atrocity. In the end, he felt it wasn't worth his effort. Something as cliquish as this couldn't last. It might pique the interest of humans for a little while, but then the craze would pass. He couldn't have been more wrong.

Because he hadn't felt it urgent to end it before it even began, three people had left this club to never be seen from again in the last two months. Two men and a woman. They were all as different in their appearance and backgrounds as could be possible, so there seemed to be no rhyme or reason to how the victims were chosen. The randomness of the chosen targets would make it more difficult for Ulric to figure it out, but he welcomed the challenge. It would make his victory all the sweeter.

Ulric felt that one of his kind, well a rogue created at any rate, had decided to use this club as his feeding grounds. It would be all too easy. Find some poor sap who idolized vampires although Ulric couldn't fathom why. Then all he would have to do is just bare his fangs to win them over and promise them eternal life. He'd have a free meal and draining the body would provide a high that would last for days.

This was the third time this week he had to suffer sounds worse than that of a wounded animal coming through the speakers of this wretched place in the hopes of catching the culprit. The longer he had to endure this nightmare only ensured the severity of the torture the rogue would suffer when Ulric discovered him.

He eyed the room, settling his attention on others of his clan. Most were there out of curiosity. They were first timers, and he could tell they wouldn't return. At least not all of his kind had lost their good sense in the sixties, but a couple were there to enjoy the thrill of being admired. They kept their true self a secret, but they reveled in the praises sung of vampires. '*Sickening*,' he thought, making mental notes of who they were in case they ever crossed paths in the future.

His focus was so blindly set on seeking out his Elementals, he never noticed the woman approaching the table until a familiar voice cut through his thoughts. "My, my, my," she sang out. "I never imagined I'd find Ulric

Larsen in a place like this."

Startled, he looked up to see Camilla's cheeky grin staring back at him. When he arrived in the city, he had hoped he might run into her again although he didn't know what he thought might come of it. His trips to the city had increased over the last year even before this business with the nightclub. It was the hope of her that brought him back again and again even if he had a hard time admitting that to himself.

She slid into the booth, inviting herself to join him. The orange wedge of her Harvey Wallbanger was barely hanging on to the edge of her glass, and he waited for it to fall on her lap. It didn't. The drink made it safely to the table with the wedge still perched. Disappointed he lost his excuse to brush his hand across her thigh to remove it if it had fallen, he closed his eyes for a moment to clear his mind. When he opened them, she was lifting the orange to her mouth to suck the flesh off the rind. *'It's always the one you can't have that you desire the most,'* he thought.

"I could easily say the same thing about you. I would think your interest in this morbid vampire fascination cult would be even less than mine," he told her.

She smiled and nodded, placing the orange rind in the ashtray on the table. "You would be correct. I'm just here," she paused, looking for the right word. She turned to him with that twinkle in her eye that warned him she was up to something, "Recruiting."

"Recruiting?" Ulric asked. "At a vampire love fest?"

Camilla grinned from ear to ear, stretching one arm across the table and resting her head on it to look up at him. "I know it sounds ridiculous, but my numbers are low. It's not exactly easy to find new members, so I've had to get creative," she said, straightening herself.

"Low?" Ulric was surprised. "How do you mean? I believe Water out populates Fire ten to one, and that, I'm sure, is a low guess."

She gave one long, slow nod. "But not in my pack. It's harder for me. I can't have children."

Ulric sucked in his breath. He'd forgotten. "You've told me. I'm sorry."

"Don't be. It's not your fault," she shrugged, looking around the club uneasy. "The only way to build my pack is to turn people," she sighed.

"It must be hard not having a lineage of your own."

"Oh, no. It's not that," she quickly said mortified. "Believe it or not, I'm not too eager about the idea of having children. It's just hard, and getting harder, to find anyone interested."

He sipped his whiskey and considered her words. Their transformation was hard, but he had always heard the first one was the worst. After that, it was no more painful than a bar fight with some aches leftover the next day. "Surely, it isn't be that difficult."

Camilla snapped her head toward him and glared. "You can't be serious."

"What?"

"It must be so easy with people lined up down the city streets for miles, praying vampires are real, and they might someday get the chance to be immortal. They can't wait to 'drink the blood,'" she said, attempting her best "B" movie Dracula impersonation. "Then change into a bat and fly off into the night."

"You know it's not quite like that," Ulric laughed.

"I do," she said, waving her hand at the room. "They don't."

It was true. Almost any of the patrons there that evening wouldn't hesitate if given the chance. It was sad, really. None of them were capable of comprehending the isolation immortality brings. It may seem like a small price to pay, but humans are social creatures. When you take their connections away, they wither.

A young woman dressed wholly in black walked by their table. A vial hanging around her neck most definitely contained the blood of her boyfriend, or girlfriend for that matter. There was a set of cheap, plastic fangs from a Halloween costume in her mouth that looked even more unsettling from the disco lights shining on them. They idolize a fairy tale compared to his reality.

Ulric finished off his drink and flagged down a waitress to order another round for the both of them. He stretched his arm across the back of the booth and shifted his body to face her better. "You come here hoping if they're into vampires, they may be into werewolves too? Is that it?"

She closed her eyes and clenched her jaw. "You know I hate that word."

"Why do you think I said it?" he teased.

After a pause, she admitted, "Not exactly."

"How so?"

"No one here wants to become a wolf."

"There must be some-"

"Ulric," she cut him off, "Ask anybody, any person, or any group you wish if they would rather become a vampire or werewolf," she said as though the word caused physical pain. "They'd choose vampire every time."

He argued, "Not every time. I'm sure most would prefer neither. At any rate, you've found three recruits so far. It doesn't sound that hopeless."

Camilla's head snapped upright, and her whole body tensed. She had never given him a number.

Ulric laughed to ease the tension, "As I suspected."

He knew the moment she claimed to be recruiting it must be she who was behind the disappearances even though he wasn't sure why.

"You're not mad?" she asked with obvious surprise.

'Mad,' he thought. *'I'm downright livid!'*

"Well, I'm not pleased," he told her, knowing he couldn't stay mad for long. Not at her.

"Four."

That caught his attention. "What do you mean four?" he hissed. "They've only reported three."

"I knew you'd be angry," she muttered in a way that implied she did regret letting him down.

He reached for his glass, forgetting it was empty. He rolled the bottom of the glass around in a circle on the table. Without looking up, he said, "Look to your left. Two o'clock. Do you see the two guys across the room, chatting alone at their table?"

"Yeah, I see them."

"They're undercover cops."

"Oh, hell, Ulric. I'm sorry."

Ulric's face flushed red with hot anger. The rage would soon wane, but at that moment, it took all his trained restraint to not draw any unnecessary attention their way. "What did you expect? Three reported missing with their last known whereabouts in this vampire themed circus. I don't know how they missed the fourth."

Camilla waited for the waitress to set down their drinks and leave before explaining. "I've made sure each of them was seen after leaving here," she shook her head. "They shouldn't have been connected to this place. I don't know why they're saying they were last seen leaving here when it is an assured fact they were witnessed elsewhere."

"It doesn't matter, Camilla. They still would have made a connection to this club if they were all here shortly before their disappearance."

She sat quietly, looking like she was preparing for the worst.

Ulric shook his head. His anger was already diminishing. There was something about her. Something he couldn't put his finger on. He felt it the first time they met, not that it would do him any good to try to pursue her. "Well, you found four new pack members at any rate," he said, trying to lighten the mood.

He took a swig from his glass, allowing the warmth of the whiskey to smooth over the residual warmth of his anger.

Camilla's continued eerie quietness unsettled him, and the way she looked at him side eyed like a child, waiting to be caught prepared him for the other shoe to drop. "Oh, Camilla," he groaned. "Don't tell me it was more than four."

"No," she assured him, looking back toward her drink and toying the new slice of orange that adorned it. "I found four recruits, but I only have one new pack member," she admitted.

He was puzzled for a moment before it dawned on him what she meant. "Did you give them the option before or after you bit them?"

"Does it matter?" she brazenly asked.

Ulric gripped the back of the booth so hard, the wood splintered in his hand. The music was far too loud and the place too packed for anyone to notice, but Camilla heard it snap behind her. She sat perfectly still awaiting what may come.

"How could it not?" he asked quietly, disdain dripping from his voice. "Since my kind began creating vampires, I have despised those who tricked humans into giving up their mortality. You, of all people, should know how I feel about the concept of choice."

"What about my lot is so hard for you to understand?" she asked defensively. "Ask any of these people how they feel about," she took a deep breath, "werewolves," she said, side-eyeing him as though the word itself was toxic. "They may have a curiosity. If I ask would they be interested in becoming one, every single one of them would say no. Then where would I be?"

She bit into the orange angrily, punishing it for the lack of enthusiasm she receives for her pack. "I could explain to them," she began, still sucking on the pulp, "what I am and the kind of life I can offer them," she said before washing the fruit down with a large gulp. "Which I might add is the only chance I have of finding that needle in a haystack who might say yes, but while searching for that person, what am I supposed to do when they say no? I would have to kill them anyway."

Camilla rested her elbows on the table and cradled her face in her hands. "Not everyone is as you are, Ulric Larsen. Not all of us have the power to erase memories," she told him sadly.

Ulric lifted his glass to his lips, but before taking a sip, he corrected, "I can't erase memories; I can only alter them." The whiskey warmed through his body, and he noticed, not surprisingly, it wasn't covering his anger any longer. It had faded like his common sense does whenever he's in her presence. "But I see your point."

"Finally," she muttered under her breath. Her body relaxed, and she sat up straight.

Even with her erect posture, she looked like she could crumple at any moment. She looked defeated, whether it be from the conversation or the task she was pursuing, he couldn't be sure. But she was silent again. The one thing he learned from the few times he'd been around her was to avoid letting her get into her own head. It would be a matter of minutes before she fled if she did.

"How do you do it?" he asked, hoping to keep her company a little while longer. "You pick up someone at random to take back where? Your hotel?"

She nodded.

"You take them to your room and bite them. Then while they're suffering the unbearable agony of the venom, you explain what is happening?"

"Something like that," she sounded beaten. "Not at random. I only select ones with some level of interest in my kind."

Ulric sipped his whiskey. "What if they don't want it?"

Camilla picked up her glass and finished it in one slow drink. "It's depressing really. Humans have this innate will to live. They will fight to overcome anything put in their path. But when faced with life as a wolf, most of them beg for mercy. They believe death would be better. So I give it to them. I give them mercy."

A waitress appeared nearby, and Ulric motioned for more drinks. "Your numbers can't be that low. How big does your pack need to be?"

She shrugged. "It's not a set number. It's safety. When the pack is large enough to feel safe, I'll be done. The biggest problem is maintaining and replacement. Most of the people I turn vow to never have children. They won't bring a child into this way of life."

Ulric thought it sounded rather reasonable, but he could see the problem it presented.

"Since a natural born is rare, the only way to grow my numbers is by turning them," she sighed. "I've had a few who couldn't handle it. They took their lives in their hands and ended it. Most of the ones I lose run off because they heard tall tales of some fabled land in the south where wolves can transform pain free," she said mockingly.

"That's not a tall tale, and you know it."

"I know it," she spat. "But it wouldn't do me any good to tell them, would it?"

Ulric smiled, "That would be tough competition." He felt the soft spot he had for her growing. "Take a guess how many more you would need to feel safe in your pack," he said, thinking maybe there was a way he could help her.

The waitress returned, and Camilla immediately picked up her drink. She sipped it and set it down with the orange slice still perched.

He watched her fascinated. She always drank Harvey Wallbangers, but never seemed to drink one the same way twice. There was nothing habitual about this creature next to him.

"I don't know. I'm starting to think I'll never feel safe."

"Why is that?"

"I can't explain it."

"Try," he insisted.

"For a while now, I feel like I'm being watched, followed. I'm constantly having to look over my shoulder. I know you're just going to think I'm paranoid, but it has me worried."

"I don't think you're paranoid at all. If you were just some girl I knew, I might jump to that immediate conclusion. But people like us..." he trailed off, shaking his head. "Your senses are sharp, and your instincts, even a turned wolf's instincts rival that of mine."

Camilla forced a smile at him. She sipped her drink and studied her nails.

The patches of silence between them were coming more often. She'd be on her way in minutes if he didn't do something quick. He wanted her to stay more than he realized.

He stretched his arms out in front of him, lacing his fingers together to crack his knuckles. "I hope you know you're safe with me," he told her, looking into her eyes. "What do you say? Let's get some shots."

"Why, Ulric," she teased, batting her eyelashes at him dramatically. "Are you trying to get me drunk and take advantage of me?"

His eyes rolled up in the back of his head. "I know better than to try."

Camilla's laughter danced in his ears and made him smile. This time it was genuine. Something he rarely experienced.

"For a dance," she offered.

"What?"

"Shots in exchange for a dance," she explained. "I think it's a fair trade."

Ulric had been so captivated by her that the dreadful music in the club had been drowned out, and the only sound he could hear was her melodic voice. He groaned, "You know I don't dance."

"Don't dance, not can't dance," she smiled. "One dance, and we drink. No dance, and I'm off to find a new source for recruitment."

He closed his eyes and rubbed his face with his palms. "Fine," he muttered. "But only one."

Camilla giggled and jumped from her seat.

Ulric slowly pulled himself out of the booth and took her hand. He led her onto the dancefloor as a slow song began blaring over the speakers. He turned to her and took her into his arms. Their bodies moved together in time to the music, perfectly in sync with each other. His heartbeat increased steadily as they danced, and he wondered if she could feel it.

She looked up at him and smiled. That's when he felt it. He was letting go. All of his anger, his sadness, his fear and the worries that he'd carried with him every day for centuries was melting away. The only thing that mattered was Camilla and holding her in his arms. Tomorrow, he would feel the pain of her absence, but tonight, he was falling in love.

Later that night, they stood on the sidewalk in front of the club, and Ulric whistled for a taxi. He turned to Camilla to say goodbye, and he hoped to run into her again soon.

She placed her hands firmly on either side of his face, launching herself up on her tiptoes to give him the deepest, most passionate kiss he'd ever had. She pulled back, and her shrill laughter filled the night air. "If only you could see the look on your face!"

Ulric stood speechless.

"Don't act so surprised. We've been flirting all night."

He composed himself enough to say, "I didn't think I was your type."

"What?" she grinned mischievously. "Because you're Fire?"

"No," he replied slowly. "Because I'm a man."

She grinned and gave him that look out of the corner of her eyes that had always made him wonder what she was up to. "It's no secret I like women. Heck, I may even prefer them, but I like everybody," she bit her lower lip.

Without hesitation, he wrapped his arm around her waist and pulled her close. "Is that so?" he asked. "In that case," he said, bringing his lips down to meet hers.

When he took Camilla back to his hotel room that night, he never would've guessed it would be over three decades before she'd leave.

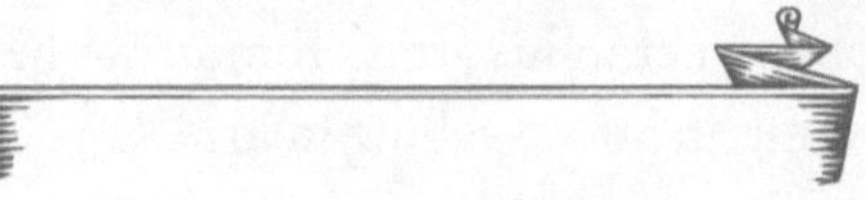

Chapter Twenty
Lilah

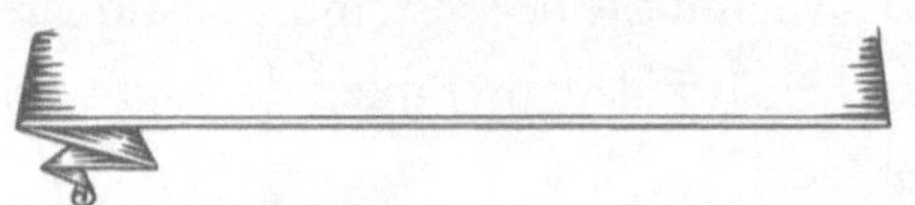

Jackson had regretted his decision to go out tonight for over three hours. He and his friends had drifted apart. They went to different colleges, one moved away, and one stayed in Fairview, got a job, and started a family right after graduation. Back at the end of high school, he and his friends had different visions for their future, but they were certain one thing would always remain the same: their friendship. Yet he'd spent most of the hour drive home from the city wondering how he'd ever been friends with them in the first place.

He'd seen them and hung out from time to time with one or the other since being back home. Things were different now that they were adults. He knew things had changed but he didn't fully realize how much. Priorities had shifted. There was more to life than figuring out how to cheat on a test or going to practice.

One of his buddy's cousins was getting married, and his buddy had invited him to the bachelor party. It wasn't his scene. He wasn't going to go. Bars, drinking, anything that might cause him to get a little too worked up was something he had to avoid until he was certain he had his emotions under control. In the end, he partly decided to go because somehow he knew deep down this would probably be the last chance the four of them had to hang out together.

Not to mention, his dad would be leaving soon. This time it would be for good. He would much rather be home spending what little time they had left together, but his dad insisted he go. It would look suspicious when his dad goes missing in a few days if Jackson canceled all his plans leading up to the disappearance.

He went knowing he wouldn't drink to keep himself calm, to keep everybody safe from what might happen if he lost his cool. Trent had already offered up designated driver services. Jackson tried to tell him to have some fun because he wouldn't be drinking anyway, but Trent was under strict orders from the wife not to come home trashed.

Jackson had convinced himself it would be good for him to go out and have a little fun. That was until Ethan got them kicked out of the Stag Night Bar. The last two hours had been spent contemplating the life decisions he'd made when he was younger, choices that caused him to think three of the seven he was out with tonight were the best friends a young man could hope to have. Friends he'd been certain he'd have lifelong. That wasn't entirely fair. Sam wasn't as obnoxious as the others. It didn't change the fact he'd spent almost the last hour counting down the minutes until they'd get to Fairview.

That was until one of the fools in the bed of Trent's pick up pounded on the cab and announced they wanted to stop and eat. It was like someone moved the finish line back a couple laps. The end was still in sight; it was just farther away.

They were almost to town when Jackson's wolf ears perked up. He could sense danger long before anyone else could. Sitting alert, he scanned the road before them, but there wasn't a car to be seen. Jackson didn't see her until after he had already grabbed the steering wheel, turning the truck to the left. It was a shape, a blur, something in the darkness ahead of them. Her clothes blended perfectly into the countryside. It was in the nick of time too as they barely avoided hitting her.

The truck veered back and forth on the county road. Its tires screeching as Trent struggled to regain control of the vehicle. The guys in the back laughed wildly and shouted into the night as the girl tumbled into the ditch. "Damn, Wolf Eyes Montgomery at it again!" Trent cried out. "How did you see that dude?"

That was a name he hadn't heard throughout college. He picked it up in grade school and hated it, but by the end of high school, he'd appreciated it more than he had thought possible. "I almost didn't. That was close."

Jackson couldn't be sure if she jumped out of the way or if she fell. With the hoodie pulled up, hiding her features, there was no way he could be certain she was a she except that he felt it. Something told him to go back to her more than to see if she was okay. Something was telling him that she was important.

The truck pulled into the restaurant parking lot, and half of the group in the back jumped out and headed to the door before the truck came to a stop. It was pretty packed for this time of night, and Trent crept to a crawl through the still unpaved side of the parking lot. Jackson waited a minute before climbing out of the cab. He looked around hesitant to join them inside. This was his home. It's where he was raised. Half of these guys would probably never step foot in Fairview again after the wedding next weekend. It would mean nothing to them to cause a scene around town, but he still had to show his face tomorrow.

If he was being honest, he knew that might be one of the motives, but it wasn't the main reason he lingered outside. His gaze drifted down the road in the direction they came. He couldn't stop thinking about her, and he never even saw her face.

The gravel crunched under Trent's feet as he walked around the front of the truck. He stood near Jackson, slapping a hand on his shoulder. "I wouldn't worry about it too much. I saw the dude get up in the rearview mirror shortly after we passed."

Jackson nodded at his friend and started walking toward the restaurant entrance. That wasn't his concern at all. His mind wasn't wrought with worry over whether she was okay. He knew she was. The thought weighing on his mind was how someone he didn't know could have so much significance to him, and the more he thought about her the more important she became.

He walked into the restaurant ahead of Trent and spotted the rest of the gang immediately in the corner booth. Most of them were sitting on the backs instead of the seats. Their obnoxious voices carried throughout every corner of the building.

A plan began formulating as he headed over to join them. Jackson was famished which was nothing new. He could eat every hour of the day and still be hungry, but there was plenty of food at home he could help himself to if he wanted. He was going to order something quick and then head home on foot when he was done.

As far as he was concerned, they were back in Fairview now which meant the party was over. He was only here with them because that's where his ride brought him. His house was within walking distance and would only take a few minutes to get there. The ride wasn't necessary anymore.

The waitress came over with two more menus for him and Trent. Jackson didn't need to be psychic to tell the waitress was thinking this would be the worst part of her shift. When the waitress offered him a menu, he held up his hand. "I just want a chocolate milkshake and an order of fries."

She nodded and left the table.

Sam blurted out, "That's a first. I have never known Montgomery to not be hungry."

Jackson leaned back and cracked his neck before shrugging at his friend. "I'm just tired."

His friend didn't say another word, but gave him a concerned look. That's something else Jackson Montgomery was not known for, lack of energy.

The waitress returned with the milkshake and took the orders from the rest of the table. Jackson sipped his drink in silence torn between trying to following along with what his friends were carrying on about and trying to determine how soon wouldn't be too soon to make his departure.

His head jerked up, and he eyed the door. Seconds later she walked in the restaurant. He had been wrong. It wasn't a hoodie after all. It was a light rain jacket. It was something you didn't typically see people wearing around here.

She scanned the restaurant quickly before heading to the counter. Jackson couldn't take his eyes off her.

Trent pounded the table a couple times with his fist lightly to get Jackson's attention. He nodded in the direction of the counter where the girl was pulling out a stool. It wouldn't have been hard to discern she was the one they had encountered on the road just outside of town. Her clothes looked exactly as you'd expect if someone had been run off the road into the ditch.

He wanted to go to her to be polite, to apologize for his friends, to ask if she was okay even though he already knew she was fine. He couldn't. As hard as he tried, he couldn't will his legs to get up from the booth. Jackson had never had a problem talking to women before, but this one was different.

Jackson sucked the warm air of the restaurant into his mouth, and it was chilled from the milkshake he'd been nonstop sipping. There was something extraordinary about her, and he just realized what it was. She was one of them. She was an Elemental. A voice inside his head told him there was something so much bigger that was drawing him to her.

She stood from the counter, and Jackson kept his eyes on her half hoping she'd leave and half afraid she would at the same time. He'd want to follow her outside if she did to say he's sorry, hoping it'd lead to more conversation where he might have a chance to see her again. Part of him believed his legs would fail him, unable to bear his weight to go after her.

To his relief, she headed to the back hallway of the restaurant where the restrooms were located. He tried to build his courage while she was gone to go talk to her, knowing his friends would probably act like a bunch of high school jocks and embarrass him if he did. They were pretty much already acting like fools.

He ran over lines and introductions in his head like he was back in junior high, building up the nerve to ask Kara to the Valentine's dance only to find out Trent had already asked her. They didn't speak for five months after that. It wasn't until the first day of freshman football practice when they finally made amends.

The memories racing around his head disappeared in an instant, and a shiver went down his spine. Without lifting his gaze, he knew she was back. Jackson raised his eyes just as she focused on him. Their eyes locked for only seconds before he tore his gaze away. Everything within him was affected by one look. His breathing became deeper and raspier. His heart raced. Jackson's already high body temperature shot up, and beads of sweat started running down his whole body. In fact the only thing that she didn't stir in him was his inner wolf. For once, that secret part of him was as quiet as it had been prior to his first transformation. No one had ever affected him like this.

'She must be a wolf,' he thought.

He'd only met a couple other wolves, and they were all older friends of his dad's. *'I wonder if he's aware there are any in the area. And where did she come from?'* he thought, remembering how she came into town on foot.

Jackson tried to follow along with his buddies' conversation. The rest of the place was quiet, probably because they couldn't hear themselves think over the ruckus being made by the guys in this booth. It wasn't the volume that made it difficult to keep track of what they were saying. He was too distracted by her. Every second he allowed himself to look away felt like an eternity. He had to glance back to make sure she was still there, to make sure she was still real.

He took a deep breath and gathered all the inner confidence he could muster. *I'm going to do it. I'm just going to walk over there and introduce myself to her. That's what I'm going to do. Just as soon as I can will my legs to move me in that direction.'*

Putting his hands on the table in front of him, he braced himself to stand up, but when he looked back in her direction, he saw that she was staring right at him. He shifted his eyes away and toyed with the straw in his now empty milkshake glass. *'She's looking at me. You idiot! Go talk to her!'* he yelled at himself internally.

It was too late. His nerve was gone. He hoped he'd have the guts to try again before she left. There was a pen laying on the table. Trent and Sam had written down the farm address and directions for one of the out of towners. He picked it up and glanced back at the girl at the counter. She was still watching him intently. It almost looked as if there was a bit of fear in her eyes from recognizing the jerks who almost ran her down.

On the corner of the paper placemat, he quickly jotted down his name and phone number before any of the guys saw what he was doing. He ripped the corner off and folded it in his palm while looking her way, both understanding he would put her off if he continued to stare and being unable to stop all the same. *"Just go give it to her. You can do this."*

If they had met up here more casually and under different circumstances this would be easier. Just same time, same place. Instead, fate brought them together because Trent hadn't seen her walking down the county road at night. If it weren't for him grabbing the wheel, who knows what might have happened. Yet, they're all laughing and carrying on as though it was nothing. That's what was making this difficult he convinced himself to soothe his ego. It wasn't that he was afraid to approach her; it was that he was uncomfortable interacting with her under these circumstances. Even as he repeated it to himself, he knew it was a lie. She was important somehow. How he knew that was still a mystery, but what wasn't hard to figure out was that he couldn't mess this up.

Something was wrong. The girl at the counter looked around the restaurant, stopping at each person for a moment before moving on to the next. *'Was she looking for someone else?'* he thought. His heart sank, and he hoped he was wrong.

Jackson couldn't have been more mistaken. Something didn't sit well with him about how she was acting. Even though she had pulled out her phone and was typing something, it looked like she was very sick.

'Trent,' he thought. *'She must have been hurt when he almost ran her off the road. Head injury. She fell, and...'*

"Is she okay? Something's wrong," he said loudly, standing up. Jackson took off toward her as she started to sway and barely made it to her before she landed on the floor. Luckily, he caught her with no time to spare.

He laid her on her back and pulled the bench over from near the door to elevate her legs above her head. It surprised him where this first aid know how came from because he couldn't remember ever having paid attention in health class.

"I'll call for an ambulance," the waitress said.

"No need," a man's voice said from behind where Jackson knelt.

He looked up at the two strangers who'd just walked into the restaurant.

"Lilah!" the woman shouted and crouched down beside her near Jackson.

'Lilah,' he thought. *'That's a pretty name.'*

"She's our sister, and she's had a bad night," the man explained to the waitress. "She'll be fine once she takes her medication."

"Who are you?" the woman asked.

"Jackson."

The woman nodded. "How do you know Lilah?"

"I don't. I saw her faint."

The girl began to stir.

"Keep still, sis," the woman said. "Don't try to get up just yet."

One of the restaurant patrons motioned for people to go back to their seats. "Show's over folks. Move on."

Lilah looked straight into Jackson's eyes and blushed. She looked back and forth between him and her sister not sure what had happened.

"This is Jackson," the woman told her. "Lucky for you he was here. He got you on your back, and your legs raised above your heart before Todd and I arrived."

The girl sat up with help from her brother. "Thank you," she whispered.

Jackson's heart began to pound when he heard her sweet voice. "It was nothing really. Glad you're okay," he said shyly, but still managed a smile.

They couldn't stop gazing into each other's eyes.

"Let's get you home," her brother said.

They helped Lilah to her feet and headed for the door. Jackson watched her as she walked away, wondering if he'd ever see her again. *'Wait,'* he thought and opened his hand. The piece of paper with his number was still tightly stashed in his palm. When Lilah stopped at the door, he grabbed her hand and pushed the paper into it.

"Thanks again," she smiled sweetly before leaving.

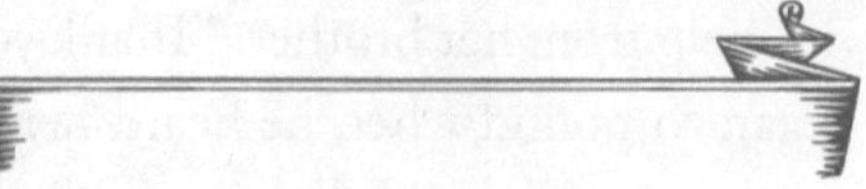

Chapter Twenty-One
Halloween

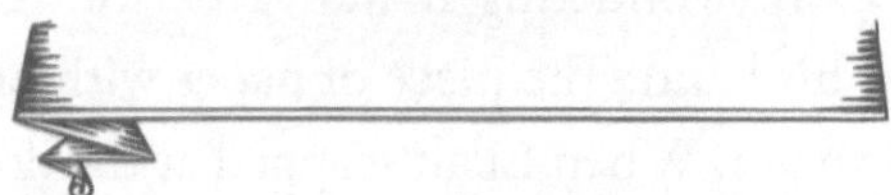

It was almost Halloween. The nights were growing longer, and the chill in the air became more brisk. The leaves changed colors and dropped to the ground, painting a carpet of red, yellow, and orange across the yard. From where he stood on the porch, a maple tree was casting vibrant orange-red hues into the mix. The light from the full moon cast a glow over the masterpiece. It was his favorite time of the year, and he looked forward to it.

Judd stood on his front porch looking around the neighborhood. Homes were decorated with jack o'lanterns, ghosts, skeletons and bats. Bright orange lights shown everywhere. Children were picking out their costumes, making the sometimes difficult choice of what alter ego they would portray this year. This was the time when he and his fellow Elements were rejoiced and celebrated.

'Well, maybe not Marcus,' he thought. Air was rather unspectacular in that regard, but vampires, werewolves, and witches were all around. They were the stars of the seasonal section at any store. They headlined every drive in movie theater. Stories of things that go bump in the night would keep children awake for hours, afraid of the monsters that lived under their bed.

The real threats never hid in their bedrooms. They walked amongst them. They were neighbors and pillars of the community, the people you'd least expect. The real monsters lived down the street, handing out candy to everyone who knocked on their door. You'd never know who they were until it was too late. The children waved to them as they rode their bikes to school. They'd knock on their doors selling chocolate to raise money for whatever group they had joined. The children never knew they were monsters because they had met no harm.

On this one occasion, Judd loved to see the little ones dressed as vampires with their plastic white fangs falling out of their mouths. Adults who idolized this blood sucking way of life mystified him, but children were innocents. It became a game. Each year, he'd tally up the number of costumes that came to his door. The wolves always lost, but they did consistently beat out Air. It was always between the witches and the vamps. On the years the witches won, Judd would skip the Return. Call it spite. Call it jealousy. Call it a bruised ego. Call it his own personal joke played out of boredom ever since trick or treating became widespread. He loved the reaction out of Anya when he arrived on the rock the years the vampires were victorious.

"So nice of you to join us this year," she would spit at him.

"Well, Fire is highly looked up to, no? I mustn't let my people down." It would confuse her and Marcus, and he would laugh because he knew the only reason he was there with them was because he was more popular. His laughter and puzzling comments would only get under her skin even more which made the triumph that much sweeter.

The years he lost he would stay home. Sometimes he'd get an angry visit or phone call from one of them, or both. Most years they didn't bother. It didn't matter if he showed when Water was never there. His absence was unimportant. He could hear the phone call now and Anya pleading, "What if this had been the year?"

Judd shook his head and walked back inside. He had told her many times the only way all four of them would ever be on that rock together is if they dragged Water, kicking and screaming the entire way. It was a tactic he'd never allow.

This year was setting up to be a record year for Fire. No less than three new vampire movies were released. He was sure they would beat out the witches by more than two to one, and he couldn't wait for Jackson to send him the tally count that night. He found it hard to take pleasure in what he was certain would be one of his biggest feats yet. He had been going to the Return for twenty years regardless of his little diversion, and this year, he wouldn't be coming back.

He went into the kitchen and started rummaging through the cabinets. Jackson would be home soon. It was late, but his son would be hungry even if he had just finished eating. If this was to be the last moments they shared together in this realm, he was going to make his son's favorite meal before he left.

JUDD TURNED OFF ON the country road that would take him most of the way to the lake. The Return was three days away. He wanted to speed up time to ensure nothing ruined their hard work, and he wanted to slow it down to spend more time at home simultaneously. Closing the front door and leaving Jackson behind was the hardest thing he's ever done and was already his biggest regret.

There wasn't much time to dwell in his own self-pity. Around a sharp curve, he saw a car crashed into a telephone pole. There was a young man near Jackson's age in the street, frantically waving his arms. Next to the car, a young woman lay on the road. It appeared as though she had been pulled from the car not thrown, but she looked severely hurt.

He slowed to a stop, and left his car parked in the road with the hazard lights flashing. The man was desperate, begging for help. "Please! I don't think she's breathing!"

Judd knelt by the woman's side and examined her. There was no pulse. It was too late. If he'd gotten here in time, he could've saved her. "I'm sorry," he said, hanging his head not wanting to be the bearer of bad news.

The woman's eyes opened and her fangs lengthened in her mouth. Judd flew back from the shock of it.

'No pulse. She's a created,' he reasoned. *'This can't be a coincidence when they're so close to the lake.'*

Ulric scanned for the man, but he had vanished. When he looked back to the girl, she was gone as well. He started to stand, but he felt two sets of hands push down on his shoulders with enough force to counter his immense strength. The pinch of the needle stung the skin in his neck.

Whatever they had injected took effect quickly. He felt weak and light headed. His vision was blurred, and he saw two of everything. He collapsed to the ground, and the blond woman from Salvador appeared over him.

"Why?" he asked.

"I believe you already know the answer."

"Who are you?" he slurred.

She crouched down over him. "You disappoint me almost as much as Water. Of the other three Elements beside that moon worshiper, I thought you would be the one to remember me."

THE EVENING WAS ALMOST over. There had only been a few stragglers in the last half hour. After the last one, Jackson turned off the porch light, and he set the dish of candy on the table in the hallway near the door. He walked into the living room hearing each foot fall loudly sound off in the empty house. This was how it was going to be from now on. It would just be him alone in this place.

Lilah didn't did make it over, but it wasn't for lack of trying. He had hoped she would be there to help calm him and take his mind off of never seeing his dad again. She said she couldn't make it because she wasn't feeling well, but he knew better. She was an Air, and he was her match. Lilah felt fine, but she needed to be with her family until they had news of the Return.

Even though she thought Jackson was a novice to all things supernatural, she had to know their connection was a two way street. It upset him how sheltered she was that her family hadn't explained it to her thoroughly yet.

He headed out back and set his cell phone on the rail of the porch, so it would stop tormenting him. Most of the evening in between trick or treaters was spent staring at the screen, hoping his dad would call. They had said their goodbyes four nights ago when he left to go to the cabin. His dad had always hidden his emotions well, and Jackson believed his dad wouldn't call tonight to say goodbye because they'd already done it. He yearned to hear his dad's voice one last time nonetheless.

Jackson stood in the driveway between the house and garage, thinking about how his dad had it paved years ago and continued the paved drive down the side of the garage as well. It was when he was very young and first took an interest in the sport. His dad put the basketball hoop on the side of the garage to make it easy for him to dribble and shoot hoops to his heart's content.

At the time, he felt so loved and lucky to have a dad who would go to such lengths to make him happy. Looking back, he realized it was to prevent him from always having to go to the park or the school to play. His dad wanted to keep him home and safe. He was loved, and he was lucky. He had a dad who do whatever it took to protect him.

The temperature had dropped rapidly for being late October. He didn't notice how cold his hands were getting or the puff of white that could be seen with each exhale. He barely noticed the snow that had covered the ground while he was counting the number of witches and vampires that came to the door for his dad. It was something he had done every year since taking over the job of handing out candy. It tore him apart to not send the text with the final count as he usually did.

Basketball was his passion. It had been the center of his life until he met Lilah. There had been many winters spent slipping on the ice because nothing could keep him from it.

His phone was still on the rail of the back porch. It was hard to say how much time had passed since he came outside, and he was curious to see how long he had been out there. It could've been five minutes or five hours. Either would be expected and would also shock him at the same time. He didn't want to check his phone for the time because it would show no new messages from his dad, and that was all he would notice.

The first year after learning about the Return he bawled when his dad left.

He wasn't quite a man yet, but he was old enough that some might think it embarrassing to see him react in that way. It was hard to accept that his dad might leave to go to the cabin and never come back home.

After that, they played it off. They had a routine. They would say their regular goodbyes as though his dad was honestly going on a fishing trip. They'd make jokes. Typical banter like telling his son not to throw any parties, or he'd have the devil to pay when his dad got home. He didn't cry, but every Halloween since that first one he would sit on the edge of a chair in the kitchen, staring at his phone, waiting on the text from his dad telling him when he'd be home.

This year was different. This year he knew his dad would make the Return. Marcus and Leena had found Water. Jackson hadn't been filled in on the details, but Water must have agreed. It was time. A thousand years was long enough. This year when his dad left, he knew it would be the last time he saw him.

Deep down he still had hope. Water could have a last minute change of heart and back out. He never wanted anything more in his life than the text from his dad tonight. The longer his phone went silent he began to reluctantly accept the Return had been a success.

Jackson fought back the tears stinging the corners of his eyes and leaned against the garage. He stared in the direction of his cell phone, both hoping it would ring and willing himself the strength to simply pick it up and look at it. The strength never came. He lifted his foot against the outside wall of the garage and pushed against it, propelling himself forward. As he moved, something caught his eye in the illumination of the street light.

He saw a hole in the wall of the shed. As if by instinct, he put his finger over the hole to cover it. There were three other holes nearby, making a square pattern with the first one. He touched each of them with his fingertips before taking a step back to study them. They were hard to make out even with the glow of the light. They looked like spots on the wall in the night time. There were four sets of four drill marks in all. They went up the side of the garage in a line. The last set was about a foot underneath where the backboard hung now.

They weren't much for sentimentality. There were no pencil marks on the frame of the kitchen doorway, recording his development. These drill marks were his growth chart, illustrating how his dad had to raise the hoop every couple of years. He had been so young when his dad introduced him to the sport, so his dad positioned the backboard fairly low.

He touched his hand to the second set of holes. He could remember being ten years old and telling his father the hoop was too low for him to use any longer. His dad appeared to be shocked, saying there was no way his boy had gotten that big.

It was a song and dance act for his benefit. He realized that now, but he didn't then. He challenged his dad to come outside, and he'd prove it. They went out to the driveway, and he was filled with determination to show his dad he had grown. It was like he believed sheer grit could add an extra inch to the soles of his shoes.

Jackson swallowed a deep gulp of air and exhaled slowly through his mouth. He blinked rapidly to quell his tears. *'No,'* he thought to himself. *'I won't allow these memories to become ghosts of the past.'*

The ringing of the phone disrupted his thoughts. His heart raced as he ran for it. He knew it wasn't his dad, but somehow he knew it was just as important, maybe more so.

He grabbed the phone and checked the screen, but he didn't recognize the number. "Hello?" he asked hesitantly.

A voice he wasn't familiar with said, "Jackson? This is Marcus."

Jackson sucked his breath in sharply. There were only two things he knew about Marcus. He was the Air Element, and he was very secretive. If he was calling, it had to be bad news. If he was calling, it also meant the Return didn't occur. Worry overtook him as he feared the worst, wondering why he hadn't heard from his dad.

"You know me, then," Marcus said, hearing his shocked reaction. "I wasn't sure how much your father had told you."

"Yes, he told me who you are," Jackson said surprised by his own voice. He wasn't sure where the words came from, but they didn't seem to be coming from him.

"Where is your father? I've been unable to get in contact with him."

"Wh-What do you mean?" Jackson asked. "I thought the Return was successful since he didn't tell me otherwise. I thought he was with you."

"No," Marcus told him, forlornly. "There was a ... complication."

"A complication?"

Marcus ignored the question. "The Return wouldn't have been completed anyway because your father didn't show."

Jackson's eyes widened, and he turned in circles as though some clue to his dad's whereabouts was within arm's reach of where he was standing. "Didn't show? That's not possible. He left. He went to the cabin. Four nights ago!"

"Son, I'm sorry. Your dad may have left, but he didn't come here." Marcus sighed. "I apologize. When your father didn't arrive as scheduled and couldn't be contacted, I assumed he changed his mind about going through with it. I should've called you sooner."

He opened and closed his mouth several times. He couldn't believe what he was hearing.

"I've got to go. There's a situation. If you hear from him, have him contact me as soon as he can, and I'll do the same for you."

"Yes, I will."

"And one more thing," Marcus added. "Don't tell anyone you spoke with me."

The line went dead. Jackson immediately tried calling his dad. It went straight to voice mail which meant it was either dead or turned off. Something was wrong. Something had happened. His breathing came in short pants, and he practiced the techniques he had been taught to control his emotions. Slow, deep breaths. In and out. Repeat. His dad was Fire. It was impossible for something to happen to him.

Jackson's phone dinged. It was Everleigh telling him about the Return. She only said it wasn't successful, not that his dad was the reason why. *I wonder if she knows.*

Without thinking about what he was doing, he made his way inside. He wanted Lilah to come over, needed her. His panicked state was getting too hot, and in the darkness, he could see the orange glow of his eyes. There wasn't much time left before he transformed.

It would be damn near impossible to get her to come out this late at night especially not after the news of Fire circulated through her family. If she couldn't get away from them earlier, there was no way she'd be allowed to leave now.

He walked into the kitchen and took a bottle of pills from the cabinet. He flicked the lid off, and it flew across the counter, bounced off the wall, and landed somewhere on the floor. Dumping the pills in his hand, he took twice his usual dose. It was a slim chance they'd take affect before his inner wolf won out.

The phone rang again. He hoped it was his dad, or Marcus telling him everything was okay. It was Everleigh.

"Hello?" he answered, hearing the growl in his voice. *'Breathe! Slower. In and out.'*

"Are you okay?"

"I will be," he said with his eyes closed, focusing on each breath he took.

"Have you heard anything more?" Everleigh asked.

"Just what you told me," he lied.

"Look, I talked to Lilah about coming out tonight, but I'm not sure it's a good idea if you're upset, and don't try to tell me you're not," Everleigh told him.

Jackson continued to concentrate on his breathing. The pills needed to work faster. "Everleigh, I don't give a damn if you think it's a good idea. She calms me. It's like her presence grounds me."

"Consider it done."

Jackson drove to the farmhouse to pick up Lilah. His emotions assuaged on the drive just knowing he'd soon be by her side. By the time he arrived, he was back to his normal self. After taking her to his house, he slipped into the kitchen for drinks, but really, it was to text Everleigh. He asked if she had heard anything else about the Return.

This time he told her he hadn't heard from his dad and was worried about him before she had a chance to reply. He expected her to say there was no news, but she didn't. She told him the truth. She told him Fire didn't make it to the Return this year. Jackson guessed she was aware of what happened when they talked earlier, but she was only telling him now because Lilah was there to keep his inner wolf hidden away. It didn't matter. He was thankful to finally have someone to talk to about it.

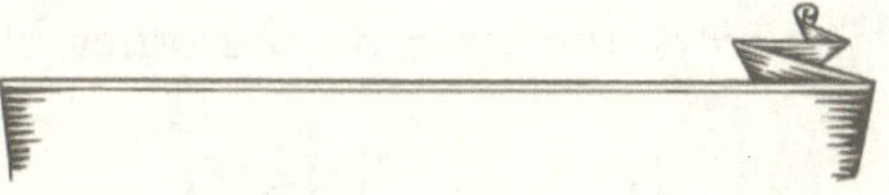

Chapter Twenty-Two
Water

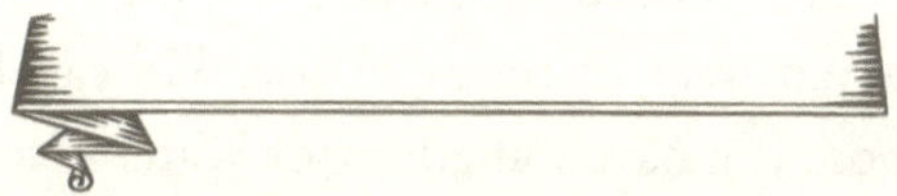

One year earlier...

Marcus looked at Fire and Earth who were gathered on the rock. Once again, Water was missing. Next year would mark their one thousandth Return attempt. Fire was hit and miss. He would show for decades in a row only to be absent for a century, but Water had never made an attempt. Only he and Earth had been at every Return since the beginning.

"Something has to be done," Anya interrupted the silence. "The state of the Earth needs us. Balance was meant to be a temporary solution for a year," she emphasized.

"Earthquakes and hurricanes are occurring at an alarming rate," Marcus nodded.

"More than that. It wasn't long ago that cyclones started hitting areas normally unaffected by such phenomena," Anya added.

"Don't look at me," Marcus told her. "You know I have no power over these things any longer, same as you."

Anya jumped to her feet and began pacing the length of the rock. "That's exactly what I mean! Water was the one who insisted on this little trek, and Water will be the one to bring about the end of the planet at this rate."

"Normally, I find your rants to be quite unbearable," said Judd with the usual tone to his voice showing disregard for everyone, "but this time I agree. It was an adventure when we started. I found the Dark Ages to be rather pleasurable, but I'm uninterested in the whiny nature of people today. I'm set to be done of this plane." This would be his whole truth if it weren't for Jackson. His son was the only reason he had to stay.

"There has to be some way," Anya looked at Marcus for answers.

"My abilities don't work the same on the other Elements. You know that."

"What about you, Anya?" asked Judd. "Don't you witches have tracking spells?"

Anya's back was to them, but Marcus could see her shoulders rise and fall as she took deep breaths to maintain her composure before answering. She turned to face Judd, "Locate, not track. We aren't dogs. We can locate someone if we have an item of theirs to use. We can locate any missing person. I don't suppose you have something of Water's lying around?"

Judd's eyes danced, and a grin turned up the corners of his mouth. "You sniff out an object to find someone. That's tracking," he teased her. He loved how easy it was to get under her skin.

Marcus stood between them. "Enough. We don't have time for this. Any minute now the Divine Spirit will send us back because we aren't whole."

Anya shook her head in agreement, "Then we'll figure it out over the phone."

"Do you really think Judd is going to answer your calls if he knows it's about the Return? Or mine for that matter?" Marcus turned to face Judd.

"We'll have a group call after we are sent home and try to figure out how to find Water before the next Return, okay?" Anya asked Judd.

Judd placed his hands on the rock behind him and stretched out his legs. "I have plans later."

They stared at Judd.

"What? Like you expected Water to actually show? Of course I made plans. I knew I'd be back." Only his plans consisted of a good night's sleep and maybe a little fishing in the morning.

Anya threw her hands up and crossed them on the back of her head as she began pacing the rock again. "You are the most infuriating excuse of a human I have ever had the displeasure to know."

"Thank you," Judd beamed. "Flattery will get you everywhere."

Anya stopped and whipped around to face him. Before she could say anything, Judd eased, "Tomorrow, Anya. We can talk tomorrow. We have a year to figure this out. One night won't make a difference anyway."

She stood silent for a moment. "How can none of us know where

Water is?"

"The wolves are making their home near the Montana and Canadian border now," Marcus told her.

"Yes, but not Water. I can find the both of you. I always found Judd by looking for those closest to him. I find you through Leena," she explained to Marcus. "But when I locate the wolves, I can never find Water."

"Same," Marcus peered out at the trees that grew along the north of the rock. He was unaware that someone lurked in the trees watching him as well. "I can focus on the vampires, and eventually one of them will say, do, or think something about Judd and lead me to him. I haven't heard a word about Water since the day we all stepped off this rock for the first time."

"Me either," Anya said sadly.

Judd sat up clearly interested in their revelation. "Wait a minute," he eyed them both suspiciously.

He stood up and searched their faces for a clue, anything that might tell him this was merely a ruse. "You are saying the last time either of you saw Water was the day we came?"

Marcus quickly glanced at Anya to see if she had his same thought. "That's right," Marcus told him.

"You've seen Water?" Anya asked.

"Not for a long while. Our paths crossed from time to time in Medieval Europe. We always had a lot to discuss what with both of us trying to save our people from being massacred." Judd looked to Anya, "You know a little about that yourself, don't you?"

Anya glared back at him. "Where's Water now?"

"I don't know."

Anya shook her head and anger swelled in her eyes.

"I mean it," Judd insisted. "It's been awhile."

"I just don't understand it. No matter how many times or how long I focus on the wolves, no one leads me to him. It's like they don't even know Water exists, but how can that be?" Marcus tried to distract them from the fight looming overhead.

"Him?" Judd was puzzled.

"Yes, Water."

Judd's eyes lit up again in amusement.

"What's so funny?" Anya asked him.

"It would appear that it's your lucky day," Judd mused. "I might be able to help after all."

"I knew it!" Anya accused. She squared off opposite Judd and brought her face within inches of his. "I knew you were holding out on us. Where is he?"

"I already told you. I. Don't. Know," Judd hissed through clenched teeth.

"Then what do you know?" Marcus gently tugged on Anya's arm, encouraging her to take a step back.

Judd turned to Marcus and raised his eyebrow, "Well for starters, I know that Water is not a *he*."

"Her name, given by the Divine Spirit, is spelled K-a-m-i-l-a-h, and its pronounced Camilla. She uses the modern version of it."

"Camilla?" Anya's eyes widened as she put two and two together. "Camilla Sabry?"

"One and the same," Judd answered, ignoring the impact of the bomb he dropped.

"Judd Montgomery!" Anya hissed. The fury in her voice pierced his skin like tiny needles.

Marcus supposed there was something he was missing. "Do you know this woman, Anya? This Camilla? Water?"

"I do not know her," Anya said. "However, her name has been mentioned in pleasant company."

"That's funny," Judd remarked. "I don't remember ever having told you her name."

Anya walked to him and towered her petite frame over him, and crossed her arms. "In what realm of existence would anyone ever deem your company to be pleasurable?"

"How do you know her name?" Marcus asked Anya.

She lost herself for a moment. She laughed out of anger and paced away from them, shaking her head. She stopped at the edge of the rock and shook out her head and arms as though preparing to box.

Anya walked back to her fellow Elements. Her thumb was bent under her chin and her finger under her nose, pressing her lips together. "How do I know her? I don't know Water. He may have been too young to remember her, but Jackson talks about his mother all the time."

The silence was deadening. Marcus and Leena processed the revelation while Anya stewed.

"It was bad enough you came to Fairview, bringing a wolf with you, but you brought Water's son. You made targets of us all."

Judd snapped back, "Don't you dare speak to me as though your bloodline is pure. We all know the secrets you hide in your home."

"How long, Judd?" Leena asked, stepping out from behind Marcus and trying to intervene before their fight got too deep. "How long did you have an affair with her?"

Judd jumped to his feet. "Affair?" he spat at Leena. "She was my wife. I was in love with her."

Leena's voiced softened. "You and Water? In love?"

He ran his fingers through his hair. "Well, you know what they say. Opposites attract."

She asked again, "How long did it last?"

"Thirty years, give or take."

Marcus punched his fists together in a rare show of emotion. "Thirty years! In all that time, you never thought to bring her to the Return?"

"Oh, I thought about it," Judd said. "I thought about it every year we were together."

"Why didn't you?" Leena asked.

"Because she didn't want to go. She doesn't want to go. Camilla has no desire to ever leave this world."

"Did it never occur to you to force her to come with you?" Marcus asked enraged.

"No," Judd answered in a matter of fact way.

Marcus balled his fists and raised his arms over his head, and slams his fists down into his legs, screaming out his frustrations. The force he emitted knocked down trees two miles away and flung them close enough to the rock that all the Elements felt it shake.

"No?" he screamed. "You came to the Return some of those years in the decades before Jackson was born. Why did you not show your teeth?"

"Um, I don't know," Judd answered sarcastically. "Maybe something to do with the idea that when a woman says no, she means no. You don't coerce her into it. Have you learned nothing in your thousand years alive?" his voice raised to a shout at the end.

Anya stepped in to keep the peace between them. "Let's take a moment," she told them.

She turned to Judd and said, "I understand why you didn't force her, manipulate her, or do something underhanded to bring her here. But why in all these years did you never tell us you knew her? Never tell us her name? Never give us one clue to go on so we might find her?"

Judd walked to the edge of the rock and sat, dangling his legs over the edge. He straddled two realms. He was in the space between on the rock, and the veil pierced enough he could see the area behind the hunting cabin where he would emerge when he left. He thought about that time twenty years ago when Jackson was barely walking. He and Camilla were supposed to come, using the cabin as a romantic getaway. He knew she wouldn't attempt the Return. He only wanted time with her away from the day to day, a chance to fall in love again.

He could feel the eyes of the three of them resting on his back, waiting for him to answer. "Because she liked me."

"Liked you?" Marcus asked. "I thought she left you."

Anya gasped, "Marcus!"

Judd pushed himself back onto the rock, and the cabin faded from view. "While the two of you only deign to tolerate me, Camilla enjoyed my company." He smiled at the memory of the good times. "I wish you could have seen us together. Then you'd understand. It was nice having someone on my side even if it was the one you'd least expect."

Anya muttered, "Like they say. Keep your friends close and your enemies closer."

He looked at her questioning what she meant.

"Come on, Judd. Even you know Fire and Water don't mix."

Judd hopped to his feet and slapped Marcus on the shoulder. "If that's the case, Marcus and I should be waist deep in a bromance by now, wouldn't you think?"

Marcus recoiled and moved away from Judd.

"Besides, it wouldn't have done any good. You wouldn't have found her."

"Why is that?" Leena asked.

"Jackson is her only child. All the wolves throughout our history have been turned. It doesn't matter who made the bite, their sire lineage traces back to her. They will protect the pack leader at all cost," Judd explained.

"Aside from the time the two of you were together when you rightfully respected her choice, you had no idea where she was?" Anya asked.

"Oh, no. I have an idea," Judd told her. He reached down and snapped a small branch off one of the trees Marcus felled. He broke it into smaller pieces, throwing them out into the darkness.

When he spun around to face them again, Marcus asked, "Are you going to share this idea of yours with us?"

"Why?" Judd demanded. "So you can lay out a trap for her? Drag her to the next Return, kicking and screaming?"

Marcus opened his mouth, but Leena stepped in front of him. "No, Judd, but I would like the opportunity to talk to her, to appeal to her. Balance is in chaos. We have to do something."

Judd mulled it over. "Maybe it is time." He pointed to the pendant around Anya's neck, "I believe she may be the bringer of the storm. I think she's in Michigan."

"That close? Why do you think this is where we'll find her?" Anya asked.

"For one," he said, sitting back down on the rock holding his knees to his chest, "there's a new pack in the northern part of the state. Their numbers have been vastly increasing the last several years. If she is preparing for war, she'll want a small army around her," Judd explained.

"And two?"

"What?"

"You said for one, she may be building an army. What's two?" Anya asked.

"Judd rubbed the back of his neck. "She has to be close. I think she's visited my house a couple times, but I can't be sure it was her."

"Leena and I will go to Michigan to see what we can unearth," Marcus said. "Can we count on you for help if we need it?"

"Yes," Anya answered without hesitation.

"Can I count on both of you?" Marcus repeated.

Judd nodded.

Leena kneeled next to him. "Is there any more you can give us to go on? What does she look like?"

Judd got a far off look in his eye. "She's beautiful," he answered. "Like none you've ever seen. She had silky, long blonde hair the last time I saw her. Her eyes are blue, and they're deep. They can melt your heart when she smiles, but if you make her angry, they can freeze your soul."

Water
The Elementals: Book Four
Available February 2021

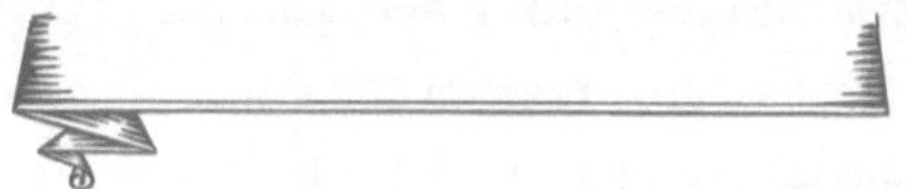

Camilla sat in a tree watching Connor running around below her, howling, carrying on, and drawing as much attention to himself as he could. For months, her wolves had been picked off. One had turned up missing or killed every full moon. Connor was bait tonight. She was going to catch whoever was behind it.

It felt like hours had passed since she first got into position on the branch. She'd been sitting there long enough her legs were starting to fall asleep and trying to change position made her backside hurt.

That's when she felt it. There was a presence she didn't quite recognize. It was Water, and it wasn't. She saw its eyes a good fifty yards off, but coming fast toward Connor. She didn't know who or what it was, but it wasn't one of hers.

Camilla waited until the timing was perfect. She jumped from the branch transforming into a wolf by the time she touched the ground. The unknown wolf didn't see her coming. Camilla picked her up with one distorted, beastly hand and bashed the wolf's head into a tree, knocking her unconscious.

The wolf didn't wake up until several hours after sunrise in Connor's basement. She had transformed back into a beautiful, young woman with long golden locks. When she awoke, Camilla looked into the most gorgeous blue eyes she had ever seen. The woman looked around startled, clutching the blanket they had used to cover her.

"I won't hurt you," Camilla told her sternly. "Not yet. I want answers."

The woman eyed the basement door and the two guards that stood between her and freedom. She fell to her knees with sobs choking out of her throat.

"Get her some water," she told Connor.

Turning back to the woman, she asked, "What do you want with my wolves?"

There was no answer. The woman's sobs grew louder.

Camilla took a couple steps toward the woman and reached down, cupping the woman's chin and lifting her head up. "My patience is growing very thin. You're lucky I've grown softer the last few years and didn't kill you immediately. This is your last chance. What do you want with my wolves?"

Between sobs the woman managed to say, "A pack."

"You make a pack, not steal one."

"Every time I try..." the woman looked down.

Camilla sighed, "You kill them. Didn't your parents teach you control?"

The woman shook her head no.

"What about your original pack? They should've taught you something."

"No."

"Where are they now? Slaughtered? Or did they kick you out?" Camilla asked, growing frustrated.

"I don't know."

"How do you not know?" How is that possible?"

The woman sadly said, "The first thing I remember is walking out of the woods. A farmer found me."

"When was this?"

"They guessed my age to be eighteen when I was found."

'Not very long ago then. She can't be more than twenty-five,' Camilla thought.

Connor returned with the glass of water and handed it to their prisoner.

While the woman took a drink, Camilla asked, "What's your name?"

"Ruby."

Camilla pinched her lip between her thumb and index finger while she debated what to do. It had been a long time since she murdered anyone or had cause to. Her heart went out to this young woman. She was an orphan. She needed a parent figure in her life, a mom. "I think I can help you."

"That takes years!" Connor couldn't believe Camilla was considering it.

"Remember who you're speaking to," Camilla warned him.

"With all due respect, you're not going to allow her into our pack, not after she's murdered three members of our family?"

"No," Camilla said, turning to Ruby. "But I will help you form your new pack and learn control." She grinned from ear to ear. "Besides, I know a shortcut."

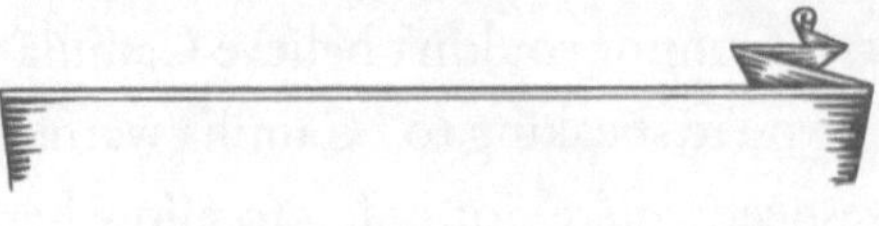

About the Author

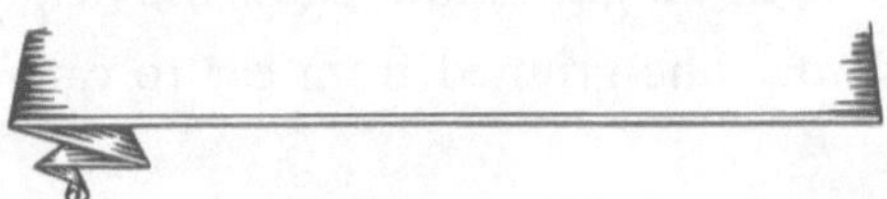

Jennifer Lush is a mother of three from central Illinois where she has lived her entire life. Aside from spending time with her children and grandchild, writing and traveling are her two main consuming passions. Luckily, they are mutually beneficial.

Writing has always been in her blood even if it took her longer than planned to do it. One of her earliest memories of longing to be an author happened in kindergarten when she told her parents what she wanted to be when she grew up. It took close to four decades, but she has finally made that childhood dream come true.

Jennifer is an entertainer at heart who is always making those around her laugh. She can turn any mundane event into a story worth repeating with flair. Inspiration for her fictional worlds comes from everywhere. There are more ideas floating through her mind than she has time to write, but she is determined to finish as many as possible.